TRUSTING A COWGIRL

CALLAHANS OF COPPER CREEK BOOK 4

NATALIE DEAN

EXCLUSIVE BOOKS BY NATALIE DEAN

GET THREE FREE BOOKS when you join my Sweet Romance Newsletter :)

Get One Free Contemporary Western Romance:
The New Cowboy at Miller Ranch, Miller Brothers of Texas Prologue - He's a rich Texas rancher. She's just a tomboy ranch employee. Can she make him see life can still be happy without all that money?

AND Two Free Historical Western Romances:
Spring Rose - A feel good historical western mail-order groom novelette about a broken widow finding love and faith.

Fools Rush In - A historical western mail-order bride novelette based off a true story!

Go to nataliedeanauthor.com to find out how to join!

ALSO BY NATALIE DEAN

CONTEMPORARY ROMANCE

Copper Creek Romances

BAKER BROTHERS OF COPPER CREEK

Copper Creek Romances Series 1

Cowboys & Protective Ways

Cowboys & Crushes

Cowboys & Christmas Kisses

Cowboys & Broken Hearts

Cowboys & Second Chances

Cowboys & Wedding Woes

Cowboys' Mom Finds Love

CALLAHANS OF COPPER CREEK

Copper Creek Romances Series 2

Making a Cowgirl

Marrying a Cowgirl

Christmas with a Cowgirl

Trusting a Cowgirl

Dating a Cowgirl

Catching a Cowgirl

Loving a Cowgirl

Marrying a Cowboy

KEAGANS OF COPPER CREEK

Copper Creek Romances Series 3

Some Cowboys are Off-Limits

Some Cowgirls Love Single Dads

Some Cowboys are Infuriating

Some Cowboys Don't Like City Girls

Some Cowboys Heal Broken Hearts

Some Cowgirls are Worth Protecting

Some Cowboys are Just Friends

Some Cowboys Fall for Hidden Stars

Some Cowboys Come Home for Christmas

Some Cowboys Brave the Flames

Some Cowboys Fight for Love

PALMERS OF COPPER CREEK

Copper Creek Romances Series 4

Mateo & Nicole

Sophia & Cameron

Roman & Olivia

Camilla & Dallas

Isabelle & Jason

Marcus & Wynter

Miller Family Saga

BROTHERS OF MILLER RANCH

Miller Family Saga Series 1

Her Second Chance Cowboy

Saving Her Cowboy

Her Rival Cowboy

Her Fake-Fiance Cowboy Protector

Taming Her Cowboy Billionaire

BROTHERS OF MILLER RANCH SERIES BUNDLE

MILLER BROTHERS OF TEXAS

Miller Family Saga Series 2

The New Cowboy at Miller Ranch

Humbling Her Cowboy

In Debt to the Cowboy

The Cowboy Falls for the Veterinarian

Almost Fired by the Cowboy

Faking a Date with Her Cowboy Boss

MILLER BROTHERS OF TEXAS SERIES BUNDLE

BRIDES OF MILLER RANCH, N.M.

Miller Family Saga Series 3

Cowgirl Fallin' for the Single Dad

Cowgirl Fallin' for the Ranch Hand

Cowgirl Fallin' for the Neighbor

Cowgirl Fallin' for the Miller Brother

Cowgirl Fallin' for Her Best Friend's Brother

Cowboy Fallin' in Love Again

BRIDES OF MILLER RANCH, N.M. SERIES BUNDLE

Though I try to keep this list updated in each book, you may also visit my website nataliedeanbooks.com for the most up to date information on my book list.

CONTENTS

1

——————

Riley

I shouldn't even be here. Therapy is for idiots who don't know what they are getting into. I'm perfectly capable of dealing with my own problems. I don't need some woman to pat me on the head and tell me she's proud of how brave I am.

Riley scowled. His arms were folded tight across his chest as he sat in a large room with half a dozen other veterans. From what he understood about this place, everyone was required to participate in group therapy on top of one-on-one therapy. Most of them were a good fifteen to twenty years older than he was. In fact, he was the youngest guy there.

Well, what did people expect when a dead-beat father kicked his son to the curb a few months before he turned eighteen? The army had interested Riley more than anything else had, like it was his calling; he wanted to protect people and defend his country. His father just couldn't accept that his son wanted to make something of himself. After that, the army was the only place that would offer him both a place to stay and a job until he could strike out on his own.

They didn't make men like him anymore. These days men were jobless, helpless, and poor excuses for human beings. They knew nothing of real-world trauma, and they probably never would.

Those were the people who should be getting therapy. Not him.

The doors opened and a few people walked in. The first was an older gentleman. He was probably in his late fifties. He was followed closely by a young woman who quite possibly was under twenty. The final person was one he'd seen around here —a man who looked to be about his age.

The young woman had blonde hair that fell down her back in waves. She wore a cowboy hat and boots, which wasn't unusual around here. He hadn't gotten a good look at her face, but there was something about her that tugged at him, whispered that she was something unique.

"Mr. Scott, would you like to share anything today?"

Riley jumped and then scowled at the man who led the group meeting. From what he could tell, the man didn't have any legitimate credentials. He was trained just like any of the other people working here. That meant he only knew how to listen. Riley hadn't even bothered to learn the man's name. What was the point? He was just another face in a sea of people who would never understand.

Already, he'd had the obligatory evals with his therapist. He'd done enough talking to last several lifetimes. He knew his diagnoses. There was absolutely nothing this guy could do or say to make any of it better.

"Mr. Scott, part of your agreement in coming here is to participate in group sessions."

Riley rubbed the spot between his eye and his nose, then

hunched over, resting his elbows on his knees. "I don't have anything to say today."

The air around them practically buzzed with expectation. He'd been the only one who refused to speak at these things, and it was getting to the point where he started feeling like an outcast.

It was just as well. He wasn't here to make friends. He'd do his time and head home.

"Well, that about does it for today." The host rose from his chair. "Thank you all for attending. We'll have another meeting in two days. Those of you who are new here, please check in with Shane at his office to receive your therapy schedule."

Metal folding chairs groaned and screeched against the floor. Riley winced, waiting until everyone had gotten out of their seats before standing. When he did, the meeting leader was right in front of him.

Riley let out a sigh. "Is there something you need?"

"You know the rules, Mr. Scott. You can't have your first equine session without first participating in group."

Riley folded his arms, his jaw tightening. "The judge only said I had to attend this group for sixteen weeks. The way I see it, I've already been here for two. I'm doing just fine."

The man shook his head. "Unfortunately, that's incorrect. The judge mandated that you have sixteen weeks of *equine* therapy. Technically, that hasn't started yet."

"That's a load of bull—" He snapped his mouth shut and pressed his lips tight enough that he lost feeling in them. He lowered his voice and tried again. "Nowhere in my paperwork does it designate what kind of therapy. It just says I have to come to this location to get it."

If the man wasn't so irritating to begin with, Riley might have felt sorry for him. The group leader shifted and flipped through some paperwork he had on a clipboard until he found what he was looking for. Spinning the board around, he jabbed his finger at a line in the document a few paragraphs above the judge's signature.

Right there in black and white it stated, "Riley Scott has refused traditional therapy and will be required to participate in mandated equine therapy for a minimum of sixteen weeks."

How had he missed that?

The glorified therapist dropped the clipboard to his side and offered a tight smile. "Perhaps you will share something on Thursday. I would really like to get to know you better."

And I'd really rather shovel horse manure.

The man was far too cheery for his taste. He patted Riley on the shoulder. It was only one tap, but it sent jolts of fire down his arm and he flinched.

"One more thing." The man, who had a nametag that read *Kevin*, dropped his gaze down to Riley's side. "You know the rules. No weapons at group. You're welcome to conceal carry around the ranch and town as discussed, just not here." He flashed Riley a smile and strode away.

Riley glowered at the back of the man's head, then charged toward the back door. The gun. The mandated therapy. All of it just added to the weight that rested on his shoulders. There were several small cabins on the property for people just like him, and thankfully he didn't have to share his place with anyone. It was off to the side, away from all the activity.

The owner here probably did that on purpose. He'd gotten the court order and made a judgment call. Even though Riley was sure the paperwork didn't label him as dangerous, that's just what folks assumed.

He hurried down the steps, relishing in the nippy air as it hit his face. Out here in the mountains, it stayed colder longer. Spring was coming, but it hadn't hit this part of Colorado yet. The temperate conditions helped to ground him. There were fewer sensory issues from smells and sounds to deal with.

Quiet.

Like when it snowed and the earth took a nap.

Riley breathed in deeply, allowing the pine and straw scents to envelop him. He didn't need therapy. He wasn't a violent person. People got depressed all the time over little things. Why couldn't people accept that his depression was just as valid? They didn't need all the details of what went on when he was overseas.

And he sure didn't need to relive them every single day of his life.

A thundering sound approached and immediately his senses were alert. His whole body tensed and he reached for a weapon he didn't carry. A beast of an animal rumbled past him, bursting from a nearby barn ridden by a rider much too petite to handle such an animal.

She was short, thin—a bare whisp of a woman. Her skinny arms could barely pull the animal to a stop. And when her cowboy hat flew from her head, a shock of blonde hair tumbled around her shoulders.

His heart rammed up into his throat and sweat sprang to his brow as he launched toward her. He could only imagine what might happen if she were to be thrown from the saddle. Where were her parents?

Riley darted out in front of the horse, who reared back then landed firmly, but not before bucking once to dislodge the pixie who rode him. She remained on the beast, but only just. Her hair blocked her face and little white puffs escaped her red lips.

He hurried around to her side and plucked her from the saddle before placing her on her feet. She brushed her hair from her face, revealing a pair of the largest green eyes he had ever seen.

Thick lashes framed those emeralds and drew him in. She was the young woman from before. They stared at one another for a moment before she folded her arms and peered at him with mild irritation. "That wasn't very smart."

He stiffened. She couldn't possibly be referring to his saving her life.

"You could have been seriously injured," she accused. Her head whipped around and she surveyed the area. "Who's assigned to you? They shouldn't have left you alone out here."

His head reared back. "I beg your pardon?"

"You're supposed to have a sponsor—therapist. You know, someone who should have taught you how to approach an animal?"

"I think you've got this all wrong." He folded his arms. "Based on what I saw, you were the one in need of help. Are your parents around here somewhere?"

"My parents?" she scoffed. "I assure you, I'm more than capable of handling this animal. I was practically born in the saddle. In fact, I work here." She patted the horse's rump causing him to sidestep. "Buster here just got spooked. He hates mice, don't you, fella?"

"*Buster* is five times your size. Shouldn't they be giving you a horse more your speed?"

Her eyes narrowed. "I'm going to forget you said that." She brushed past him and effortlessly floated into the saddle. At least that's how it looked from his vantage point. When she was situated, she glanced down at him. "I wasn't kidding though. Your sponsor needs to teach you some horse etiquette. I can handle myself. But you might have gotten seriously hurt."

She clicked her tongue and Buster moved forward, tail swishing like he was as gentle as a giant teddy bear.

Riley's pulse continued to race, still locked in fight or flight mode. While his exterior was calm and collected, his insides were screaming to release the pent-up anxiety that had just blasted through his chest.

It didn't matter what that woman said; she had been in danger and he wasn't about to let another person die if he could help it.

He'd already been responsible for too many unnecessary deaths.

2

———

Grace

Grace hopped down out of her father's truck and waved goodbye before trudging through the icy parking lot toward the country club. According to Shane, the guest who was assigned to her was being rather stubborn in his group therapy and hadn't made it past the threshold to be assigned a horse.

That didn't mean she would just not show up. On the off chance he was ready, she needed to be there.

The veterans she'd met on-site were all really nice. She still didn't understand why Dianna was so concerned about her working with them.

Granted, she hadn't met all of them, and there were new ones arriving every day. There was also that guy she'd nearly trampled who had seemed a little rough around the edges. He seemed to be holding onto something and refusing to share it with anyone.

It wasn't any wonder that he needed additional help.

She pushed open the door to the country club and glanced toward the group of veterans sitting in a circle with Kevin. He met her gaze and smiled briefly but immediately turned his attention to the group.

A quick trip down the hall toward Shane's office and she'd be able to head out for her daily ride. Her knuckles made a staccato sound against the wood door when she knocked. Shane glanced up and smiled warmly.

"Great! Just in time. Your client finally participated in group last week—the bare minimum—but at least he opened up."

Her eyes widened and she moved into the room. Heart beating a little faster, she took a seat and sat on the edge of the chair. "Really? So what does that mean now? Do I take him out riding and have him tell me how he feels? Has he got any training? Or do I need to start with the basics?"

Shane chuckled. "First, let's take a breath. Mr. Scott is a little skittish when it comes to therapy. You'll recall, he didn't want to come in the first place. When you begin your sessions, don't push too hard. I don't expect he will want to open up at all. Remember, this is an introduction to traditional therapy. A lot of the vets who end up here have refused help for a long time. It's not until they connect with an animal that they realize they need it after all."

She nodded. "Of course. Nice and slow. Like a timid bunny."

He grimaced. "I would suggest you don't use that term. It might come off—poorly. These men served our country overseas and in terrible conditions. They saw things we can't even fathom. Patience and kindness. That's all you need to provide for now."

Grace flushed, staring at the lines in her hands. She understood animals. That was easy. Men were a different species altogether. Her father had really done her a disservice when he'd kept her from dating during her teenage years. Now she was like a fish out of water—not that she was trying to date anyone

—she just had a hard time talking to them without sounding like a bumbling idiot. She lifted her gaze, willing her blush to fade, but it wouldn't behave. "Are you sure I'm ready?"

Shane shifted in his seat, leaning back and gazing at her with a thoughtful expression. "You're kind-hearted. You know how to listen. And best of all, you're the most non-threatening person I know. I think you're going to do just fine. These therapy sessions are mostly to let the men work through their own problems. Just—listen."

"I think I can do that."

"You'll have ninety-minute sessions daily. Mr. Scott is required to work with us for four months. If you can't make a session, please notify me so I can get a substitute."

"Of course."

He smiled reassuringly. "Your first session will start in about a half-hour." Shane reached for a file and flipped it open. "Looks like he's been assigned to work with Dolly. You can show him the ropes—how to put the saddle and bridle on. If you have time afterward, go on a short trail ride." He closed the file, then set a pair of serious eyes on her. "If at any time you don't feel safe, you notify me right away. We'll get you a replacement."

That last statement caused a fresh wave of nerves to assault her. Hopefully it wouldn't come to that. She had it in her mind that she would be able to prove herself. She could do this. It didn't matter that she was on the smaller size. She had a big heart, and she could handle herself.

Grace rose from her chair and offered Shane her hand. "Thank you for the opportunity."

He stood as well, shaking her hand firmly. "You'll do great."

MOST OF THE veterans around here were older. Each of them was probably closer to her father's age than her own. It wasn't that she was worried about working with someone who was older. She got along well with her father and his friends.

The thing that made her nervous was having to work with someone who suffered from experiences they'd had while serving her country. She still didn't know how she would be able to look him in the eye and tell him that he was going to be okay.

How could she say something like that?

Shane's words were the only thing that gave her comfort. Just listen. That's all she needed to do. Don't focus on their trauma; focus on the symptoms of the PTSD.

Grace squared her shoulders and lengthened her stride as she headed toward the barn. Warmth swallowed her whole the second she entered the building. She rubbed her cold nose and focused on the stall where her client was supposed to be waiting for her.

No one was there.

Her brows creased and she slowed, hesitating. Had Shane told her wrong? Buster and Dolly were each in their stalls. She continued down the aisle but didn't see any signs of someone waiting for her. Shane had to be mistaken.

Grace spun around and collided hard with someone who was much taller than her. The hat on her head tumbled to the ground and a gasp tore from her throat. Her hand flew to her chest as she looked up and met the eyes of the man before her. His familiar blue eyes pierced right through her.

She shivered.

"Callahan?" he muttered gruffly.

Grace nodded. "Mr. Riley Scott?" She peeked around him. Where had he come from? No one was in here a second ago. She swallowed hard and met his gaze again, a timid smile filling her face. "I guess I know why you didn't have a sponsor with you last week."

He grimaced. "Do you have to call it that?"

"Therapist then."

"Worse."

She pressed her lips together. "Then what would you prefer?"

"Callahan works." He edged away from her, putting quite a bit more space between them. "I'll call you that."

"You can call me Grace."

He studied her for a moment. "If it's all the same to you, I'd rather not. I'm not here to make friends. I'm here to complete my duty and then I'll be gone."

Shane wasn't kidding when he'd warned her about this one. It was clear Riley didn't want to be here. She reminded herself to keep a smile on her face as she tilted her head. "This is going to go a lot smoother if you'll just—"

"I'm not dangerous," he muttered.

"No one ever said you were."

"I don't need therapy."

She forced a small laugh. "Well, obviously not everyone agrees with you."

His dark blue eyes flashed. "This is my life, and while I agreed to come here for the next four months, I'm doing it my way."

Grace folded her arms, reminding herself that this outlook was to be expected. Riley would figure things out. She just had to give him time. "You can do whatever you want when it comes to the therapeutic side of things, but when it comes to the horses, you have to follow my rules or you're going to get hurt."

He huffed. "Like how you nearly broke your neck last week?"

Of course he would try to throw their first encounter at her. He wanted control.

Grace scooped her hat from the ground and dusted it off, then brushed past him. "You're completely right. I'll go let Shane know you would like a more seasoned cowboy—"

His hand reached out, pulling her to a stop. She stopped and looked down where his large hand lightly wrapped around her upper arm. His touch was warm and gentle despite the way he'd caught her off guard.

Slowly, she lifted her gaze to meet his and cleared her throat before pulling away from him.

"Sorry," he said, with the rough edge gone from his voice momentarily. "I'm happy to work with you."

Eyes narrowing, she lifted her chin, hoping that he would notice that she wasn't willing to be pushed around. With pursed lips, she gave him a short nod and then motioned to the stalls where their horses were stabled. "Then let's get started."

Normally she could hear when someone walked behind her. But not Riley. He was as light-footed as a rabbit in the woods. It didn't matter how much she strained her ears; she couldn't tell if he was five feet or six inches behind her.

Grace slowed to a stop in front of Dolly's stall. When she faced Riley, she let out a yelp at his close proximity. Once she caught her breath, she reached for a brush and placed it firmly in his hand. "The first thing you do before you saddle a horse is give her a good brushing. This helps prevent any sores from developing. Make sure to get rid of any dust and dirt. Pay attention to her back and her girth."

He stared at the brush in his hand for a moment, then moved into the stall.

Out of the corner of her eye, as she brushed Buster, she watched as he meticulously ran the brush down Dolly's back. He murmured something she couldn't hear. It was sorta sweet, the way his features softened.

Riley looked up at her and she sucked in sharply, spinning until he couldn't see her face. Oh great. She wasn't supposed to stare. That was one of the big no-nos. That, and pretending not to see them.

She brushed Buster with a little more fervor, eliciting a snort from her steed. She relaxed her pace and rubbed his neck. "Sorry, buddy." A few minutes later, she snuck a glance in Riley's direction again.

No longer brushing, Riley rubbed his hand down Dolly's nose. He had a soft kind of smile on his face, and it was the most relaxed she'd seen him since they'd interacted the previous week.

Grace ducked her head back to Buster and completed her brushing. Maybe this wasn't going to be so bad after all.

3

iley

THIS WAS JUST GREAT. Not only did he have to do one-on-one therapy at this ranch place, but he also had what looked to be the most inexperienced person of the bunch as his therapist. There were all kinds of cowboys wandering this place and the owner couldn't find anyone better than a tiny woman.

Riley wasn't even sure she was equipped to handle the horse, let alone someone who suffered with PTSD. What was this country coming to?

There was only one good thing to come from this session.

The horse.

Dolly didn't have a temper at all, from what he could tell. She had the most soulful brown eyes he had ever seen. When he brushed her, she turned toward him, nuzzling his arm with her nose.

Okay, so maybe being here with the horses wasn't so bad. But that didn't mean he needed to sit and talk about his feelings. Talking wasn't going to change anything. It wouldn't bring back the people who'd died. It wouldn't ease the guilt that flooded his chest, making him feel like he was drowning before he even woke up in the morning.

More than once he'd caught her staring.

What did she expect? That he was going to sprout horns and turn into some kind of monster? That's probably *exactly* what she thought would happen. Well, she'd be disappointed because he wasn't a monster. Not even close. He would be amicable and do exactly what they told him to do. Then he'd get out of here, head home, and make sure he didn't drink so much.

That's what got him into this problem in the first place.

The scowl on his face deepened. How could a judge think that coming out here in the middle of nowhere and riding horses would do a lick of good? It would be hilarious if it wasn't so backwards.

The space grew quiet.

Too quiet.

The hair on the back of his neck stood stiffly at attention and he whirled around only to come face to face with Callahan's angelic face. Her arms were folded over the side of the stall and her chin was placed atop them.

Here it was—the moment she started asking her therapist questions. And if it weren't for the fact that those large green eyes were so clear and innocent, he might have told her right where to shove it.

Where the rain don't shine, that's where.

But that strange feeling returned with a vengeance.

People weren't supposed to behave like magnets. Human bodies were capable of so much, though. He probably shouldn't even be surprised that something about her seemed to call to him.

Wait. She was talking.

Riley cleared his throat. "I'm not in the mood to talk about what happened to me."

She smiled. But it wasn't a typical smile. The one she wore was like the ones his teachers used when he answered a question wrong in grade school. What had she asked?

He swallowed down a curse and turned his attention back to his horse.

But instead of pointing out his mistake, she moved on. "Have you always had a way with animals?"

Riley stiffened. The muscles in his arms twitched, flexing as if to ward off an incoming torpedo. "What kind of question is that?"

His brusque tone didn't seem to bother her. "Most people who come here like animals, that's all. Dogs are a big one. Do you have a dog?"

"No," he grunted. "I don't have time for a dog."

"Maybe you should reconsider."

Before he could argue with her on what it actually meant to not have time for something, she draped a pad over the wall that separated them. "We need to inspect this and make sure there isn't anything that could rub against Dolly to hurt her. You're putting your whole weight on her back and even the tiniest little prickly thing could cause major damage." She tilted her head and a thoughtful look crossed her soft features. "Kinda funny how we can draw parallels to our lives, don't you think?"

He clenched his teeth. If she was suggesting that what he went through equated to a tiny prickly thing, then she was more out of touch than he thought.

The look on his face must have been enough to make her reconsider her words because the woman wouldn't stop talking.

"What I mean is that there are things that we realize will harm us and yet we don't remove them from our lives. You know, like triggers. I bet there are a few things that really just get under your skin, huh?"

"Like you."

Her features faltered.

There was a small part of him that felt bad for what he'd said. Hadn't he just told himself he would be the model example of how this was supposed to go? He was supposed to keep his head down and stay out of trouble.

All it would take would be for this woman to go running to the boss and he'd get in trouble.

He nearly apologized, but something held him back. She wasn't talking to him because she cared about him. This was her job. She clocked in and clocked out just like anyone else in this godforsaken town.

The pad was clean, free of twigs and burrs, which was what he assumed she meant by prickly. Rather than ask her how to put it on, he focused on how she placed it on the back of her horse. It was a few inches away from the base of the horse's neck.

With the pad placed on the horse, he waited for her next instructions. She didn't speak as she wandered around the back of her horse, keeping her hand on his rump. It appeared she was checking how even the pad was, but heck if he knew. She might just be avoiding having to say another word to him.

Next, she strode out of the stall and headed for a wall upon which hung several saddles. Should he follow? Was she even going to tell him what to do next? Irritation flooded his chest, poisoning his otherwise mild attitude. "If you're not thick-skinned enough to deal with a guy like me, then maybe you're in the wrong profession."

She peeked at him before yanking a saddle that probably weighed more than her from the wall. "This isn't my job." Callahan brushed past him, still carrying the saddle. He nearly reached for it to help her out but thought better of it.

"What do you mean, this isn't your job? Shane hired you, didn't he?"

"*Technically.*"

"Then this is your job."

She tossed the saddle onto her horse's back and then faced him. "This is a temporary gig I took on to help out my sister's boss. I didn't have to do it. I wanted to. You might not believe me, but I have a deep respect for anyone who is willing to risk his life for my freedom. I'm here to help. But if you don't want it, then you might as well leave now."

"I can't. It's court-ordered."

"I assume it was court-ordered in lieu of something else. If this place is so bad, then go find a different solution." Her voice wasn't demeaning. It wasn't harsh or judgmental, either. But it was firm and demanded respect.

Suddenly he felt very small. He might not agree with what this place offered. He definitely didn't believe it would help him whatsoever. But he could at least try to be accommodating. Ticking his jaw from side to side, he folded his arms and put all his weight on one foot. Even if he had a choice to go somewhere else, he'd have a hard time bringing himself to do such a thing.

He could do so much worse than dealing with Callahan on a daily basis.

Riley let out a groan and his hands dropped to his sides. "Fine. I'm sorry."

"I didn't ask you to apologize," she said, turning back to her horse. "I don't think it's appropriate the way you've been talking to me about what I do here, but you're entitled to your opinion."

"Then what do you want me to do?"

She didn't move right away. He continued to stare at the back of her head, wondering if she was so uncomfortable she couldn't meet his eyes. Then finally, she glanced over her shoulder. "I want you to try."

"*Try?*"

"Try," she repeated. "You obviously like the horse. If I had to guess, I would say that you probably would enjoy most if not all of your time here if you'd be a little more open-minded."

"Try," he muttered. The word left a sour taste in his mouth. To try would mean that he would have to believe this would help him to some degree. He glanced at the brown horse in the stall he'd just vacated. Callahan had a good point about him liking animals. They didn't judge. They didn't pretend to understand what he'd been through. If *trying* meant he didn't have to deal with a *real* therapist, then maybe it would be worth it.

He rubbed the back of his neck and faced the wall of saddles. They were all different and yet the same thing. How was he supposed to know which one he was supposed to choose?

"I take it that you are willing to do what I ask?"

Riley shot a look at her out of the corner of his eye. "I never said that."

"You're not riding Dolly today if you don't at least agree to answer my questions while we go for our first ride."

The breath he released felt heavier somehow—like it was a form of dense gas that didn't have the chemical makeup to float. Instead, the second he released it, he could practically imagine it sinking to the ground at his feet.

"One week." He half-expected her to argue with him, tell him that wasn't good enough.

But once again, she surprised him.

"Sounds fair enough." Her voice came from directly behind him, causing his heart to jump-start. He tensed and his jaw clenched. "You really shouldn't sneak up on a guy in my position."

"Who's sneaking?" She pointed to a saddle closest to him. "Get that one. Check it like you did the pad, and then put it on your horse. Make sure the pad is equal on both sides, and if it isn't, *don't* drag it against her hair. You have to lift it or you'll agitate her skin." She spun around and headed back toward her horse.

Even after his gruff nature, after his rude words, after his body language practically yelled at her to keep her distance, she didn't seem scared. Grace Callahan was a force to be reckoned with, and it wasn't all that difficult to see it.

While she might appear soft and sweet on the outside, she was strong, like a lighthouse in the storm. She didn't let him ruffle her feathers—something that might serve to be good or bad in the future.

Good or bad for what?

He grabbed the saddle and moved toward his horse.

It wasn't like he was here for anything besides his court-mandated therapy sessions. He wasn't going to let this Callahan woman get under his skin. It had taken years to meticulously build the walls he had around him. It would take a lot longer than one day talking about horses to make that fortress crumble.

4

———

 race

GRACE TIGHTENED her grip on the reins she held to quell their shaking. She'd known this was going to be hard. From the very beginning, her family and even Shane had made statements making her wonder if she was capable of doing this job.

Her whole life, she hadn't met a person who was so intent on being left alone. It made sense. She couldn't fault him for his feelings. But there was a small part of her that *had* hoped he would have at least been okay with just interacting like acquaintances.

She wasn't so dumb to assume this was how he treated everyone.

He just didn't want to be *here*.

Grace wasn't proud of it, but when he'd called her a trigger that got under his skin, she nearly walked away right then. The only thing that kept her there was her own stubbornness.

It paid to be a Callahan in this situation.

The cold nipped at her cheeks as they took one of the open trails around the property. She knew she couldn't ask him intrusive questions. At this point, she wasn't sure what they would talk about if he wasn't up for actually making conversation.

Stability.

That's what Shane had said she was offering. Listen to him, offer stability, and no judgment. Should be easy enough.

"So?" his gruff voice broke through her reverie. "Are you going to get started?"

Grace glanced at him. "We have."

"No. I mean, are you going to ask your questions and then tell me how I should feel?"

Her brows furrowed. "Is that what you think this is about?"

"What's it that you call it? Right. *Breaking*. You break horses. You find a wild horse, an animal that doesn't want to be tamed, and you put a saddle on it. Then you force that animal to go against every instinct it has ever had. You make it listen to you so you have an obedient little machine that you can ride to your heart's content. That's what you're trying to do out here, aren't you?"

She could argue with him, tell him every single reason he said was wrong. She could insist that he didn't know what he was talking about. But she didn't. That's not what this was about. He was lashing out like he'd been doing since he'd arrived.

Her heart ached for him—for the person he used to be before he'd walked through his own personal hell and came out on the other side, unwilling to trust anyone. But that was just what was on the surface. This went deeper.

Grace took a deep breath and focused on their surroundings. "You're not a horse to be broken. You never will be."

He huffed and she ignored it, praying for guidance in how she could phrase what was in her heart.

"Did you know when a horse is broken, it just means it's safe to ride?" She glanced at him again. "What you are referring to—the obedient horse—that comes with training. However, we're not making mindless robots out here either. There's a relationship between a rider and his horse—a bond. I think you might understand that part of things, even if it is only a little."

Was he upset? His silence wasn't expected. From what she'd experienced so far, Riley was usually quick with a retort about most things. Right now, he didn't even wear that stone-faced expression.

He caught her staring and she offered a smile.

Just like that, his expression darkened and his jaw set tight. He didn't say anything, but she could tell his fury rested just beneath the surface.

Chills swept through her body and she let out another sigh. She'd made another mistake somewhere along the way. In theory, she was ready to help him get past the hurdles he was dealing with.

Actually helping him in real life was another story altogether.

They rode in silence for a few more moments. At some point he'd pulled behind her, making it hard to observe him while he rode Dolly. With each passing minute, her muscles tightened. She could feel his eyes on her like he was surveying the situation and preparing something.

But their ninety-minute session ended up being uneventful. They made it back to the barn and she walked him through the steps to remove the saddle, brush down his horse, and give her a reward.

Those were the moments he seemed to let his guard down more. He continued to speak to the horse in quiet, calm tones.

His touch was gentle and his features softened. Riley preferred the company of his animal more than he wanted to spend time with another human being.

Her heart continued aching for him. The lines on his face showed exhaustion and frustration. His experiences had hurt him. While he had a rough exterior, she had managed to catch glimpses of something that ran deeper.

Something sharp and festering flickered to life deep down. It was short-lived, but she'd felt it. She wasn't *angry* with him. That wasn't what it was. It was something else. A helplessness, maybe? A yearning to be that thing that could break through the walls he'd built around himself? He treated that horse better than he treated the people around him, and there was just something depressing about that.

He glanced up at her, once again catching her staring at him.

Oh great. Why did that keep happening?

Grace tore her eyes away from him, attempting to shift her thoughts to something happier. Unfortunately, that didn't seem likely. Riley's face had been burned into her mind, a problem to be fixed. She knew if he would just open up to her, he'd feel so much better.

"Can I ask you something?" His curt voice ripped a hole in the serenity that had once surrounded her. He was right behind her, the stall wall the only thing that separated them.

She peeked at him over her shoulder. "You can ask me anything you'd like."

"How old are you?"

This time she turned to face him. Her age was probably the only thing that she was insecure about. She was well aware that she was the youngest one out here working with the veterans. Shane had initially offered to let her work with the children, but she refused. Her eyes narrowed and she folded her arms.

"When I said you could ask me anything, I didn't mean something personal."

"How is your age personal?"

She thought she saw a hint of a smile, but upon giving him a closer look, she realized that wasn't possible. "Anything you might want to use against me, I would consider personal. This therapy is for you to do the talking."

"Well, I'm talking now."

"Yeah, about me."

"Some people would consider that an improvement based on how much we talked while we were out riding," he shot back.

She pressed her lips together tightly. "Tit for tat, Mr. Scott. You tell me something, and I'll answer your question."

This time one corner of his mouth lifted. "Fine. I'm thirty-two."

Her brows creased and she moved closer to him so there were only about two feet between them. "But you're a retired veteran."

"Yes," he drawled. "Is there a problem? Am I not allowed to be here if I'm not over the age of fifty?"

She shook her head. "I knew you were younger. I guess I just thought you had to work a certain amount before you could retire from the military."

"I served my country for fifteen years. Is that not enough?" There was a bite to his tone, the humor completely disappearing.

Grace shook her head and moved forward another inch. "You must have really started young."

"I was seventeen when I signed up for the US Army." He said it like he was trying to defend himself for his life's choices.

If only he knew that she had no intention of judging him. Stating that out loud would only serve to put distance between them again. She'd finally gotten him talking, and there was no way she'd jeopardize what little progress they'd made.

"Your turn. How old are you?"

Doing her best to show him he didn't scare her, though at this point nothing could be farther from the truth, she squared her shoulders. "I'm twenty-two."

And just like that, the walls came up. He scoffed at her, shook his head and moved back to Dolly's side. "I knew you were young, but I didn't think you were *that* young. Are you even legally allowed to be working with me?"

She shot to the edge of the stall she was in and nearly flung herself over the wall. "I have a bachelor's degree in psychology and I went through training to be here. I'm not a traditional therapist, but I'm more than capable of helping out someone who thinks they're too good to just *talk*."

Grace clamped her mouth shut, her face turning bright red. She'd lost her temper. It was a small outburst and nothing like what he'd dished at her, but it was still against the rules. She was supposed to show him that he could trust her. She needed to create a safe space. And she'd just destroyed whatever progress they'd made.

Riley kept his back to her while he worked at brushing Dolly down. His shoulders were stiff and he wasn't arguing back.

Well, if she had already messed this up, she couldn't make it any worse.

"You think that just because you can manage to live day to day with your dark thoughts, that you're okay. Well, let me tell you something. *None* of us is okay. You might have a deeper kind of trauma. And you might be entitled to feeling like you're this outcast that no one will ever understand or know what you've been through, but you're doing that all on your own. There are hundreds, if not thousands, who are just like you.

Maybe you should take a good, long, hard look in the mirror and ask yourself if you're happy."

She huffed and moved to the stall door, yanking it open and slamming it shut but only successfully causing Buster to react. She'd have to apologize to him later, when Riley Scott was no longer in hearing distance.

Pausing in front of the stall where Riley stood, she couldn't help herself. She threw one more accusation at him. "If you're so okay, then none of this would bother you. And maybe, just *maybe,* you would be willing to look outside of yourself and realize you could do a lot of good. There are people who have been through exactly what you have and they could use someone to talk to."

Grace stormed down the long aisle toward the barn entrance. She didn't have anyone else she was supposed to work with. And at this point she didn't even know if she still had a job here anymore.

Not likely.

She could see it all now. Riley would storm into Shane's office and demand that she be removed as his sponsor. He'd tell her boss that she shouldn't work with anyone anymore because she couldn't handle one statement about her age.

The worst part was that Riley was probably right. She shouldn't have been so quick to anger when it came to that particular issue. What had gotten into her? She was *qualified.* She knew better than to lower herself to his level. She let out a groan and a growl at the same time, stomping her way toward the parking lot when she realized she hadn't driven to work that day.

Smart move, Grace, she chastised herself. If she called her father to pick her up early, he'd know something was up. There was no way she would go back to that barn to get a horse to ride when Riley was still there. Her only option was to find a place to hide out in the country club until the time when her ride arrived.

Grace had prided herself on being the level-headed one— the person in their family who could see the bigger picture and not react right away.

What was it about Riley that had gotten under her skin so easily?

It wasn't him. It couldn't be.

She was probably just insecure and not quite ready to work here. That had to be it.

Instead of going into the club and finding a seat at a table, she made a beeline for Shane's office. She might as well tell him now before he had a chance to hear from Riley just how bad it had been.

Grace pushed open the doors and plopped down onto the chair facing Shane. "I quit."

He didn't react immediately like she'd expected. Shane was rather predictable. He'd either get concerned that she was upset, or he'd get upset that she was breaking her commitment when he needed her most.

But she was wrong.

When she'd arrived, he'd been reading something on his computer screen. His eyes darted to her, void of surprise, which had taken her off-guard, but she'd quickly recovered. Now he leaned back in his chair, studying her as if he could read what had just occurred out in the barn with Riley.

"Does this have something to do with Mr. Scott?"

She pressed her lips together. For once, she wished she could lie. To tell Shane that Riley had said something or done something to make her want to leave would be so much easier than admitting she couldn't control herself.

Lying wasn't an option.

"Yes, but not in the way you might be thinking."

Shane steepled his fingers together and rested his lips against them. He sat like that for what felt like an eternity, then he dropped his hands and leaned over to pull open one of the drawers in his desk. He retrieved a folder and dropped it onto his desk with a flourish. "Mr. Scott can be difficult to work with."

She shook her head. "No, you don't understand. This wasn't his fault. It was mine."

His brows creased and his eyes narrowed. "Would you care to elaborate?"

Heat exploded in her face, making her feel like she'd been shoved into a sauna. She dropped her gaze to avoid his scrutiny. "I lost my temper."

Shane lifted a brow and his lips quirked upward. "*You* lost your temper." He said it like he didn't believe it was possible, which only made the heat in her face intensify.

"*Yes*. I did. I got short with Mr. Scott and there's no excuse for it. I have the education and the training to know better. I shouldn't have—"

"And you want to quit because..."

She threw her hands in the air as she stood up and paced in front of his desk. "Because he's going to come through that door any moment and tell you that I'm not capable of working here. I'd rather quit than get fired."

Shane chuckled. "What if he doesn't? Come through that door and ask that you get fired, I mean?"

"Oh, he'll come. I know it. He doesn't want to be here, and he definitely doesn't want me to be the one to help him if he stays. I'd be happy to stay if you still want me to, but you'll have to assign me to do something else. Maybe I can exercise or train the horses with Sean."

Shane slowly rose from his chair and moved around the desk. He placed his hands on her shoulders and offered her a smile. "I think you're right where you need to be. *If* Riley comes to see me to request a new therapist, we'll figure things out at that time. Until then, you make sure you come back tomorrow for your next session."

Her heart still pounded with all the sensations that continued to battle for attention. The anger, irritation, anxiety, worry, and disbelief were sucking up all the oxygen in her lungs. She fought the dizziness that tried to flood her mind and closed her eyes.

"Grace," he said quietly.

She opened her eyes, hating the way Shane could make her concerns slowly melt away when she felt like she needed to hold onto them, despite the way they made her sick to her stomach.

"I'm not going to force you to stay if you don't want to. I can find another therapist to work with Riley if pressed. But if we can make this work, I'd prefer that he sticks with someone he's already gotten to know."

"That's just it, though. He doesn't know me."

"He knows you more than anyone else here."

Shane was right. Riley hadn't really interacted with anyone else that she was aware of. The steps the vets went through before seeing a therapist followed a pattern. She took in a deep, calming breath, then let it out. "Okay. But if he comes in here to ask for someone new, I think you need to give him what he asks for. Don't try to convince him he's wrong. He won't like that."

He chuckled. "I think I can manage that."

5

RILEY PACED in front of Dolly's stall and pulled out his phone to check the time. Callahan was supposed to be here for their appointment in two minutes.

Unless she quit. That was a possibility.

Though, if that were the case, he would have thought that someone would have told him. It seemed like bad business for him to just be sitting there, waiting when his therapist wasn't going to arrive.

He checked the time again. One more minute and he'd be heading over to that office to demand an explanation.

Was he too harsh the other day?

No.

He'd gone over the conversation again and again. He'd definitely hit a sore spot with her, but he was well within his right to have such opinions.

Riley muttered an expletive just as the numbers on the

clock shifted. He would have left yesterday and never looked back if he had known this was what would end up happening. He knew better than to believe a bunch of people who insisted they could take care of his court-ordered therapy.

Glancing once more at Dolly, he murmured, "Sorry, girl. Looks like we're going to have to wait on our session." He turned toward the door and a shadow filled it. The person was a good several yards away, but he would have recognized that silhouette anywhere.

His heart hammered a little harder but shifted from the fury he had felt before to something else entirely.

Callahan hadn't quit. Though technically she was about a minute late. Back when he signed up for the Army, if he had been even a second late, he'd end up on the ground doing reps.

Riley leaned against the stall, his arms folded. She was lucky he hadn't given up and had a talk with Shane about her tardiness.

She passed him, not looking at him directly.

Still sore over their last conversation? Probably. His eyes followed her as she entered the stall beside him and grabbed a brush from where it sat on a shelf. She kept her back to him, brushing with more purpose than anyone ever should.

Riley hesitated. Maybe he should apologize.

He wracked his brain for everything he'd said. Had he been overly harsh? He hadn't thought so, but now that he was thinking about it, he couldn't be sure. She didn't seem mad. But then, these people weren't supposed to act mad.

Getting the lashing yesterday had been the one time during their session that she seemed normal and not so much like a robot. Riley headed into the stall with Dolly and went through the process that he'd done the day before.

Every so often, he glanced over to Callahan and his frown deepened. What did she want from him? She hadn't uttered a single word. Finally, he let out a sigh. "Well?"

She looked at him over her shoulder. "Well, what?"

"Aren't you going to start?"

Callahan shook her head. "Nope."

"Why not?"

She stopped, faced him, and placed her hands on her hips. She didn't look upset. In fact, there was no emotion present in her expression. She could be furious or thrilled and he wouldn't know. "I'm not going to force you to do something you don't want to do. I was wrong yesterday in asking you to try. Do what you want. Say what you wish. I'll listen. If you have any questions about the horses, I'll answer them. How does that sound?"

Yesterday he would have thrown a little party. That would have been exactly what he wanted.

Today?

Today was different. He didn't like this new person who stood before him. This shell of a woman who didn't smile and didn't give him a piece of her mind. He wanted that therapist back.

That realization hit him like a load of bricks.

He actually wanted to stay.

And he wanted the person working with him to be her.

Riley cleared his throat and shifted closer to her stall. But words failed him. He wasn't good with explaining himself, not like he probably should be. Just the thought of saying something to her about his feelings made his stomach drop, but not in a good way. His chest tightened and his breathing accelerated like he was back out with his squad chasing down a target.

To admit that he wanted to actually work on something was to admit defeat. He still thought it was a load of bull. Talking didn't fix things. It wouldn't change the past. Deep down he knew it wouldn't help.

But he was stuck here whether he liked it or not. He might

as well make the situation as tolerable as he could. That meant keeping Callahan as his *sponsor*.

Bleck. He still hated that word.

She stared at him expectantly.

He forced a smile and raked a hand through his hair, his gaze darting to the side. "I joined the military when I was seventeen. My dad kicked me out of the house when I told him." Riley let out a dry chuckle. "He was *not* pleased."

Riley pivoted and yanked a brush from the shelf and immediately set to work grooming Dolly. The last thing he wanted to do was get a look at her face and see the pity there. That's how it always started. Over the last fifteen years, he hadn't managed to find even one woman who didn't immediately tell him she felt bad for him.

He didn't need that.

He didn't want it either. Joining the army had been a way for him to take back the power he thought he had lost. But no one he'd met saw it that way.

"Sounds like you were willing to go after something you believed in, even if it meant making an insurmountable sacrifice," she said.

His head snapped up and he stared at her, but she'd turned away, back to brushing Buster. "Yeah," he mumbled. "Yeah, I did."

"That's not a trait you find a lot these days." She glanced over her shoulder and offered him a faint smile. "Did you ever regret joining the army? Especially considering the feelings of your family back home?"

He shook his head and continued using the brush, letting the swishing sound continue to soothe his heart rate. "It was an honor to serve my country, to fight for freedoms others don't get." That didn't mean it wasn't hard a lot of the time. "I joined in the spring as soon as I could. After the attacks in New York, I knew that's what I wanted to do." He peeked at her. "There was a lot of camaraderie back then—when the country pulled together against a common enemy. I guess I still feel that today."

It had been years since he talked about when he joined the army. It was a different time back then, and every soldier he worked with over the years had varying memories of that day. Kids joining the military these days did so for *other* reasons.

Money, early retirement, benefits.

Those who wanted to serve for deeper reasons were few and far between.

"When did you retire?"

Riley refused to meet her eyes, though he could feel them boring into the back of his head. They were finally both to a point where they could relax and just have a conversation. Maybe the problem had been him this whole time. He tipped his head side-to-side, stretching his muscles. "About six months ago."

"Was it hard becoming a civilian again? I hear it's hard."

He fought the instinct to close up again and push her away. She hadn't asked anything he wasn't prepared to answer. But the more questions she asked, the harder it was to believe she wouldn't at some point ask him something too intrusive.

Riley forced his churning stomach to settle as if willing it to happen would solve all the problems he was quickly realizing he had swept under the rug. "Sometimes yes. Sometimes no."

Thankfully, she didn't pry.

Releasing a breath of relief, he glanced toward her. "What about you?"

"What *about* me?"

"You grew up around here, right? What was that like?" He needed the attention off him. One step at a time. He shared, and now he needed to be done. Hopefully she could understand that.

Callahan nodded. She faced him and placed her wrist on

her hip, holding the brush in that hand. "My mother passed away shortly after I was born. I don't even remember her. Being raised by my dad on a ranch, you'd think I'd turn out like some kind of hillbilly." She let out a laugh.

The sound was like sunshine and wildflowers. Her face flushed and she looked away. "But you know? I think it all worked out. I didn't have the easiest father to live with either, but he's getting better." She tilted her head slightly. "Do you have any siblings?"

He shook his head. Besides his father, he didn't have any family—just one more reason why people in his life pitied him. "You?"

"Six sisters."

Riley about choked. His eyes widened as he sucked in oxygen that had been withheld from his lungs. "You're kidding. You're not in one of those religious cults, are you?"

She laughed again. The sound was utterly delicious, feeding his soul in ways he never thought possible, and he found himself planning ways to hear it more often. "No." She snickered. "I *am* a Christian. Though I suppose there are some people who consider any organized group of people a cult." She peeked at him, the smile from yesterday returning. "You ready to go for another ride?"

He couldn't remember the last time he *didn't* feel tightly wound. He'd been so on guard for so long that having even one brick removed from the wall he maintained around him offered so much relief. Riley returned the brush to the shelf and dusted off his hands. "Sure."

She gestured toward the pads and the saddle. "Let's see how much you remember from yesterday."

～

Despite the whole state of Colorado being in a perpetual state of dull gray-green since the last snowfall of the season, the world felt a little brighter, a little lighter.

Riley hadn't been brainwashed. He wasn't going to credit this place with that change of thinking. It was just a nicer day. The sky seemed a little bluer. That was all. Life would soon spring anew, the vibrant greens of springtime arriving just around the corner.

He took in a deep breath and released it. At some point his eyes had closed and he allowed himself to be surrounded by the sounds of this place.

The clopping sound of the horses' hooves, the occasional bird, the rustle of the nearby bushes. The farther they got from the country club, the more relaxed he became.

"That's a really good habit to get into."

Callahan's voice sounded almost timid. But what did he expect? They hadn't exactly started out on the right foot.

Riley opened his eyes, and that overwhelming peace dissipated, reminding him where he was and what he was doing there. A gray fog returned to his mind and he glanced in Callahan's direction. "What?"

"Meditation." She didn't even miss a beat.

He rolled his eyes. "You know meditation is something someone made up so people would pay them to do nothing while they sat in a room listening to bells or whatever the heck they recorded, right?"

She didn't laugh. He couldn't tell if the return of his sour mood was because of his own internal problems or because he didn't get to hear that laughter he found he enjoyed so much.

Instead, she offered him a smile and shook her head. "I suppose we can agree to disagree on that one."

They plodded along in silence for a few more minutes. He nearly thought this was how their whole ride would go, but then she spoke up again.

"I'm curious, why is your therapy court-ordered? I mean, you don't have to answer that question if you don't want to." Her face flushed and she looked away. "I know I'm not supposed to ask any super personal questions."

Riley worked his jaw. That was actually one question he didn't mind answering. But it was something that would open doors to more questions—there was not a doubt in his mind about that.

Was it worth the risk? Could he open himself up to her on this and just hope that she wouldn't pry further?

A sigh burst from his chest and he tightened his hold on the reins. The even clip-clopping of the horses seemed to soothe him more than he would have ever expected. "I was arrested for disorderly conduct."

The utter lack of response was deafening. It might even be worse than her asking a hundred more questions about him. He was almost willing to spill all just so she would start talking again.

Almost.

Instead, he slouched in the saddle and scowled at the trail.

"Once, the sheriff caught my sister sneaking into a bar when she was underage. He threw her in a cell and called my dad."

"You're joking, right?" Riley turned to glower at her only to find her fighting back a smile. "You are joking." Mild irritation anchored deep within him. This wasn't a game. He actually had a court date.

Callahan shook her head. "I'm not joking. And while it might be the worst thing—"

"Worst thing? I just told you about my court appearance and why I've been saddled with this sorry excuse for penance, and you tell me a story about your teenage sister being locked up for a few hours?" He'd lost the ability to keep his tone light.

"You don't know my dad." She straightened in her seat and

moved her horse closer. "Let me give you some perspective. My father practically raised us by himself. Up until last year, he wouldn't let any of us out of his sight—well, no dating. We could go to school and church and all that. The rule was I couldn't get married until all of my older sisters were married."

He huffed. "Sounds like your dad was just trying to protect you."

"You forget there are seven of us."

That gave him pause. "Okay, so he was being a little over-protective. If I thought it would help my daughters from not getting scooped up by the latest sorry excuse for a human being, I might do the same."

"I'm the youngest."

He glanced at her. "Oh."

She let out a heavy sigh. "So, you can see that if he was so *protective* that he wouldn't let us out to even go to a school dance, then what do you think he did when he found out my sister was in a prison cell for trying to pass off a fake ID in the next town over?" Callahan snickered. "Boy, was he mad. My father actually had one of his ranch hands sit outside the front door for a whole week straight just to make sure she didn't sneak out."

"Did she?" He couldn't help it; he'd been sucked into this story as if against his will.

"Oh yeah. Brielle doesn't think we know it, but she's up to all kinds of mischief. I think I even heard my father refer to her as the mustang of the group."

"You don't seem the type to sneak out." His statement was more of a musing. She was ten years younger than him, but somehow it didn't feel like that long of a stretch.

"You'd be right on that." Her cheeks blossomed with a pink color that only accentuated her eyes. "I guess I'm just happy with what I've been given. Sometimes we have to take a step back and find the things we're grateful for." Her smooth features pinched and her eyes darted away. "I'm sorry. That probably sounded preachy. I'm not suggesting that you don't have gratitude or that you aren't being grateful—"

"It's fine." He'd never admit it to the likes of her, but she had made a decent assumption. He had a hard time looking on the bright side. It was part of his diagnosis. After dealing with some of the stuff he'd gone through, he just didn't see the point in any of that.

race

ONE WHOLE WEEK.

Grace had been arriving for their scheduled therapy sessions for an entire week and she still couldn't seem to get past his defenses. She knew just as much now as she did last week.

Riley was a single child to a father who didn't agree with him signing up for the military. He served fifteen years and was charged with disorderly conduct and given early retirement.

Beyond that, he hadn't opened up much.

There were moments when he made her feel like she was just a silly little girl, which only made her want to talk less. How was she supposed to connect with him on a topic she knew nothing about?

That was why she sat in Shane's office before her session today. He'd been out chatting with one of his employees and told her to wait for him. But the longer she sat in his empty office, the more she felt like she was being ridiculous. She had the education. She had the training.

Telling Shane she didn't feel equipped to work with Riley was like saying she didn't think she should even be working here. What did that say about her? One week and she wanted to quit?

She shot out of her seat, prepared to slip out and tell Shane she'd figured everything out, but then he entered the office and shut the door. His hands were full of files, and he had a genuine smile on his face that seemed to make his eyes that much brighter.

Working for Shane had been more fun than she had expected. The job wasn't just being someone for Riley to talk to. It was more than that.

Risking losing it all wasn't something she was prepared to do.

Her eyes followed Shane as he walked around her and toward his desk. "Now, what can I do for you, Grace?"

A lump snagged her throat and she shot a fleeting look toward the door. How could she play this off as a mistake? What could she blame her being here on?

"Nothing. I was just—"

He gestured toward the seat she'd just vacated. "Have a seat. What's going on?"

Slowly, she lowered herself into her chair and forced a smile. This was a mistake. She shouldn't have come. She should have known better than to think she'd make a difference in one week. But now that she was here, there didn't seem to be anything she could do to change it.

Heaving a long, slow breath, she stared at her hands. "I wanted to talk to you about my client."

"Mr. Scott? Oh, that's right. I was going to call you in to talk about him."

Her head snapped up and her heart fell over itself.

Great. What had Riley been saying about her? He probably complained about her being judgy. That would be the biggest thing. She wasn't supposed to even suggest that the clients needed to change their outlook, especially not this soon. They needed to come to that opinion on their own.

Might as well rip off the Band-Aid. She'd done her best, but it wasn't good enough. "I'll understand if he wants to see another therapist—"

"What? No. That's not it." Shane dropped his file on the desk and pulled out his chair. "I had a nice talk with him the other day, albeit short." The chair creaked with the effort it took to hold a human body. Shane leaned back in his seat and clasped his hands behind his head. "There was only one thing he wanted to tell me, no matter how I tried to change the subject and check in on how he was doing since he'd arrived.

Pins and needles were a drastic understatement.

Shane didn't appear to be upset or disappointed at all. If anything, he appeared thoughtful. "I don't know what you've been doing, but it's working."

So many emotions and sensations burst through her body at the same time. Her heart stopped and started all at once. Her breathing hitched and her stomach dropped. "Pardon?"

Shane shrugged and leaned closer to his computer. "Yeah. I asked him how things were going. He said they were going as well as could be expected. When I pressed for more information, the only thing he said was that he liked you."

She blinked. It was the only thing her body could do to react to his statement. Riley liked her? She hadn't done much of anything for him that she could tell.

Her boss chuckled. "Don't look so surprised. I knew you would make a good fit for him. It just took some getting used to."

"I'm pretty sure he just doesn't want to have to wait for a

new sponsor to be assigned to him. You remember the last conversation we had."

"I do."

"Riley—Mr. Scott is only here to fulfill a requirement. If he had it his way, he'd be out of here faster than a horse shot from the starting gate."

Shane's gaze lingered on her for a moment at the use of Riley's name. Then he turned back to his computer screen. "That may be. However, his group sessions have seen a mild improvement as well."

Grace leaned forward and her eyes widened. "They have?"

He nodded and faced the monitor in her direction. There were several little notes taken by Kevin regarding Riley's participation. His first two weeks, Riley refused to talk about anything. Now he was commenting on what others were discussing. "He might not be opening up about his own traumas, but he's giving validation to the people around him. That's a good sign."

She sat back in her seat and folded her arms. That *was* a good sign. He was relaxing, allowing his walls to come down even if it was just for a little while.

"I'm sorry. What was it you wanted to discuss with me today?" Shane chuckled. "Sometimes I get so wrapped up in something I forget that there are other things that need to be touched on."

Grace shook her head. "Nothing. I was just checking in."

Shane smiled. "Great. Let me know if there's anything else you need."

She nodded, getting to her feet. Her whole body felt numb, as if she'd been shot with a stun gun. It was a miracle she could even walk at all. Her perception of how her sessions were going was utterly different from Riley's, and it made her realize one thing.

She didn't have to be so careful about what she said to him.

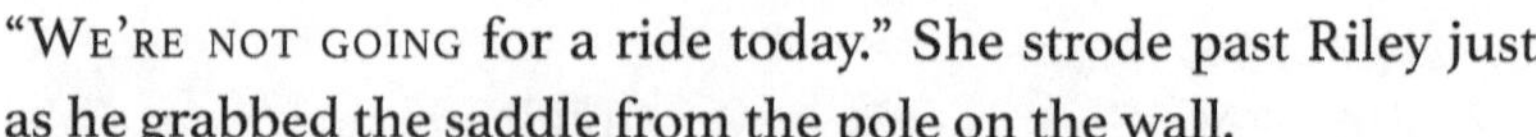

"WE'RE NOT GOING for a ride today." She strode past Riley just as he grabbed the saddle from the pole on the wall.

His head snaked around, following her as she reached for a lead rope. "We're not? But I thought—"

"Nope. We're going to have some fun."

"Riding is fun," he argued as he put the saddle back. "Riding is actually something I look forward to every day."

Grace tossed him a lead rope and grinned. "This is going to be more fun than riding."

His features pinched and he scratched his head. "I'd rather ride if it's all the same to you."

She let out a groan. "Come on. There are more things we can do with our horses than ride them. You've got a good handle on the grooming and saddling. Now, let's get to know Dolly the way you ought to."

His jaw was set, but he didn't argue with her. He lifted the lead rope and waved it at her. "And if this isn't as *fun* as you claim it will be? Then can we come back here and saddle them?"

She rolled her eyes. "Where's your sense of adventure? Just put the lead on her and let's get going to the arena."

Brows lifting, he looked toward the door as if he'd be able to see the arena building from where they stood. She hadn't taken him there yet. Mostly because it was being used by people who couldn't handle a daily ride.

Grace pushed open the stall door and wandered down the aisle, not bothering to look back at Riley to see if he was following. The only indication that he did was the additional sound of the horse hooves hitting the concrete of the stable.

The walk in the cool air was short-lived. The moment they entered the building, a burst of warm air hit her face. She removed her jacket and draped it over a bench near the bottom of the bleachers. Then she waited for Riley to catch up to her.

Once he was by her side, she held out her rope. "Hold onto Buster for a second. I'll be right back." She took off toward a storage door on one side, unable to wipe the smile from her face. She grabbed onto a large inflated ball that was half her size and threw it into the arena, then tossed another one.

Confusion was plastered all over Riley's face and he frowned. His gaze followed the balls as they bounced and rolled to a stop as if they had a life of their own. Dolly was the first to bob her head and shift her weight. She pawed at the ground, which only added to Riley's hesitancy.

Grace laughed as she jogged toward him. "You can unclip them now."

"What? You want me to let them go? I'm sorry. Do you actually expect me to believe these horses will behave like dogs? What do you think they're going to do with those balls?"

Breathless, she laughed again. "Dogs aren't the only animals who know how to play. Trust me." She took Buster's rope and nuzzled his forehead. "You're excited to have a fun time, aren't you?" Then she unclipped his rope.

Buster immediately galloped toward the nearest ball. He lowered his head and nudged it forward. The lightweight toy bounced and bobbed against the dirt floor. He trotted after it, then nudged it again, but this time ran around to block it from moving too far.

Grace stood beside Riley. Her arms were folded and she glanced up at him with a little grin on her face. "See? Horses aren't too different from any other animal. They like to have fun just like the rest of them."

His lips were parted, hanging open in shock. "I don't think I've ever seen anything like that."

"No, I don't suppose you would have."

Riley faced her. "Seriously. I didn't think horses could do much of anything besides be trained to ride."

Dolly let out a sharp breath between her lips and tossed her head. Riley jumped as if realizing that she was still there and she was missing out on all the fun. He jumped into action and unclipped the lead rope.

His horse was off like a shot. She chased down the other ball, pushing it forward and darting in front of it.

For the first time since she'd met Riley, she heard him chuckle. He wore a grin similar to her own. When his features were relaxed this way, it was a lot easier to see the man behind the angry mask. He wasn't a veteran who had a chip on his shoulder. He wasn't hurting or dwelling on his past. He was present. Not only that, but he was actually really handsome.

Her stomach flipped and she pulled her gaze from him.

Inappropriate.

There was more to this man than his looks; even she could see that.

Her attraction to him was childish at best. It was just a crush. He was ten years older than her, for heaven's sake. It didn't matter that they could spend time together in comfortable silence or have small talk. Even if the age difference wasn't an issue, he was a client.

Her face burned beneath the surface and she set her jaw tight as she watched the horses.

Just a silly childish crush.

Dolly kicked at the ball with her front leg and it rumbled toward them. Riley chuckled again and rolled it back. These antics lasted most of the session, and Riley barely spoke to her.

The old her would have thought she was still doing something wrong. But now she understood a little better. Riley needed a safe place so he could start tearing down the walls he'd created.

Once the horses tired out, they walked them back to the

barn. Rather than talk to Grace, Riley focused on talking softly to Dolly. A heaviness in Grace's heart gave her pause. As she watched him with his horse, she almost felt jealous. But that was ridiculous. It was just one more bit of proof that she was letting her fantasies get away from her.

Grace put away the ropes and the brush and then waited on a bench outside of the stall for Riley to finish. He was sweeter with his horse than a lot of the cowboys around here. The way he took his time to brush her gently and speak to her tugged at Grace's heartstrings even more.

Deep down he was a softy.

Riley stepped from the stall and froze. His eyes met hers and the softness of his expression faded into something unreadable. "What?" he grunted.

She got to her feet and shrugged. "Nothing. I'll walk you out." She turned, doing everything in her power not to let her feelings affect her. The last thing she needed was for him to know she liked him. She'd probably never hear the end of that.

And another thing. She needed to work on not staring at him, too.

He hurried after her, his voice gruff. "No. Not Nothing. What's the matter? I can tell you're hiding something. You know that, right? I was trained to read people."

That did it. Her face burst with heat. She turned to look over her shoulder, away from him so that he couldn't see *that*. "Really. I was just waiting for you. That's all."

His hand landed on her shoulder, successfully stopping her from being able to turn or walk away. Seeking any form of escape, she set her gaze on the ground.

"Did I do something wrong?" His voice was quieter now, so much so that she snapped her head up to meet those blue eyes of his.

"No. Of course not."

"Then what's the matter?"

"*Nothing.* For heaven's sake, Riley. I was just waiting for you to be done so I didn't leave you in there alone." Why couldn't she get this blush to dissipate? They were out in the cold now; she should be able to get some kind of relief.

He didn't look convinced. The way his eyes narrowed as he studied her, she could tell he wasn't going to give up easily. He wanted to know what was going on. She couldn't blame him. He had trust issues. It was understandable that he'd want to know everything upfront.

Grace gnawed on her lower lip and forced a smile. "You want to know why I was staring?"

"That's why we're standing here, isn't it?"

"I thought you were good with her—Dolly, I mean. You clearly adore her."

"She's just an animal."

She shook her head. "It's more than that. You have a strong capacity to love, and it shows." That was probably too forward —too on the nose. Once again, her skin betrayed her and she blushed violently. "I know we've been over this before. But I'm here for you. You can tell me anything without judgment. You don't have to hide any of it, and I won't tell anyone either."

His brows lowered. "If I don't like dealing with my past, why would I want to put that burden on someone else to carry?"

Before she could answer, he strode away toward the cabins.

One more reason for her to like him. He would rather suffer with his own demons alone than ask someone else to live through them. It wasn't healthy, but it was chivalrous in its own little way.

7

———————

Riley

THE SMALL CABIN was nicer than a lot of the places Riley had stayed in before. It only had one bedroom, but there was a quaint little kitchen nook and living room attached. If he didn't have a small apartment back in Denver, and if this place wasn't reserved for clients, he might have liked to stay. It was cozy, calming, and made him feel like he could hide away from the world.

Riley pushed his foot into his boot and tied the laces. He stared at his shoe. Even though it wasn't the exact one he wore when he was last deployed, it was similar enough to dredge up some of the old memories and the craving for some whiskey to go with it. He winced, shoving the darker ones aside. It was better to focus on other things. That was why he was here, wasn't it?

No more booze. No more dark thoughts. The whole concept

was laughable—until Grace had made him start to believe otherwise.

She was getting to him. Riley had to admit that first before he could figure out a solution. Why did she have to be there at every turn with something smart to say? He was quickly losing his battle to keep a handle on what he had locked inside.

Grace didn't want to know what he had hidden. She was kind and patient and... innocent. She was everything good that he didn't have, and he refused to drag her to the depths of the despair he dealt with on a daily basis.

Day after day, he got closer to spilling something about himself that just wanted out. That couldn't be normal. Who was he kidding? It *wasn't* normal.

Sure, one day he might find someone who loved him for who he was, and he'd love her. They'd grow closer and he'd end up telling her some of the things that kept him up at night. Grace wasn't that person.

Grace.

When had he started referring to her that way instead of by her last name?

Strange. Using her first name actually felt *right*. He attempted to shake off the thought, but it wouldn't leave him alone.

Would it be so bad to use the name she told him to?

Yes. Because it would weaken that line of professionalism he'd drawn in the sand.

Grace—Miss Callahan was barely a therapist, but that was what she called herself so that was how he'd treat her.

And clients couldn't be interested in their therapists. There was some kind of rule about that. Just because he was getting attached to her didn't mean he wanted something more from her. Except when he grabbed his jacket before leaving the cabin, he couldn't deny the way his heart skipped just for a moment.

It was okay that he looked forward to seeing her. He didn't have to blame this change on anything. Generally, people who struggled with depression could make it better when they had a change of scenery.

That's all it was.

The dirt path was worn and led straight past the barn. He'd get there before Grace did, as usual, which allowed him to spend additional time with Dolly. The closer he got to the building, the heavier his thoughts from their conversation the other day weighed on him.

Grace wanted him to open up to her—to tell her how he felt. Even if he thought she could handle that kind of conversation, he didn't want to saddle her with any of it. There was already so much pain in the world. It was better for him to deal with this the way he always had.

Riley stepped into the barn and froze in his place. Grace was already there. She had a different horse saddled, one he hadn't seen before. While she smiled at him, she didn't look too happy about what she was about to do. Immediately, Riley's defenses went up. He edged closer, slowly. "Where's Dolly?"

"Dolly is our introductory horse. She's meant to give us a feel for what your needs are. She's been at this for years. This is Maple, and she's going to help you to identify your feelings."

Riley stiffened. "I don't need to identify my feelings. I'm not a child!"

Maple's ears swiveled back and forth swiftly and she yanked against the lead rope. Grace glanced at her and patted her neck. "It's okay. You'll be fine."

His heart rate increased even more. "I keep telling you. I don't need therapy. This is ridiculous." Riley folded his arms. "I'm not doing it."

Maple snorted and pawed her hoof to the ground.

Grace smiled sweetly and handed Riley the reins. "If you can get Maple out to the corral and do a few laps, I'll let you have Dolly again. She needs some exercise today since she hasn't been out yet."

"Fine." Riley pulled on the lead, prepared to stomp out of the barn, but the rope went tight and he stumbled back a step. Turning, he found Maple stubbornly standing her ground. "Come on, Maple, let's go," he muttered.

She tossed her head and her ears continued twitching.

"I don't think she wants to go with you," Grace said.

"You think?" Riley shot her a dark look. "Funny, isn't it? When people don't want to do something, they push back. Guess horses are the same."

Grace leaned her shoulder up against a pole and tilted her head. She nodded to Maple. "What do you suppose she's feeling right now?"

Riley threw his hands into the air. "I don't know."

"Look at her. How is she behaving?"

"She's being obstinate."

"That's an accurate observation. Wonder why."

Riley let out a frustrated sigh. He knew what she was getting at. She was pointing out that the horse was being difficult just like he was.

Grace continued, "One of the reasons we use horses in therapy is because they don't usually hide anything. They can mirror our behaviors. You're just trying to help her. Exercise is good for her. And you're just doing what I've asked in helping to facilitate that. So why is she being obstinate?"

His shoulders drooped and he willed his heart to calm. Taking a deep breath, he really looked at the horse. "She's being stubborn. Maybe she doesn't know that it's good for her. Or she just doesn't like the way I'm leading her."

"Both good observations. She can sense your anger and aggression. When that happens, she digs in her heels. Maybe you need to try a different approach."

Riley moved closer to Maple, holding out his palm with

slow movements. He clicked his tongue and murmured, "Hey, girl. How about we try again?"

Her ears twitched forward, then to the side. He rubbed her nose and then moved to run his hands down her neck. Maple pawed at the ground once more, then stepped forward.

Riley shot a surprised look at Grace. "No way. It can't be that easy."

She lifted a shoulder. "Maple is special. She's been trained to set boundaries. She won't do anything with someone who is showing outward signs of aggression or anxiety. Labeling what you're feeling inside is important to the healing process."

His jaw tightened and he moved toward her with Maple following closely behind. He had the training. He could show outward patience and calm. "You want to know what I'm feeling inside? What I deal with on a daily basis?"

Grace pushed away from the pole to stand straight, but she still had to look up at him. "That's why you're here, isn't it?"

Riley took a deep calming breath. "Depression. Guilt. Anxiety. Oh, and lest we forget, anger. There? Happy? I can label how I'm feeling at a given moment. Does it *fix* anything? No."

He said all of that with a cool voice, then brushed past her toward the corral. He'd like to say she pushed him into a corner, forcing him to admit all of that, and it only infuriated him more. But surprisingly he didn't feel any more or less upset about any of it, which was unexpected.

Grace didn't push him to speak to her anymore. She watched from the sidelines as he took Maple into the corral and had her trot some laps. Each time he stewed, Maple could sense it, and it was harder to get her to continue her laps which only proved that Grace had been correct. Maple made him more attentive to how he was feeling. What should have been a quick ten-minute exercise ended up being three times as long.

"You can let her wander," Grace called out. She climbed up

onto the bars that separated him from her and perched there, beckoning him to come over.

He unclipped the rope and trudged over to her, resigning himself to the knowledge that once again, he was proven wrong. "Before you say anything, I know."

She tilted her head in that way that both infuriated him and made him want to... want to what? Whatever it was, it took him off guard.

"I'm in a perpetual state of aggression or something."

"I didn't say that."

"You didn't have to. Maple made that perfectly clear." He leaned against the bars beside her and dragged his focus over to the horse. "I don't know how you guys do it—training a horse to behave that way."

"We didn't have to. It's something in her nature. Most horses have that instinct. Some more than others."

He looked in her direction, then brought his focus back to the horse. "So what now? You want me to talk about my *feelings*? You proved me wrong and now you get to make me do something else?"

She snickered. "You make it sound so bad. *No*," she drawled, "I'm not going to *make* you do anything. Our work together will remain what it is. I simply wanted you to see what I see. Because your perception of yourself will differ from what others see. Maybe that's what the judge noticed. Maybe not."

He huffed. "That judge was being a—" He cut himself off. Calling the judge a name wasn't going to do him any good. He was stuck here. And any argument he made, he had a distinct feeling that Grace would disprove anyway.

The breeze around them ruffled his hair and helped cool his heated face. Riley heaved a sigh, breathing in the nature around them—the smell of an oncoming rainstorm, the new growth of vegetation, and a slight floral scent that could only have been Grace herself.

He peeked at her. "I guess I should apologize for how I've been acting around you."

Grace didn't move. She didn't look at him or make him feel small for admitting any of this. It was like he'd been making a big deal about nothing.

Riley knew better. This was a big deal. But the fact that she wasn't making it out to be warmed him. He took another long breath. "I don't think I've been truly happy for a few years." His voice shook and his chest constricted. He hadn't even told his therapist back home about these feelings. There was just something about Grace that made him want to connect, even if it was just a little bit.

This time she met his gaze. Her beautiful green eyes didn't land on him with pity. She wasn't concerned either. If he had to pin down the emotion that she held behind them, it would be affection. But that was even more ridiculous than him developing an attraction toward her.

His throat tightened and he tore his gaze away, staring at the dirt beneath his feet. He folded his arms and muttered, "But that's not going to change any time soon."

"Why do you think that?" she whispered.

"Because things don't work out for me. I've done things... things I'm not proud of. I'm just—let's just say I don't think God wants me to be happy."

"You know what's funny? I don't think God wants any of us to be *happy*."

He snapped his head around so fast he thought he might have given himself whiplash. His mouth dropped open, but before he could utter a word, she continued.

"God calls us to *holiness*, not happiness. By proxy, when we honor him with our good choices, we find happiness. That's what repentance is about, is it not? Changing our behaviors and learning from our mistakes so that we can grow and become better." Her eyes found his, a crease forming between her brows. "That's not to say that happiness isn't important. I'd say God doesn't want us to suffer either. It all comes back to having gratitude and finding joy however we can." She pulled her lower lip between her teeth and nibbled on it as if waiting for her words to sink in. "I guess the question here is, do *you* think you deserve to find happiness again?"

Emotion burned hot behind his eyes and in his throat. How was he supposed to tell her that he couldn't bring himself to forgive the things he had done... or rather, didn't do?

He broke eye contact and muttered thickly, "I don't know."

race

GRACE'S HEART ached painfully for him. It was in the quiet moments like this when she could almost see through the walls he'd put up.

Almost.

He wasn't giving her much to go on, but at least she had a starting point now. She could do something about the emotions he had bottled up inside. She just needed him to believe that she could make a difference. Talking about those kinds of things helped, if only to feel like he no longer carried the weight on his shoulders alone.

Her hand gripped the bars on either side of her legs. This was one of those times when she felt like she didn't have the proper words to help him. If he didn't think he deserved happiness, she would never be able to change his mind.

She wished she could climb down from her perch and wrap

her arms around him, tell him that even though it didn't feel like it, everything would get better.

Normally those kinds of conversations were easy. In the past all she had to do was point out the good in the person's life. If they had a family, a spouse, children—all of those were reasons to live for. On top of that, a job or their health was important to point out.

But as far as she could tell, Riley didn't have much he felt he could be grateful for—a notion that only made her heart sicker.

So instead of doing *anything*, she sat there like an idiot, wishing she could find the words to help him.

The air around them had turned sour. She yearned for the happiness from yesterday.

Grace climbed down beside him. She was so close she could almost feel the warmth coming off him. She folded her arms and shivered despite not feeling chilled at all. "What do you want to do with the rest of our session?"

She didn't look up at him, but she could feel his eyes on her all the same. Grace shifted under his stare, refusing to meet his gaze because she knew if she did, she'd be bound to say something else that wouldn't help.

"You're going to let me choose what we do?"

Lifting a shoulder, she let a small smile steal across her face. "Sure. I'd say you earned it."

He didn't speak right away. She almost thought he wasn't able to come up with something and she'd have to make a few suggestions. But then he surprised her. "*Anything*?"

She dragged her eyes up to meet his. "That's what I said."

"Could we postpone our session to later tonight?"

The hopefulness in his voice reminded her of that of a child. It was soft, and there was a hint of longing that rested beneath the surface. There was no way she'd be able to tell him no. Not with the sweet look on his face.

"What do you have in mind?"

"A sunset."

Her brows shot up and her stomach flipped for no other reason than because this was the most extraordinary request a guy like Riley could have made.

"It's okay if we can't. I'm sure there are rules and—"

"I'm sure we can get special permission. I'd have to talk to Shane about it. But if that's what you would really like to do, I don't see why not. I think it sounds like a wonderful idea. There are studies that suggest sunsets improve a person's mental state and relieve stress..." Her voice died off and she flushed. He didn't need any more reminders that he was here to get that kind of help. "You stay here with Maple. I'll run back to the club and check with Shane."

He turned away from her, focusing on Maple again. His voice grew gruff, edged with emotion. "Thanks."

She placed a hand on his forearm, a gesture of support but was taken aback by the muscular tension in his arm. Beneath the jacket, he was built like a cowboy. He probably could have been one in another life.

Grace yanked her hand back and let out a strangled laugh, then hurried away. That was a bad idea. What was *wrong* with her? Letting her thoughts run rampant wasn't allowed. If this was how things were going to keep going, she might have to consider a different path when it came to the therapeutic work she was doing.

The whole way to the club, she repeated in her head the rules she needed to follow. Number one being that she couldn't fall for the guy she was helping. Number two was that she couldn't fantasize about him either.

Her heart fluttered, her head argued, and her stomach knotted, causing the rest of her body to feel out of sync.

The worst part was that Riley hadn't even been here very long. She was going to be stuck working with him close enough that it would only get more difficult to focus on being professional, given her current track record.

She pulled herself to a sharp stop at Shane's door and turned around in a circle. How had she gotten here so fast? It was as if she'd been on autopilot the whole way from the corral. She couldn't even remember coming through the doors to the building.

Grace shook her head and let out a sigh before knocking on the door. Quiet voices drifted toward her, and then the door handle turned and Brielle materialized in front of her. Grace stiffened and her brows creased. "Bri? What are you doing here?"

Brielle glanced over her shoulder, then shut the door behind her as she stepped out of the office. "I had to visit with Shane about something."

Eyes narrowing, Grace shot a look at the closed door and a sly smile touched her lips. "That's still going on, is it?"

Her older sister rolled her eyes and pushed past her. "Absolutely not. I have zero interest in Shane Owens." She turned around, her hands on her hips as she faced Grace once more. "And don't you even think about spreading that kind of gossip. You'd be no better than all those women in town who can't think of anything better to do with their time than ruin the lives of young women like us."

Grace snorted. "You're not getting any younger."

A gasp ripped from Brielle's lips. "Grace! That's a terrible thing to say."

"Well, you aren't. Don't you think it's about time you figure out what you want and go for it? All of us have something we're doing now that Dad relaxed some of his rules."

Brielle shifted her weight to the other foot and folded her arms. "I don't have to do anything. I am perfectly content helping Adeline around the ranch. But in case you're wondering, I'm offering my services to the Keagans. Their ranch needs a lot of repairs. On top of that, it's a disaster inside. I'm helping Annabel get things figured out so they can be ready for spring."

"How does that have anything to do with Shane?"

"He's the one facilitating it—financially. I was just giving him some updates on how the projects are going."

Grace cocked her head, placing one hand on her hip. "Sounds to me like you're just looking for an excuse to come visit him. Are you sure you don't find him attractive?"

"Shane? Sure he's attractive. But there's no way I'm going to settle down with a guy who has more ego than I have shoes." She flipped her hair and strode away, leaving Grace to laugh at her.

Brielle wasn't going to last as long as she thought she would. If it wasn't Shane, she'd find someone else. The Callahans weren't made to grow up lonely.

Perhaps that was why Grace was suddenly finding herself infatuated with Mr. Scott. If that were the case, it would be an easy fix. She just needed to go on a date with someone.

Grace knocked on the door again, but this time she quietly opened it and poked her head inside. "Shane? Can I ask you something?"

He motioned for her to come in and placed the paperwork he had in his hand on the desk. "What can I help you with?"

"Riley—Mr. Scott would like to postpone the remainder of our session today to later. He'd like to take the horses out to see the sunset."

If Shane was surprised, he didn't show it. He studied her for a split second and gave her a short nod. "If you are able to fit that into your schedule, I see no problem with it. We have several great locations on the property that aren't very far at all. Just make sure to tell one of the ranch hands that you'll be going out so they can wait for you. I don't want you to get lost in the dark on the way back."

She nodded. "Thanks. Does it matter who?"

He waved her off. "Just whoever has the evening shift is fine."

Smiling, she pulled the door closed behind her. Riley would be so excited. A thrill erupted within her. She was going to see the sunset with Riley.

It wasn't a date.

The little voice demanded to be heard.

This is just part of your session. Not a date.

She *knew* that.

Okay, maybe she needed to find a real date so she could get this guy out of her head and stop feeling these wayward emotions.

Still, her heart skipped like a little girl coming home from her first day of school. The excitement was still there, however misguided it was.

"Good news," she called before she was even close, "Shane signed off on it. Sunset is around six-forty this time of year so we're going to need to have the horses saddled and ready to go no later than six-fifteen. Otherwise, it will be lost behind the mountains by the time we get to the lookout."

She arrived at the corral, breathless and rested her folded arms over the top bar. Riley's smile was even better than it had been in her head, and she couldn't help but feel like she'd been the sole reason it was there. She'd made his day and it had taken barely any effort.

Grace jerked her head toward Maple. "How about you bring her back to the barn, and I'll make sure everything is set for later tonight?"

He nodded and strode over to the horse. Grace felt lighter somehow. It was in her steps. Or maybe it was the way her heart felt like it had been let out of its cage. She could breathe easier now.

The barn lights were still on and only one ranch hand was working. She couldn't remember his name, but he was about her age. He glanced up when she entered and a smile split his face. "Grace. How are you doin' this afternoon?"

"Wonderful, how about you?"

"Oh, you know, stayin' busy." His focus shifted over her shoulder. "Where's your ward?"

She followed his gaze. "Oh, Riley's on his way. He's getting Maple. She's been exercised today." Swinging her eyes back to the young man in front of her, a thought popped into her head. Maybe he could be the one that helped keep her mind off Riley. Her face flushed warm and she offered him a small smile. "I'm so sorry, but I've forgotten your name."

He didn't even hesitate. "Don't worry about that. I'm still new." He wiped his hand on his coveralls and then held it out to her. "Sonny."

She shook his hand. It was warm and strong. Just the kind of handshake that she would have expected from someone who worked for Shane. But she didn't feel the spark she had felt when she'd placed her hand on Riley's arm.

Grace dropped her hand and pushed it into her pocket. "Do you by chance know who'll be working tonight around seven?"

Sonny nodded. "That'll be me. Why, do you need something?"

"I'm taking Riley out on a ride to see the sunset. Shane wanted me to let someone know in case we get lost."

A wry smile crossed Sonny's face. "I think Shane underestimates you."

She blushed once more. "That's sweet of you, but I think it's more for Riley's safety, not mine."

He chuckled. "Perhaps you're right. Sure, I'll keep a lookout for you."

"Thanks, Sonny." She turned and gasped, finding Riley close behind her. How on earth had he entered the barn with the horse and she hadn't even heard him? Sonny didn't even indicate that Riley had come in. Was she so twitterpated that she blocked out the most important parts of living out on a ranch?

Riley glanced from her to Sonny, then back again. "You want me to brush her down?"

She swallowed at the lump in her throat and pleaded with her body to behave. She didn't need to blush every single time Riley was nearby. Nodding, she gave him a tight smile. "That would be great. I have some work to do back at my family's ranch, so I'll meet you back here around six. I think we can get them saddled in fifteen, don't you?"

He shot another look at Sonny. "Yeah. That shouldn't be a problem."

She patted his upper arm as she moved past him.

Big, big mistake.

A strange electrical current seemed to flow from him into her at the point of contact. She sucked in sharply and continued walking. To stop and stare would have been to admit something had happened, and she wasn't willing to admit to that just yet.

Nope. Nothing strange was going on. Nothing at all.

As she reached the doorway, she slowed and set one last fleeting look on the man who seemed to have a strange hold on her. He wasn't paying attention to her, which was all the better. It gave her a moment to try to make sense of the churning sensation in her stomach.

Turned out that was a lost cause.

She might never figure out what was going on.

9

—————

iley

HOT, ugly, fiery jealousy sparked in his gut. Riley knew it from the second he experienced it. When he'd entered the barn and he saw Grace speaking with that cowboy, it was like a switch had flipped inside him. He didn't want to admit it, let alone would he ever act on it, but deep down he would find a mild amount of pleasure in running the kid out of town.

His cheek twitched and he shook his head sharply to ease the tick. Maybe he needed more help than anyone actually realized. He was developing an attachment to Grace—and an unhealthy one at that. What would Shane say if he knew?

He'd probably reassign Grace to someone else.

The tightness in Riley's stomach worsened. He couldn't allow that. His attachment was normal, right? She was actually the one thing besides the horses that he looked forward to seeing each day. If she got fired, he didn't think he'd be prepared to continue his sessions.

Riley glowered at the cowboy in question as the kid waved, walking past him down the aisle with a horse he was probably taking to the corrals himself. The kid immediately yanked his attention elsewhere.

Good riddance.

The funny thing was that Riley knew he wasn't supposed to care this much. He didn't even know if Grace liked the kid. They certainly looked to be about the same age. It would make sense for her to be drawn to someone who fit that description.

It also made sense for her to be interested in someone who didn't cart around all the baggage he had.

Riley gave an exasperated grunt and continued brushing Maple down. She snorted and her ears twitched as she shifted out of his reach.

"Hey," he muttered, "get back here."

She pawed at the ground and shifted again when he reached for her.

Great. Now the horse was being stubborn again, which only meant one thing. His emotions were showing.

Ridiculous. He glared at the animal. "I'm not mad at you, you dumb animal. I'm mad at something else."

She blew air out of her lips and tossed her head.

A groan left his lips this time. "I'm mad at myself, okay? I don't like what's happening." He leaned against the wall and slid down it into the straw. His forearms rested on his knees and he peered up at Maple. "You're lucky, you know that? You don't have to worry about anything besides your food, shelter and training." His tone softened a little. "What wouldn't I give to have that kind of life."

But then he wouldn't have met Grace. He wouldn't have the brief flickers of what could possibly be happiness.

He wouldn't hear her laugh or see her smile. He wouldn't be able to just spend time in the sunshine that she exuded without even trying. Maybe being human wasn't all bad.

A few minutes later, Maple seemed to settle down. Her ears weren't swiveling back and forth, and her restlessness had ebbed. She was like a living, breathing mood ring.

He got to his feet and inched closer to her, only somewhat surprised when she allowed him to touch her this time. It was still ridiculous, but he could see the perks to training a horse to do what she'd been able to.

Now he just needed to get a handle on these growing feelings for Grace that refused to abate.

AT ABOUT A QUARTER TO SIX, Riley sat crouched down in front of his motorcycle. The blasted thing was giving him trouble again. At this point he had no idea what it could be. One thing was for certain. He'd need to get it looked at before he drove it back to the city. The last thing he needed was to have it break down when he was halfway there.

Riley placed his hands on his knees and got to his feet. He checked the time, just like he had two minutes ago. Seconds continued to inch along until he could head to the barn to start getting Dolly ready.

The pounding in his chest mimicked what was going on in his head. When he'd suggested the sunset, he hadn't meant for it to be a date, but the more he thought about it, the more he wanted it to be—especially after watching that cowboy with Grace.

Pinching the bridge of his nose, Riley admonished himself. This was a session. Pure and simple. Grace would never blur the lines of their working relationship, which was also something that he admired about her.

Another look at the time and he'd had enough.

Riley swung his leg over the motorcycle and turned the engine over. After a few tries, it sputtered to life. He rolled it over to the side of the cabin to park it. Then he headed inside for a warmer jacket.

He could arrive early at the barn. Grace didn't have to know that he couldn't wait to see her. Riley shoved his hands into his leather jacket and trudged toward the barn. Even if he didn't start getting Dolly saddled, he could talk to her. Grace had been right about one thing; he really did like the horse they'd given him to start with. She was mild and sweet, and she didn't reflect the emotions he hated seeing in himself.

The property was considerably less crowded around this time. The lights at the country club were all lit and he could hear faint music coming from the building. He'd seen something about nightly music and refreshments. He wondered if Grace liked to attend those events or if she preferred to stay at home, seeing as that was how she'd been raised.

She probably had her pick of guys. She was pretty enough to be getting that kind of attention. The jealousy returned to his stomach, slithering like a venomous snake. If they weren't currently in the throes of a therapist-client relationship, he would have no problem showing her just what she could have if she picked someone like him.

Riley stopped, his breath ripped from his lungs when his eyes landed on Grace. She stood in Buster's stall, already prepping him for the ride. Her head lifted and those beautiful green eyes locked with his.

"Riley, what are you doing here so early?"

"I could ask the same thing of you." Oh boy. Even when she said his name it did things to him—things it really shouldn't. He cleared his throat and jerked his chin toward the door. "Sounds like they're having a party up at the main building."

She tossed the pad over Buster's back. "Yeah. I think they do that every night."

"You ever go?" Inwardly, he grimaced. That was a personal

question. Off-limits. He shouldn't be asking her about that kind of thing.

Grace didn't appear to be upset about it, however. "Sometimes. Shane plans these really fun Christmas parties. He has mistletoe hanging everywhere..."

It was like he blacked out the second she mentioned mistletoe. His eyes dipped to her lips and he found himself wondering what it might be like to kiss them, to taste them.

"You okay?"

He jumped. "What?"

"You look... a little pale." She tilted her head and came to the edge of the stall. "If you're not feeling well—"

"I'm fine," he blurted, "just distracted, that's all." Without further explanation, he darted into Dolly's stall and began prepping her for their ride.

He'd experienced these kinds of feelings before. There was only one way to remedy them. His gaze bounced to Grace, where she continued working only a few feet away from him.

Riley needed to get her out of his system. He needed to satisfy this curiosity he felt. The only problem was that doing so could ruin everything he actually cared about at this time in his life.

He let out a groan and tossed the pad over Dolly's back. She shifted but didn't fight back like Maple did. Even still, he knew better than to treat his favorite horse that way. At least now, he did.

Taking in a deep breath, he counted to five then let it out. Already he could feel the difference. The anxiousness dimmed though it didn't disappear all the way.

One more glance at Grace, and he knew without a doubt he needed to do something. He just couldn't figure out what, exactly. A kiss was too forward. But perhaps his hand could brush against hers. If he felt something, then he would have to deal with that when the time came. If he didn't, all the better.

Though a large part of him didn't think that would be possible.

They emerged from the barn as the sky was quickly shifting from blue to purple and red. Grace made a soft sound and he glanced at her, finding her staring at the sky.

When she met his gaze, she grinned. "You know, a lot of people talk about how pretty the sunrise is. How it signals a new day—a fresh start—but I prefer the sunsets."

"Why's that?" His stomach continued doing that dance which made him antsy. In all his fifteen years of serving in the military, the only times he could remember feeling this on edge was in the very beginning.

He wasn't a teenager anymore. He was a grown man who just happened to hate talking about his feelings. And there was nothing wrong with that.

Grace tipped her head back, showing off her slender neck. "Because a sunset signals the end of a day and a promise that the next one will be better."

Riley chuckled dryly. "I don't think you're getting that quite right."

She scoffed at him. "Well then, *mister*. Why do you like sunsets so much?"

He didn't even blink. "Because sometimes you can only find peace in the dark."

Boy, that sounded morbid. Riley wasn't about to take it back though. It was the truth—at least for him. When the sun went down and the world got quiet, he could let the void swallow him and let everything else fade away.

Riley avoided looking at her. She'd grown especially quiet. He'd scared her off. He should have known better than to show that side of him. Women didn't like hearing about the dismal stuff, not even the therapists. They listened out of obligation, nothing else.

His hands gripped the reins tighter and he nudged Dolly

into a trot, relishing the way the pain of his rump hitting the saddle could make him forget the strange feelings that churned inside him.

It was just his luck that he'd end up finding his therapist attractive. The one person who would be off limits was the one who seemed to have the magical powers to break through his walls.

Buster moved up beside him and Grace grinned at him. "That doesn't really look all that comfortable. I thought you knew how to ride better than that."

"It's a trot. There's no other way to ride."

She shook her head and snickered. "You stand up in the saddle instead of bouncing against it. Move *with* the horse, not against her.

"That doesn't make any sense."

"Well, then at least make her go a little faster. Just looking at you makes my backside hurt."

He couldn't help it. His lips curled into a grin as he watched her push Buster to a faster speed. The fluid way she moved was almost mesmerizing. She had this way of making it look purely magical.

Maybe he was being too hard on himself. What kind of guy wouldn't find her attractive? What kind of man wouldn't develop feelings for her after even one conversation?

He dug his heels into Dolly's flanks and quickly shot forward to match Buster's pace. Grace led them along the trail to wherever she planned to have this session take them with no complaints from him.

With the lack of conversation, his thoughts shifted back to those darker places. Someone like Grace wouldn't want to be with a guy like him. If she only knew...

Riley shook his head sharply and focused on the darkening sky, the way the wind whipped through the horse's mane. The way Grace's smile could brighten even the dimmest night.

The sky continued to change colors, and every so often, he'd lose track of what he was supposed to be doing. It was probably a good thing Dolly knew what was going on. Otherwise he might have gotten lost.

Clouds moved in, making the paint pallet in the sky that much more hypnotic.

Wait. They weren't just light, fluffy clouds.

These were storm clouds.

Just as he realized it, a flash of lightning skittered across the sky. His heart leaped into his throat and he shot a worried look in Grace's direction. "Maybe we should head back," he called.

She tossed back her head and laughed. "What are you so afraid of? I didn't take you for the kind of guy who was scared of getting a little wet."

He shook his head. "These storms are—"

"Have you forgotten I'm a local? That storm is farther away than you realize. It's gonna get caught up in the mountains and all we're going to get is some rain." She pulled her horse to a stop suddenly, causing him to have to slow and turn Dolly around to meet up with her again. She tilted her head to the side and her eyes danced. "You might think that the darkness is when you can find peace. But I challenge you to really see what it feels like to have all your worries washed away by a spring rain."

As if summoned by her words, a large fat drop of water landed on his hand. Then another and another. She turned her face to the sky and laughed again. Surprisingly, the rain was warmer than he expected. It was like they were in this bubble of cold temperatures but above them had been warmed by some supernatural force.

Warm drop after warm drop pelted him. The horses didn't seem to mind in the least. Grace's eyes remained closed and a small smile was plastered to her face. Her voice was quiet and he almost couldn't hear it over the sound of the water hitting the dirt beneath their feet.

"When things get tough, you know it will be okay when the storm clouds roll in."

He snorted, and she lowered her face so she could meet his gaze.

"Do you even hear what you said?" he said.

The smile didn't leave her face, and she just stared at him expectantly.

"Storm clouds are synonymous with bad things happening. Have you ever heard the saying 'when it rains, it pours'?"

She shook her head and looked up again. "You're wrong. Rain is healing. People say it symbolizes darkness, but it doesn't. It brings life and rebirth. Without it, you don't get roses or rainbows."

He stared at her dumbfounded. Once again, she'd put him in his place.

The rain shifted from drops to sheets and she let out a squeal. "Okay, *this* is a bit much." She held her hand over her head and met his gaze. "We should probably head back before either of us catches a cold or something. I'm sorry we have to cut our session short." She had to yell that last bit because of how loud the rain had become.

Riley nodded. She pulled her reins around, forcing Buster to head down the trail toward the country club. He didn't follow right away. Instead, he looked up at the sky, allowing the rain to wash over him. He heard her words echo in his head. *Rain is healing.* A shiver raced up and down his spine and he opened his eyes. He could almost feel the pain from his past being washed away.

Almost.

race

GRACE PEEKED at Riley over the back of Buster's saddle. He worked at brushing Dolly down in her stall. There was one good thing about tonight. She'd managed to get him to open up, even if it was only a little bit. He had some dark passengers that rode on his shoulders daily.

But within time, she knew she'd be able to help knock them to the ground.

He seemed more relaxed after they returned. She couldn't put her finger on it, but he was doing better somehow. It wasn't a big change, but things like this never were. She smiled to herself, proud of how she'd managed to listen to him and not make him feel like she was only there to be his therapist.

Well, that's how it felt at the moment.

No, she wasn't supposed to turn him into her best friend. But with people in his situation, it was better for him to think of her as more than just someone who was being paid to listen to him vent.

The sound of the rhythmic brushing was interrupted when Riley cleared his throat. She looked up and jumped, finding him peering over the stall. "Can I ask you something?"

"Of course."

"Those parties at the club. What goes on there?"

Grace lifted her mouth into a half smile. "Mostly it's just mingling and dancing. It's sorta the way we enjoy spending time together out here. When the weather warms up, they might start a bonfire, too."

"Do you..." He rubbed the back of his neck. "I think it would be nice if we..."

She arched a brow. It almost sounded like he wanted to ask her to go on a date with him. Her heart fluttered and she froze. That was definitely against the rules. She knew better, and she got the feeling so did he. So why was he asking her?

Riley blew out a breath and met her gaze again. "I'd like to go, but I don't know if I'm allowed. Would you mind coming with me? For moral support?"

Her brows furrowed. "Why wouldn't you be allowed to go? You're staying here. You're a guest. In fact, I'm fairly certain you get more perks because of that."

He lifted a shoulder and broke eye contact again. "I'm not really great in social situations. I don't... get along well with other people."

She let out a laugh. "I think you're doing great. But if you'd like me to walk you there, I would be happy to." Grace gestured toward her clothes. "I don't think I could stay due to the fact that I'm incredibly soggy."

His eyes trailed down her body and he grimaced. "Right. Of course. I wasn't thinking. We can go another time."

Grace closed the distance between them; the wall was the only thing that stood between them. "No. I think you should go. It would be good for you. Like you said, you aren't great around other people—" She grimaced. "I didn't mean to say that. What I meant was that this would be a great way to get some practice and spend time around people in a group setting."

"I get to see people in a group setting on a weekly basis. That's what group therapy is for."

She rolled her eyes. "That's not the same and you know it. Come on, I'll walk you to your cabin and you can change, then we can head over to the club before I go home."

"Will you come back?"

Grace smiled at him. She couldn't deny that it felt good for him to be concerned about her not being there with him. It was nice to be needed. But going to the club with him seemed to blur the lines of their professional relationship. "I don't know if that's a good idea—"

"As a support system," he blurted. "That's all."

She pulled her lower lip into her mouth and nibbled on it for a moment. "Maybe I can see if one of my sisters would be able to bring me a change of clothes."

His features brightened, and that was all it took for the flutters to return to her insides.

Grace really needed to do better about ignoring the things that caused that to happen.

Like the way Riley could smile at her. Or the way he would listen to her and actually pay attention to what she was saying. He was beaten down, but he wasn't broken, and she loved to see that he was actually attempting to improve during their sessions.

GRACE STARED AT HER REFLECTION. Brielle was the only one who was willing to bring her something to change into, and she'd managed to find the one outfit that wasn't all that appropriate for her to wear at a club with a patient.

Her dress was low cut, one she'd worn in high school. It was made of fabric that looked more like bandanas than anything else. And it showed off her curves. Since graduating from high school, Grace had grown more conscious of the clothes she wore. She'd grown up, and she didn't want people to look at her as just the youngest Callahan. She was more than that. She was smart and capable, and she already knew what she wanted from her life.

Grace sighed and turned to look at her profile. Well, she wasn't here with Riley on a date. He knew that she hadn't picked the outfit; it was probably going to be okay. She'd dance a little, get something to eat, and then be there to support him in case he needed someone to ground him.

At least the dress paired nicely with the boots. And Brielle had brought her a fresh hat to cover her damp hair. That didn't mean she was going to get away with this. Grace already had plans in place for her sister, and Brielle wasn't going to be thrilled about it.

She slipped out of the bathroom and headed toward the main area where all the guests were gathered. The upbeat country music met her first, and then the room opened up and showed all the guests who'd arrived for socializing. The bag in her hand weighed heavily, filled with her soggy clothes.

Immediately, her eyes found Brielle, who smiled at her and waved with her fingers.

Heat seared Grace's face and she grabbed the arm of the first man who walked past her. He stared down at her with surprise.

"Hi. I'm Grace."

He touched his hat. "Wade. Wade Keagan."

She nodded her head toward Brielle, who was no longer looking at her. "You see that woman over there?"

He glanced over his shoulder toward her. "Brielle?"

Of course. All the locals knew Brielle. Her reputation preceded her everywhere. Maybe her plan wasn't going to work after all. "You've dated her."

He chuckled. "No. Should I have?"

She brightened. "Oh. Well, maybe that's why I heard her talking about you."

Wade arched a brow. "She was?"

Grace nodded. "Absolutely. She thinks you're cute. She said that she wasn't interested in seriously dating, but if you were to ask her out, she'd definitely say yes."

He glanced over at her sister once more and a frown touched his lips. "You'll have to tell her sorry. I'm not looking for anything at the moment."

Grace's shoulders sagged. Well, there went that idea. He shifted to move away from her and her fingers tightened on his arm. "Maybe you could just ask her to dance at least once? I'm sure that would be more than enough."

Wade gave her a strange look. He knew something was up. That much was clear. He just didn't know what was going on. If he had, he'd probably tell her to go jump off a cliff. His brows furrowed and he opened his mouth just as Riley materialized beside them both.

Grace shot Riley an uncomfortable look and released Wade's arm. She crossed her arms over her chest, but it wasn't going to do any good considering the outfit she wore. "Hey, Riley. I was just going to come find you."

Riley's eyes ran up and down the cowboy in their group then he held out his arm. Grace smiled in spite of herself and accepted his offering. She looked up at Wade as she brushed past him. "Just think about it, will you?"

Wade touched the brim of his hat, indicating a farewell, but Grace never saw whether or not he ended up over at Brielle's side. Riley escorted her several yards away before facing her. "Was that guy bothering you?"

Her head reared back and she laughed. "Wade? No. *I* stopped *him*."

Riley glanced over her shoulder, presumably to find Wade and stare him down again.

She touched his forearm, bringing him back to the present. "I told him he should ask my sister to dance."

His features relaxed. "The sister who brought you some clothes?"

She flushed again. "Yeah. That sister."

Riley stepped back and let his gaze sweep over her, making her feel even more embarrassed. She folded her arms again and let out a huff. "She thought she was being funny. This isn't something I normally wear."

"I think it looks great."

It took a lot of effort not to let her jaw drop to the floor. But then she should have known he would say something like that. He was a guy, after all. She swallowed and willed her blush to fade, though based on the heat in her face, it wasn't going away anytime soon. "It's not professional."

He made a funny face and tipped his head slightly. "But you're not working."

"*No*, but I'm out with a client so I should be abiding by the guidelines I'm supposed to be following when I'm at work."

Riley leaned forward, his voice lowering. His mouth stopped mere inches from her ear and his warm breath caused hairs to stand up on her neck. "I won't tell anyone if you don't."

She jumped back from him, stumbling as she bumped against something. His hand shot out and grasped her wrist. Wow, his reflexes were like that of a cat. Grace stared at him for what felt like an eternity before she pulled her hand away from him and held up her bag. "I'm going to put this in Brielle's truck."

Grace spun around and charged through the crowded area until she made it outside. The rain-soaked earth immediately settled her nerves—nerves that shouldn't have been on edge in the first place.

What had come over her? She was getting into her own head about something that didn't matter in the first place. Riley wasn't interested in her. He was a good ten years older than she was. Not only that, but she was the person who was making his life miserable—through therapy. Why would she pretend that there could be something brewing between them? The idea was ridiculous.

She ran toward Brielle's truck and yanked on the door. It wouldn't budge. Of course it wouldn't budge. She turned around and leaned against it, letting her head hit the glass as she stared up at the darkened sky. To go back inside and get the keys from her sister would make her look like an idiot. She'd escaped that room like her tail was on fire.

"What do you think you're doing?"

Grace jumped at her sister's voice. Brielle stood a few feet away, her hands on her hips. The look on her face was murder.

"Did you just tell Wade Keagan that I was in love with him?"

Grace snickered. "I didn't say *love*. Is that what he said?"

Brielle threw her hands into the air. "How many times do I have to say this? I'm not interested in dating *anyone* right now. I've been there, done that, and I've lost my taste for it."

Pushing away from the truck, Grace set an irritated look on her sister. "I'm only giving you a taste of your own medicine."

"What is *that* supposed to mean?"

Grace gestured to her outfit with angry hand movements. "*Really*? *This* dress? Couldn't you have picked *anything* else?"

Brielle smirked. "Oh. Didn't you want to look good for your veteran client?"

A groan escaped her lips and she threw her head back with

frustration. "I don't need to look *good* for him. I need to look professional and capable. *This...*" she said and gestured again, probably looking more like a crazed bird than a woman, "makes me look like I'm about to throw myself into his arms and ask him to take me away from this place."

Brielle laughed. "You're right. That's exactly how you look. I didn't see it at first, but I see it now. It's awesome."

Grace stared at her sister with a flat expression. She didn't share her sister's sense of humor in this situation in the slightest. "How am I supposed to go in there and go dancing with him, or anyone else for that matter, and not get some of the weirdest looks."

Brielle shrugged. "Not my problem, baby sister. Maybe you should have thought about that before you asked me to bring you some clothes. You really should clean out your closet, you know. There's a lot worse I could have brought you."

"I doubt it."

Brielle lifted a brow. "Oh yeah? I seem to remember a time when you were really into My Little Pony. Aren't there a few onesies that still fit you?"

Grace gasped.

"See? I could have brought that."

She shook her head. "You know I wouldn't have worn it. I would have made my excuses to Riley and gone home."

Brielle snickered. "Exactly. I could have brought it, but I didn't because I wouldn't do that to the guy you're seeing."

"I'm *not* seeing him," Grace argued.

"Treating, seeing, same difference." She spun around and headed for the building.

"No, it's not!" She stared at the bag in her hand and called out again. "Hey, unlock the truck. I have to put my clothes in there."

The headlights flashed and she yanked open the door,

tossing the bag of clothes on the floor. The lights flashed again and the horn honked, signaling it was locked once more.

Grace stared up at the building before her one final time before she trudged toward the entrance. It wasn't her clothing that mattered. She could still look professional while wearing this dress. It was the way she carried herself.

Riley stood by a fireplace. Flames flickered within the brick box, dancing to the beat of the music. Grace stopped and watched him while he was unaware. He wasn't like the guys who lived here. That was for certain. There were several men here who were broody and unwilling to open up to the women they dated, but his quiet brooding was different.

Nope, there was something else that hovered beneath the surface—something she wanted to figure out. It was strange, the pull he had on her. It probably had more to do with the way she viewed him as a client. She wanted to dig deep and help him overcome whatever it was that had spurred him to be *disorderly* in the first place.

He must have felt her gaze on him because he spun around and his eyes locked with hers. She should have expected the reaction inside her. It had been happening a lot as of late.

Heart, lungs, stomach—all vital organs went haywire. She wasn't a rule breaker, and yet as they studied one another, she started to wish she was. What would happen if she allowed herself to get closer to him in that kind of way? Would it royally mess up his progress?

Or would it be just the thing to make him trust again?

Her stomach blossomed with heat and she clasped her hands behind her back tightly, if only to steady herself. He smiled at her and she moved forward.

The room and all the occupants disappeared like the stars in the sky as soon as the sun made its appearance. Riley took a few steps toward her and they met in the middle. The corners of his lips twitched. "That took a little longer than I expected."

"My sister's truck was locked and I needed the key."

He lifted his chin, understanding filling his eyes. Then he shifted his focus to the room. "This place is really busy. Does it always fill up like this?"

She followed his gaze. "Actually, I don't know. This is probably only the second or third time I've come."

Riley lifted a brow. "Really?"

Boy, she hated the way he could make her blush with just one word. Grace ducked her head, staring at her feet. "Don't forget my father and his overprotective nature. Events like this were a breeding ground for his daughters to find suitors so we weren't allowed."

He gently lifted her chin with the crook of his finger. The gesture was so simple and yet so much more intimate than she would have ever guessed. There was this spark where his skin touched hers that made her feel like her insides could start on fire at any second. And yet she remained frozen in her place. "Well, then, I guess we should take advantage of this opportunity. Would you like to dance?"

Her throat went dry and she couldn't find the words to let him down easy. Because that was exactly what she should do. He wanted her there as a support system. He didn't need a romantic interest. And she didn't want to lead him on, despite wanting nothing more than to explore the way he was making her feel.

Riley didn't wait for an answer. The second a slow song started, he reached for her hand from behind her back and tugged her toward the dance floor. He placed her hand on his shoulder, then put his at her waist.

There was no turning back now.

11

RILEY KNEW BETTER. And yet, he was ignoring the little angel on his shoulder anyway. He'd convinced her to come to the club under false pretenses, and he was thrilled with how everything was working out.

He should feel guilty. But that familiar twisty feeling had yet to return. He was allowed to enjoy himself. He was allowed to find happiness.

And if that meant he spent some time with Grace when she wasn't in therapist mode to get it, then so be it.

Grace lifted her other hand to his neck and they swayed back and forth. Around them, cowboys were leading their girls into simple two-step dances. He didn't quite measure up to those men. Not in his dancing talent, and definitely not in the way he viewed the world.

It was still a dark place, but Grace seemed to have helped

him find a way out of the tunnel he'd been trapped in since he'd returned from the desert overseas.

His muscles flexed and his shoulders were tight. Just because she was in his arms didn't mean he was able to truly relax. He'd been on edge from the moment he saw her speaking to that other cowboy about her sister. Their conversation had seemed strained even from a distance.

Then again, that might have been wishful thinking.

Riley had this strange inclination to protect her. It was probably a residual frame of thinking from when he served. It wasn't terrible. In fact, it made him feel closer to her somehow. He had a purpose again. He wasn't just a piece of driftwood out to sea anymore.

His focus shifted to the angel in front of him. She smelled like fresh rain and flowers. It was both sweet and earthy at the same time, and it reminded him of simpler times before he'd joined the army—moments when he'd been more carefree.

Grace wasn't looking at him. He couldn't tell if it was the close proximity or if it was something else. He'd most definitely crossed a line somewhere. Well, if she wanted to get away from him, all she had to do was take a few steps.

The fact that she wasn't running was a good thing.

Unless it wasn't.

"I meant what I said," Riley murmured. "You look great."

Grace peeked up at him. "You really shouldn't be saying stuff like that to me."

He chuckled. "Is there something wrong with being honest?"

She shook her head. "No, but we have to maintain this professional—"

Riley hated the way his heart sank to his knees. "Even people who work together can compliment each other," he said.

"I suppose you're right." Her lashes danced, fluttering as she peeked at him once more. "But maybe keep that to a minimum."

"If that's what you want."

"It is."

They continued to dance in silence. The music didn't seem nearly loud enough to cover up the pounding of his heart, and the dance would end sooner than he wanted it to. He had to get her talking. "Tell me about your childhood. Were you always good with horses?"

A small smile touched her lips, signaling that it was the right thing to ask.

"I've always loved riding horses. I've always loved animals."

"Have you ever considered being a veterinarian?"

Grace shook her head. "First, I have sisters who were already interested in that sort of thing and I wanted to stand out. Second," she said and grimaced, "don't judge me."

He shook his head. "How can you even assume that? Look at who you're talking to. I'm sure there are several more things that you could judge me for than I could judge you for."

Her smile returned. "Well, I can't stand seeing an animal in pain. You know how people who become social workers get burned out really early because they have to deal with children who are struggling day in and day out?"

Riley nodded.

"Well, I think I would get burned out by having to take care of hurt or sick animals." She let out a soft laugh. "Oh, and I despise needles."

"I don't blame you there." He joined in with her laughter. Then he sobered, returning to the comment she made about social workers. "But what you do—therapy—doesn't that burn you out?" He could very well be the cause of something like that. Normal people could only take so much negativity before they just couldn't anymore.

Grace cocked her head thoughtfully. "I suppose that is a

possibility. But honestly? I don't think so. Working with adults —people like you—gives me purpose. It makes me feel like I'm making a difference in the world. You will eventually heal from the pain of your past and get to live a fulfilling life. Some of those children will continue to struggle, and there's not much we can do until they leave home."

Riley's features faltered. He had been one of those kids. With his mother gone and his deadbeat dad barely making ends meet, he had to do a lot to survive. At the time it had felt natural—something he was supposed to do. But now he knew better. The difference in his situation was that he didn't view his childhood as something negative. He'd grown and learned a lot as a kid.

Her brows knit together and her hold on him tightened slightly, drawing his attention back to the conversation.

"Did I say something wrong?" she asked.

"What? Of course not."

"But you look like you're upset about something."

He shrugged it off. "I've seen a lot of bad in this world. It's not something I would wish on anyone."

And just like that, they came right back to the darker subjects. What was wrong with him? Why couldn't he just be normal? Had serving in the army ruined him so much?

No.

That wasn't it. He'd always been more serious, even as a child. He'd had to be.

Now, he was grown and he didn't have to worry about those kinds of things. He should at least attempt to be optimistic— especially if he wanted her to enjoy his company more.

"Tell me more."

"More what?"

He offered her a crooked smile. "Tell me more about growing up on a farm. Did you milk cows?"

Grace nodded. "I did."

"What about taking care of chickens?"

"Oh, they're terrible."

He laughed. "What else?"

She bit down on her lower lip, pulling his focus. Her lips looked so soft—so plump and inviting.

Stop it. Be better.

"I guess since I don't have much to compare it to, I don't know how to describe it in a way that would be interesting."

He opened his mouth with the intention of insisting that anything she might want to say would hold his attention, but the song ended and the couples broke apart. Another slow song started up, but before he could ask her for another dance, the cowboy from before tapped her on the shoulder.

Riley stiffened as Grace turned and lifted her eyes to their intruder. "Wade."

"Would you like to dance?"

She glanced at Riley with a smile. "Thanks for the dance. Maybe you could find someone else to partner with?"

He didn't have a chance to answer before Wade pulled her into one of those fancy dances. Riley's hands curled into fists. This was one of his many issues. He felt things so fully and with such ferocity that he could go from happiness to fury in a matter of seconds.

Taking a deep breath, he released it. Grace wasn't his date. Not really. He couldn't expect her to turn down an invitation to dance. But there was no way he was going to find a girl to dance with when the only one worth holding in his arms was in the arms of another man.

He strode toward the bar and asked for a beer.

A small voice in his head cautioned him.

Alcohol makes it worse.

If he could have a conversation with that voice, he'd yell at it to shut up. The occasional drink wasn't going to hurt him. He needed a buzz—something to help dull the ache he felt watching Grace dancing with a man who was taller and probably a lot more stable than he was.

Riley knocked back a drink, allowing the bitter liquid to race down his throat and coat his stomach in that heat that also dulled the senses. He slammed the bottle on the counter and asked for another.

Two. He could have two beers and be perfectly fine.

The buzz took effect shortly after. He hadn't had a drink in he didn't know how long. The judge had requested he take a break, and he'd done just that.

Social drinking wasn't going to ruin anything. It just made it easier for his body to succumb to the heat and relaxation the alcohol would provide.

The second the slow song ended, he expected Grace to walk off the dance floor, but instead, she stood there with the cowboy. Their conversation was taking far longer than was necessary.

It might have been the beers talking, but Wade looked like he wasn't enjoying the conversation. Riley peered at them. Wade was definitely not being the gentleman he should have been. Grace turned to leave and he reached out to stop her.

That was all it took.

Riley stormed across the room and stood between the cowboy and Grace. He wasn't entirely drunk, but he wasn't as sharp as he usually was. He probably shouldn't have knocked back two drinks so quickly.

He poked Wade in the chest. "You don't touch her like that."

"Riley!" She tugged at him. "It's fine."

Wade laughed. "Who are you?"

"I'm her date."

"*Riley!*"

Wade shot a look at Grace. "Sure seems like she doesn't agree with you."

Riley puffed out his chest. "I asked her to come. She said yes. I'd say that makes her my date."

The tall cowboy folded his arms. "I asked my sister to come. Does that mean we're on a date?"

"If the boot fits."

"For heaven's sake. I'm so sorry, Wade. Thanks for the dance. Sorry about earlier." She grabbed Riley's forearm and tugged him off the dance floor and toward the side of the room where no one stood nearby. She set angry eyes on him. "What has gotten into you?"

He shot a dirty look over his shoulder. "Wade shouldn't have touched you that way."

"What way?" she asked with exasperation. Her face was flushed, and he could only assume it was because she hadn't had the best interaction with her dance partner.

"Want me to go back over there and put him in his place?"

"What? Of course not. Are you drunk?"

"I'm getting there." He paused and thought over the words he'd just said, then laughed. "I mean, no. I had two beers, but it's not a big deal."

"You can't be more than a hundred and sixty pounds. Do you even know what happens when you drink that much alcohol in such a short time?"

"I was a pretty heavy drinker. Alcohol doesn't react the same way in my body as it does to other people."

She looked absolutely adorable with her hands on her hips and he leaned closer to her.

"You're cute."

"So you've said," she grumbled. "I think we need to get you back to your cabin. It's probably not a good idea for you to be here like this."

"Like what? I'm fine. I want to dance with you."

She looped her arm through his and moved across the

dance floor and toward the back door. "I don't know what you were thinking when you took those drinks—"

"I was jealous."

"Jealous of what?"

"I didn't like the way that guy was looking at you." They exited the building and he took in a deep breath. "You were right, you know."

She let out a sigh.

"Rain is kinda nice."

"If I had known that you talk so much more when you have a few beers, then I would have given one to you sooner." Her tone was light and teasing. Maybe he hadn't ruined everything.

He leaned closer to her. "Alcohol makes it worse."

"Makes what worse?" Her brows furrowed. The farther they got from the main building, the harder it was to read her expression.

Riley didn't answer right away. Just thinking about her question was all it took for his emotions to take a dive into darker waters.

"How does drinking make it worse, Riley?"

He scowled and pulled away from her, shoving his hands into his pockets. He picked up his pace, not caring that she had to jog to keep up with him. The buzz was gone. The anger spread like a virus from the top of his head to the tips of his toes. Flashes of memories from his time in the service tore at him, hooking their claws into his heart and dragging him back to the pit of misery he'd been in when he'd arrived here.

Grace touched his arm. "Riley, talk to me. What's going through your head right now?"

He jerked away from her touch. "Don't pretend you know me. You're only here because you *have* to be."

She stopped as he continued to storm down the path toward his living quarters. That's what alcohol did to him. It loosened his tongue and it made him feel deeper. Those memories were the most important part of him—the thing he couldn't shake. It was everything he hated about himself, and if he let it go, then what would be left?

A shell.

Riley made it to the cabin and stormed inside. Grace wasn't brave enough to follow him. That, or she didn't care enough to finish this conversation. Either way, he needed to stop fawning over her. She wasn't his and she never would be.

12

———

race

ONCE AGAIN, Grace didn't know if she should have even arrived for her session on Monday afternoon. Friday night's strange conversation raced through her head over and over throughout the weekend. Riley didn't reach out to her—but no calls from Shane either.

There was a strong possibility Riley didn't want her to be there.

On the same front, she couldn't wrap her head around what he'd said about her. He was jealous. He wanted her to be there with *him*.

That didn't mean he could act out like he had.

Then there was the fact that she'd been waiting in the barn for the last ten minutes and he still hadn't arrived. The whole time they'd been having sessions, he had never been late. This was uncharacteristic.

She had half a mind to head out to his cabin and pound on his door to demand an explanation. But that wouldn't be very therapist-like.

Instead, she busied herself with preparing the animals and straightening up. The longer it took, the more livid she became. She deserved respect. She wasn't just some person he could push around and demand things from.

If his ranting had been honest, and he was interested in her, then they would deal with that the way they were supposed to.

They'd shut it down.

Before Friday night, she might have entertained the possibility of ignoring everything she knew was right and actually give into her attraction for him. But watching the way he over-reacted had made her realize that would be a *very* bad idea. He wasn't ready for something that serious yet, no matter how much she was drawn to him.

Riley had made *some* progress, but his actions last weekend made it clear he was still working through some stuff. She couldn't decide if she would play the concerned friend or the angry one. But by the time he entered the barn, she'd made her decision.

She was fuming.

Grace pushed open the stall door and moved down the aisle, brushing past him without saying a word. She couldn't be his therapist while feeling this way. She needed to cool off.

He turned toward her. "Grace—"

"We need to reschedule."

His footsteps echoed after her. "Grace. We need to talk."

One of the ranch hands entered the barn and gave them a strange look. Grace offered him a small smile, then shook her head. "Maybe tomorrow."

"I'm sorry."

Grace froze, then spun around. She waited for the ranch hand to leave the building and then strode toward Riley. The temptation to poke him in the chest and tell him that what he did was wrong felt strong. But she was mature. She knew better.

Instead, she crossed her arms and her eyes narrowed. "Okay."

"Okay? That's all you have to say for yourself?"

"I could ask the same thing of you."

He sighed. "I get it. I screwed up."

Grace tapped her foot, giving him the opportunity to elaborate. For all she knew, he was apologizing for being late. The balance of power between them was now skewed. There were probably some rules when it came to this kind of stuff.

She should have gone to see Shane before their session to let him know. But for once, she went against that thought and did something selfish. She still wanted to have an excuse to see Riley every day.

He stood before her, fidgeting like he was coming off of something, but his eyes were clear. Whatever reason he had for acting so skittish, it wasn't because he'd been drinking or taking anything.

Another cowboy wandered into the barn, passing them and heading for something toward the back.

Riley lowered his voice and moved closer to Grace. He grasped her hand and pulled her toward the side of the barn, then released her as he leaned against the wall. "Friday night... I made some mistakes I'm not proud of."

Good. At least he was fessing up to whatever that crazy night had meant.

"I should have never asked you to come with me."

Her stomach bottomed out and she stared at him with confusion. Maybe she was wrong about all of this.

"I should have just let you do what you said and drop me off. I put you in a weird position, and it wasn't fair of me."

"I wasn't upset about going with you," she blurted against

her better judgment. "I had a good time... until... well, you know."

He made a face, his eyes dropping to the ground.

"What I don't understand is what happened when I was dancing with Wade. What triggered you to—"

Riley let out a groan. "I really don't want to talk about that. This therapy thing isn't about my stupid choices when it comes to women I'm attracted to. It's about how I feel after trying to get back to a normal way of life after serving in the military."

Her mouth dropped open, and when he met her gaze, he froze. She could practically see the cogs working in his head as he went over the words he'd just spoken to her. Then he grimaced.

"Why do I keep doing that? I'm not even drunk." He pushed away from the barn wall and strode deeper into the barn but then stopped and came back.

Grace couldn't move. Stuck in the headlights, she was like one of those deer they show on those animal shows on television. Riley continued to get closer until he stopped just inches from where she stood.

When he spoke, it was just above a whisper and his voice was laced with something she couldn't place. "You want to know the truth? Everything I said on Friday was real. When I take even one drink of anything alcoholic, I can't control the words that spew from my mouth. I can't control my thoughts or how I react to them."

He breathed heavily enough she could feel the warmth of it on her cheek. He was close enough that it would take nothing to reach out and touch her, to pull her into his arms. But he didn't. She couldn't decide if she was disappointed by that or not.

Riley shut his eyes tight, then opened them, and the ache she saw behind those windows to his soul tugged at her own heart. "I can't explain what is going on with me. I can't tell if you're the reason I'm finally opening up about my life and the way I see the world, or if it's this place. I barely got any sleep this weekend. There were several times when I nearly got on my bike and just drove away. But I'm here."

Still frozen, Grace just watched him as he continued to work through the feelings he had and the thoughts that plagued him.

"Will you say something?"

As much as she wished she could do something about his feelings, she knew deep down that she couldn't. Her eyes narrowed and she folded her arms. "What do you want me to do?"

He raked a heavy hand through his hair and a sigh burst from his lips. "I don't know."

"Well, I can tell you this much. A relationship between us isn't going to happen." Grace looked away, not willing to put herself through the emotions she knew she'd experience if she got even a glimpse of disappointment from him. "There are several rules about stuff like this. Even though I'm not an official doctor, I know better." Her voice cracked. She pressed her back against the wall so she faced away from him. "You are attracted to me because I'm one of the first people to help you that you've connected with. It's understandable and—"

"*No.*"

She looked in his direction. "No?"

Riley shook his head. "It's more than that. I can't stop thinking about you. I have this obsessive need to take care of you, to make sure you're safe."

Grace bit back a derisive laugh. "That doesn't sound like you have feelings for me. That sounds like you have a hard time letting go of your past life and you're trying to project those feelings onto someone new." She cringed as the words escaped her throat. She could have said that so much better if she'd only thought about it for a moment longer.

Riley faced her, placing his hand against the wall over her shoulder. His eyes flashed with intensity. "How *dare* you."

She remained still. He wasn't scary. While the vibe around him was passionate, she didn't feel like he'd harm her. On the contrary, his tone and the way he continued to insist on this conversation had awakened something deeper within her.

"I'm an adult, and I'm more than capable of reading my own emotions. I know when I am sincerely attracted to someone and when it's just an infatuation. Along those lines, I would definitely know if my feelings for you were based on my attraction to someone who can relate to me." He leaned closer still so their noses almost touched, and his voice softened. "As much as you'd like to think you can empathize with my situation, you can't. You will *never* understand what I had to go through—what my team had to experience on a daily basis. I don't blame you for that. But I'm smart enough to accept what I can and can't change about it."

Grace's heart beat so loud, she could hear it in her ears and feel it in every finger. No one had ever spoken to her like this. Maybe that was why so many girls preferred to date men who were older than they were. It was nice not to have to be left guessing.

"Now," he continued, "can we please talk about what's going to happen next?"

Her throat was dry. Her legs weak. She didn't know what they were going to do next. Ethically, she couldn't date someone she was treating. On the other end of things, this wasn't the same patient-therapist situation that mandated those kinds of strict rules.

The equine therapy that Shane ran was less formal. Most of the people who worked for him didn't even have degrees in this field. She wasn't even sure if he had hired her because she had the education or because he knew her sister.

Grace pressed her lips together in a firm line. "What do you want me to say?" Her voice cracked. "I'm not supposed to—"

"Say you feel it too."

She snapped her mouth shut and looked away. "That doesn't matter."

He let out a muttered curse. "It *does* matter. Did you know that people who suffer from PTSD benefit so much more if they have a stable relationship with someone or with family?"

Her head snapped back so she could meet his gaze. "Of course, I know that."

"Tell me you're not interested and I'll drop it. Tell me that I'm crazy for being drawn to you and the small moments we've spent—"

Friday's events came back with a vengeance like a slap to the face. "You said I was only here because I was being paid to do so." She pushed against his chest with her fingers and moved past him, then turned to face him. "I'm not going to be bullied or manipulated. I'm here to help you get better, that's all. And today, you were late. I didn't even have to wait for you, but I did. If you have a problem with rescheduling, take it up with Shane."

She charged from the barn, her whole body humming with electricity. That had been the hardest conversation she'd ever had in her entire life. Never had she expected that she'd have to tell someone who admitted to feelings for her that they couldn't act on them.

Like always, Grace had been the good girl she knew she was supposed to be and she'd told him no.

So why on earth was she still reeling from the conversation and feeling like she made the wrong choice? Deep down she knew he was special. He was the kind of guy who had layers to him, which made him interesting. She didn't see the scars. All she saw was a man who needed a little bit of support to be lifted up again.

Grace got a few yards from the barn and then she started sprinting toward the main building. She couldn't stay here today. She needed to get her head on straight.

Did that mean she was going to tell Shane about any of this?

Absolutely not. There was always a time and a place for stuff like that. And that little devil on her shoulder was still chanting that she needed to do whatever it took to maintain stability in Riley's life.

She could continue to work with him and not develop stronger feelings for him. That would be easy, right? All she would have to do is make sure he never got close to her again. Oh, and she couldn't let him touch her. There would be no more dancing, and every conversation had to be about progressing toward one of his goals.

Geez, none of that sounded fun at all.

13

———————

iley

ANOTHER WEEK PASSED, and every single day he made sure to be on time. He'd lost precious time with Grace last week on Monday. He wouldn't risk losing any more.

Riley had no intention of backing down. He'd always considered himself one who had amazing instincts. It didn't matter if it was out in the field or if it was back on US soil; he was good with reading what certain feelings meant.

And the way he felt about Grace hadn't left him. With each passing day, his feelings for her grew. From the way she spoke to him to the way she handled a horse. He didn't bother going back to the country club for their dances. Grace had made it clear she wasn't interested in that sort of stuff, and being there might only make things worse. He couldn't afford to take another couple of drinks and end up doing something stupid again.

Instead, he continued doing everything she said—well, that he could actually accomplish.

Grace didn't make him use any horse other than Dolly. He must have passed that part of their therapy sessions with flying colors. He'd been able to rein in his anger and irritation. He even opened up about his home life a little more.

Today they had another "fun" session. They were back in the arena, and Grace had gotten the balls for the horses to play with. They sat a few feet away from one another on the railing of the fence that separated the dirt floor from the stands.

As usual, Grace was the quiet one. He didn't even catch her looking at him as much as she used to. There was a strong possibility that he'd lost his chance with her.

That didn't matter. He'd come up with a plan for if she stuck to her guns and didn't allow anything romantic to occur between them. He'd already discussed his options for housing with Shane.

The man was a saint. He had offered Riley a job if he completed his therapy sessions with flying colors.

But Grace didn't need to know any of that.

He glanced at her, finding her focused on the horses, and he let out a sigh. "What are we going to discuss today?"

She didn't turn toward him, nor did she smile. It was one of those mornings when he knew something bad was brewing. Perhaps that was why she'd suggested the arena. Her hands gripped the bar on either side of her legs. If it weren't for the occasional blink and the way her chest rose and fell with each breath, he might have assumed she was a statue.

"Grace?"

She jumped and glanced in his direction. "What?"

"What are we going to discuss today?"

Her brows furrowed and she returned her attention to the horses. "How about you tell me about your most recent tour of duty."

He scowled. "I thought I didn't have to discuss details like that—only about the symptoms of my PTSD."

"Fine, don't talk about it. Apparently, you already know all of it now."

Riley stilled. Her tone of voice wasn't in her character. She was mad about something else. "What's wrong?"

She sighed. "Who's the therapist, Riley?"

He bit his tongue to prevent himself from saying that neither one of them were. That would go over about as well as anything he'd said last week or the weekend before. "I'm just suggesting that you're in a pretty bad mood."

"Yeah. I am. My truck broke down again. There's nothing I can do about it either. I don't have the money to get a new one, but fixing it is costing more than I can afford—" She sent an apologetic look in his direction. "I'm not supposed to be venting to you about any of this. These sessions are supposed to be about you."

He sliced his hand through the air and forced a chuckle. "Don't worry about me. I'm fine." She gave him a pointed look and he chuckled again. "You know what I mean. You can vent to me about anything."

Once again she gave him that look. "Then why don't you vent to me? I know there are months of issues just begging to crawl from the recesses of your mind."

"I'll share if you share. It's only fair."

She rolled her eyes. "I already told you what I'm dealing with."

"True. But you didn't tell me how you *feel*."

Grace gave him a flabbergasted look, and he laughed. "Kidding. But really." He reached over and placed his hand over the top of hers. "I can be a sounding board if you need me to. I've got some vehicle troubles of my own to figure out. Maybe you could tell me where you take your truck."

"It's literally the only mechanic's shop in town—unless you decide to drive all the way out to Colorado Springs."

"Is the guy any good?"

She shrugged. "I have nothing to compare it with. How am I supposed to know?"

"Okay. New subject. How is Brielle doing?"

Grace shot him a strange look. "Why are you curious about her?"

"Wasn't she the one your father caught sneaking out and doing things that she shouldn't?"

"Yes," she drawled. "But I don't know what that has anything to do with—"

"Wasn't she the one who brought your dress the other night for the dance?"

Grace's expression made it clear she knew exactly where he was going with this.

"Maybe she could give you some pointers on how to bend the rules, if only for a few weeks."

She withdrew her hand from beneath his and crossed her arms. "I'm not going to date you, Riley. And if you mention it again, I'm going to be required to report it to Shane."

He edged closer to her and his voice dropped to a whisper. "I think you would have already done that by now if you were going to do it."

"Fine. I'm still not going to date you." Her voice was lighter than it had been in previous discussions that were similar to this one.

In fact, if he was correct, he was pretty sure he saw the corner of her lips twitch into a faint smile. It was short-lived, but there was a huge possibility her defenses were weakening.

Riley shifted his attention to Dolly, who seemed to be having an incredible time chasing that ball. "Where is the mechanic in town?"

"On Main Street. You can't really miss it."

"Would you mind driving me when you get your truck back? I could use a ride home."

She nodded. "Okay."

Well, there was one opportunity where he'd be able to spend some time with her without the possibility of someone walking in on them. "Do you have an idea of when your truck will be fixed?"

Grace nodded again. "It's gonna be ready by tomorrow."

"Thanks."

"For what?"

He smiled at her. "For being willing to help."

"It's what I'm here for." Her voice bordered on being lifeless, and he hated seeing her this way.

"Hey, you know what I'd like to do when we're in town?"

"What?" she said dryly.

"I heard they have the most amazing fudge at a candy shop in town."

Once again, he caught a twitch or something around her lips. "That is actually true."

"I'd like to get some."

"I guess we can do that."

"It's a date."

She shot him a sideways glance. "It most definitely isn't."

He chuckled. "Okay. It's not a date."

14

G race

GRACE PARKED as close to the cabins as she could and then waited for Riley to exit his home. His motorcycle was parked out front, and she had a ramp in the back of her truck in order to get it in the bed.

She didn't dare climb out to go knock on his door for fear she'd let curiosity get the better of her and she wouldn't decline if he were to give her a tour. Instead, she pulled out her phone and sent him a quick message. Then she tossed the phone on the seat beside her.

Within minutes, he was out the door and rolling his motorcycle toward her. It took minimal effort for him to get the bike in the back of her truck, and he hadn't needed her help to do any of it.

Riley climbed into the truck and held out her phone as he

offered her a smile. Why was he suddenly in a better mood than he'd been before?

You're a good therapist. The words ran through her head over and over without stopping. Grace kept her hands on the steering wheel, tightening then relaxing her grip if only to keep her mind off the fact that Riley was in her truck. She was taking him to town.

What was she doing? She was taking him to town in her truck and they were leaving the safety of Shane's property.

She had to have lost her mind.

Grace shot a look at him out of the corner of her eye. It wasn't that she didn't trust him. She did. He was a decent guy, and he'd never done anything to make her nervous. It was her own emotions she couldn't trust.

Her heart flipped every single time he shifted and looked in her direction. Her palms grew clammy.

Keep your focus on the road. That's all you have to do. Drop off the motorcycle. Bring him back. And above all else, stay professional.

Oh, wait. They were going to the sweets place. It wasn't going to be a short trip after all.

What had she gotten herself into?

Grace let out a sigh which ended up sounding like an explosion of sound due to the quiet in the cab. She should have turned on the radio before he climbed in. Turning it on now would only draw more attention to the fact that she was on edge.

Her face filled with heat and she fumbled with the dials on the dash to turn down the heater. It had been cold when she'd started her truck, but now it felt like a sauna. There was no rhyme or reason to the change... except her passenger.

His words last week entered her thoughts. Riley's insistence that there was something brewing between them and that acknowledging it would only benefit his treatment had set her on edge all week. She'd had to force herself to ignore just how close he was to the truth. She was drawn to him. She had been since the first day they'd met.

The question now wasn't whether or not she should give in. It was why she was fighting it so much. Was it because she thought it would be unethical? Or because she was scared he was right?

"You doing okay?"

She jumped and glanced in his direction. "Mhmm."

Riley chuckled. "You don't have to lie to me."

"I'm not lying," she squeaked. *Good one, Grace.* She definitely didn't sound like she believed her own words. Why would he?

That warm laugh escaped his lips again and he settled back in his seat. Thankfully, he didn't argue with her further. "Would you feel better if we turn this into an extra session?"

Grace snuck another surprised look at him. "You can't be suggesting that you would willingly submit yourself to a session while we drive to town."

"I believe that's exactly what I'm suggesting."

She shook her head and set her sights on the road again. "I don't believe you. You've been against this from the start."

He shifted in his seat, turning his face away from her as he looked out his window. "You're not wrong. I don't really like talking about my time as a soldier. There's nothing I can do to change that part of my life. Why dwell on it?"

"Because it helps."

He huffed, but it didn't sound as harsh as it had in previous conversations. "I have yet to see evidence of that."

Grace couldn't help it. She rolled her eyes. "Do you remember your first day here? Our first session? Compare it to how you are today. I'm sure if you thought about it hard enough, you'd be able to see the difference."

He didn't speak up right away. And when he did, he shifted around so he could look at her. It took everything in her power not to meet his gaze. Once more, she tightened her grip on the steering wheel, preparing for what he had to say.

"You make a decent point."

It felt like she'd been hit over the head. Had Riley actually admitted he agreed with her sentiment? She chanced a look in his direction and her throat closed up, finding his gaze on her. She moistened her lips and forced herself to return her eyes to the road. "Good. I'm glad you can see reason."

"I didn't say you were right."

A bark of laughter escaped her lips. "Of course you didn't. But actually, you did."

Riley shook his head. "I said you made a good point. But let me make one. Don't you have good days and bad days? When you aren't feeling your best, aren't you a little more cranky and would prefer to just be left alone?"

"Yes..." she drawled. "But even when I'm having a really bad day, you won't catch me breaking the law." Grace knew she shouldn't have said that the second the words escaped her lips. She flinched. "I didn't mean—"

"It's fine. You're right on that one, too. Looks like you're winning this one."

She sighed. "Riley, it's not about winning and losing. If you're improving, then we're both winning."

He grew quiet.

That's when she knew she'd made a mistake. She shouldn't have brought up his past—at least not like that. He probably thought she was judging him—again.

Grace bit back a groan. Why couldn't she be more eloquent with her words? Why couldn't she see where a conversation was headed before it got there so she could take a detour? "Riley, I'm sorry."

"Don't be. Really. You're completely right. I didn't behave in a way that was acceptable. Perhaps it's not my PTSD that needs to be treated. It's my personality."

She gave him a disheartened look. There was nothing she could say to fix this. Somehow she could sense it. They needed to get on another topic of conversation. But what?

"Do you know why I decided to learn about therapeutic services?"

He didn't respond.

"I wanted to help people. I would imagine you joined the army for the same reason. You said you joined about fifteen years ago—that's after the terrorist attacks in New York, right? You probably wanted to be in the army since you were a kid."

He glanced at her again but kept quiet.

"It got me thinking. From what I've read, a lot of men and women who joined after that tragedy did so because they wanted to fight for a cause. Not because it was their only option. You're a good man. I don't think you give yourself enough credit. Yes, you were assigned to therapy here. But you want to know what I think? If you weren't a good guy, you wouldn't have come. You would have just given the proverbial middle finger to the people who sent you this way."

She peeked at him, thrilled to find his features softening and the corners of his mouth lifting into that smile that had the power to send her stomach reeling. She grinned to herself. Good. They'd avoided the catastrophe.

The strangest part was that every word she'd said had been confessed honestly. Riley *was* someone she admired. It took guts to go through therapy. One of the hardest things to do as a human being was to admit being wrong and accept help. There were several people she knew in town who probably needed therapy and who would never consider even seeing a therapist. Riley was already a step ahead of each of them solely due to his attendance and involvement in Shane's equine therapy services.

Was it possible Riley had made his own good points over the last week? Maybe he'd come into her life not only so he could be helped, but because she needed someone like him in her life. If she kept it quiet, perhaps she could experiment with the idea. A few dates wouldn't hurt.

Besides, Riley would be heading out of town when this whole thing was over. On top of that, there were perks to having a solid support system—someone he could trust.

The heat in her body returned as she contemplated what it might mean to date a guy like Riley. He was older. In some ways he was more mature. The flutters in her stomach exploded as she chanced another look in his direction.

There was one thing for certain.

Grace wasn't going to chase after him. But if he decided to ask her again...

She wouldn't say *no*.

Riley

JUST WHEN RILEY thought that things would work out between himself and Grace—if he were to try—she went and said something that proved she was way out of reach. It was fine. Any normal person in his position would agree that pursuing a girl like her was problematic.

It wasn't just because she was his therapist. There was the age difference. And then the obvious—she would never understand what he went through or how to help him. Not really.

The only people who had been able to get close to empathizing with him had been therapists who were once in the military themselves.

At the time, Riley had been so against therapy he'd burned every bridge he'd had. No one wanted to work with him back home.

No, they didn't turn him away. But he could see it in their

faces. They weren't invested in helping him and he didn't want their help anyway. So why waste his time?

Grace pulled her truck into a parking lot that had half-a-dozen cars parked there. The place was small and run-down, like it had been erected when the town was organized. It had to be the oldest building on the street. If not, it came really close.

Without looking at Grace, he climbed out of the truck and headed around back. He wasn't surprised that Grace didn't follow him. The space in that cab had felt tight. They were suffocating with the awkward position they'd put themselves in. Grace had put him in his place without even trying. He didn't begrudge her for it. She was right, after all.

Riley just wasn't cut out to find a relationship with a girl as amazing as she was.

He got the bike out of her truck and walked it toward the front of the shop. Then he headed inside. An older woman popped her head up from her computer and smiled at him. "Good afternoon. How can I help you?"

Riley thumbed over his shoulder toward the door. "I have a bike that needs to be looked at. I was hoping you guys could fit me in?"

She turned toward a door that led to the garage portion of the shop. "Bridget!"

A woman in coveralls and grease marring her face and hands wandered in from the back. Her hair was pulled back into a messy ponytail. She glanced in his direction with a wide grin then moved over to the woman behind the counter. "What did you need?"

"This young man has a—"

"Harley Davidson. It's giving me troubles and I have to drive it back to the city in a few months." His chest constricted. He'd done so much to prepare to stay, but at the current rate, he might be heading home after all.

The grease monkey wiped her hands on a rag, her focus on the windows behind him. "You staying with the Callahans?"

Riley jumped and looked back at the truck, clearly visible. "No. I—er—I'm staying at the country club."

Understanding filled Bridget's gaze. Apparently, it wasn't any secret what Shane was cooking up at the club. Riley wasn't surprised. If people were coming from out of state to a small town like this, there was bound to be talk.

He cleared his throat and gestured toward his bike which was also visible. "Do you think you'd have time to look at it this week?"

Bridget turned to the receptionist. "What's my schedule like this week, Ms. Jacobs?"

She turned to her computer and clicked her mouse a few times. "Looks like the earliest slot is on Friday."

They both turned to him expectantly. "Grace said this is the only place in town. It's not like I have many options."

Bridget snorted. "Of course she'd put it that way. I'll have you know I have more experience fixing cars than ninety percent of the guys who work in shops like this one."

"I don't think she meant anything by it. She still brings her truck here," Riley hurried to add. "I'm perfectly happy to wait until Friday."

At least Bridget's smile still appeared to be genuine. She didn't look too upset by their conversation. In fact, her smile seemed brighter. "You tell Grace that I appreciate the referral. And if her truck starts acting up again, I'll give her one on the house."

Confusion washed over him. "Okay. I will."

Bridget chuckled. "That truck is on its last leg. I don't know how much longer she's gonna be able to drive it. But that's what happens when a truck gets handed down from sister to sister." She gave Ms. Jacobs a wink. "I might be a magician when it comes to cars, but I'm not that good." She offered a wave to

Riley. "Give your information to Ms. Jacobs, and I'll call you when I figure out the problem."

She disappeared through the door, leaving Riley with Ms. Jacobs. She motioned for him to come over and he complied. She held out a contact sheet. "Fill this out and we'll get you in the system."

It was one-sided, barely any questions. She could have typed this information in if he'd given her the info verbally. To be fair, the longer he spent in the shop, the more time he had to get his head on straight. He needed to decide what he wanted to do and just stick with it. He couldn't let his feelings of uncertainty hold him back.

There was one thing he knew for certain, and it might be harder than he thought it ought to be. Grace was the girl for him. He could come up with a thousand reasons it wouldn't work out with her, but the most important reason to try to make it work trumped all of them.

She made him feel different—worthy—somehow. Even when she tripped over her words. Grace had an innocence about her that he missed in his own life.

Riley handed the sheet of paper back to the nice front desk lady and headed for the door. If he wanted to win Grace over, he couldn't let anything stand in his way.

THE SIGN above the door boasted *Fantasy Fudge,* and the display in the window proved the name fit the business. Stacks of fudge bricks were arranged in a way that put the candy shops in movies to shame.

A blast of hot air hit them both as they entered the fudge shop. The smell of caramel and chocolate wrapped around him like a warm hug. There was a "sweets" shop he used to visit when he was a kid, and everything about this place reminded him of it.

The displays were chock-full of chocolates, truffles, fudges, and anything else he could have imagined. There were specialty candy canes in glass jars on top of the display cases. And shelves of candied and caramel apples.

A round woman in an apron beamed at them when they entered and bustled to the edge of the counter. "Grace! I haven't seen you in a while. How is your father?"

Riley glanced toward Grace, who had her hands shoved deep into her pockets. There would be no brushing his hand against hers just so he could touch her. She smiled at the woman. "He's doing okay. But he would be livid if he knew I was here and didn't get him any chocolate turtles."

She laughed. "Oh, I believe it. I'll make sure to wrap some up for him. What can I get you both?"

Grace made eye contact with Riley but only briefly. "I'll have a tutti fruitti candy cane," she said.

The woman nodded. "Of course. And for you?" She turned to Riley. "Are you a candy cane kind of guy?"

He shook his head. "I'm a chocolate fudge kind of guy."

"Oh, a man after my own heart." She hurried over to the shelves that had the fudge. "What kind do you want? I've got cookies and cream, peach, pralines—"

"I had my eye on the mint you have over to the right."

She jumped into action. "How much?"

"Half a pound would be great."

The woman hurried back and forth, gathering the sweets and getting them into a bag. She headed toward the register, but before she could ring them up, Riley stepped forward.

"Put it all together."

She lifted her eyes, darting her focus from Grace to Riley a few times. "Of course."

Grace reached out to him, placing her hand lightly on his forearm. "You don't have to do that—"

"I asked you out here. It's my treat. Besides, you're taking me around since my motorcycle is out of commission." Riley pulled out his wallet and moved forward before Grace had a chance to stop him. He handed the woman some cash and offered her an appreciative grin. "Keep the change."

She blinked, holding out the bag of candy. "Thank you."

The second they were outside, Grace bumped her shoulder into his. "That was really nice of you."

He reveled in her praise.

"Ruth and her husband have been working that shop since before I can remember. John passed away about two years ago, and she's been doing it all on her own ever since. I thought for sure when John died that she'd pack up and move away—you know, to be with her children or grandchildren. But she didn't." Grace unwrapped her candy cane and stuck the open end in her mouth.

The way she was talking, it was as if she'd forgotten all about their conversation in the truck on the way there. They were no longer therapist and client. They were two people who were wandering down the street of a small town right outside Colorado Springs.

A breeze ruffled his hair and tugged at his jacket. "When does it start to warm up out here? It's March. Doesn't that mean it's supposed to get warm and things start growing again?"

She chuckled. "It's the beginning of March. We've got another month and a half at least before the temperatures get into the mid-seventies. Haven't you ever heard of the phrase 'in like a lion, out like a lamb'?" Grace peered at him, still enjoying her candy cane.

Riley tilted his head thoughtfully. "Sounds familiar."

"Well, as the weather starts to warm up, the winds pick up. It's got something to do with the pressure in the atmosphere. So it's cold and usually rainy—and almost always blustery. I'm surprised we haven't had much rain so far. But then I guess if the clouds were to dump anything, it would end up being a mix of snow and rain." She glanced at him again. "Where you're from, do you have a longer winter?"

"It's not much different, I suppose. I've just noticed it feels colder because we spend so much time outdoors." Riley pulled out his fudge from the bag and attempted to tear off a piece which ended up being harder than he thought.

Grace laughed when all he got was the tip of the corner. "I think you're supposed to use the plastic knife she gave you."

He frowned. "But I just want a taste."

She shrugged. "Fine. Do it the hard way. I suppose that's the way you prefer to do things anyway."

Riley scoffed. "What's that supposed to mean?"

Grace lifted a shoulder, but the hint of a smile touched her lips. "You're forgetting that I'm trained to notice things about you—learn what makes you tick and how to help you through things when you put up walls. So if I say that you're doing something the hard way because you're being stubborn, it would probably be in your best interest to listen to me."

He stopped walking, forcing her to turn around and look at him. Once again, she made a good point. She hit everything on the nose with her little speech.

Grace frowned. "Great. Did I say something wrong again? I don't know what's gotten into me. I used to be so good at being able to phrase something in a way that—"

He closed the distance between them and placed his hand against her upper arm. "No. You didn't say anything wrong. In fact, you've been nothing but honest with me since the moment I got into your truck. I'd be lying if I said that I didn't need that kind of brutal honesty sometimes. I just don't get that with anyone else."

"But you need compassion and—"

"*No*," he drawled. "I need someone to be straight with me and tell me when I need to redirect my actions in another way." The way she was looking at him made it clear she didn't believe a word that had come out of his mouth. His hand squeezed her arm slightly. "I'm not referring to the PTSD. That can be tricky. But I'm dealing with it. The stuff that you're helping me with—by being blunt—that's something different. It's helping me understand why I've been so *stuck*."

The confusion in her features was adorable. She wasn't grasping what he was trying to say. He'd been so miserable in his life.

Alone.

Stubborn.

Refusing to let anyone in.

And it had everything to do with the way he judged others or himself before they had a chance to prove he was wrong to do so. He'd been looking for love in all the wrong places. Finding a girl who would be there for him was one thing.

Finding a girl who was willing to put him in his place and point out his flaws was something else entirely.

No wonder he was so drawn to Grace. She was exactly what he'd wanted and everything he didn't know he needed.

They stood mere inches apart as his head continued putting all the pieces together. The tension continued to grow as they stood outside of the small storefronts on this street. Then Grace looked down where he still held her arm. Before she could pull away, he released her and stepped back. He offered her an apologetic smile. "Maybe we should—"

"Do you want to get some dinner?"

He froze. To assume her offer was anything more than a dinner between friends would be dangerous, but he didn't care. This could be the door he'd been waiting to open. All he had to do was step through it and find the happiness that waited on the other side. There was only one right answer. "Sure."

race

GRACE DIDN'T KNOW what had gotten into her. One second she was feeling guilty for saying the wrong thing.

Again.

The next she felt like she was being pushed by some outside entity, insisting that she needed to do something or she might miss out on something great. It was the strangest sensation.

Once she asked him to dinner, there was no turning back.

Not that she wanted to.

They continued walking down the street quietly in their own thoughts. A thrill rocketed through her. The warmth of his hand on her arm lingered and her stomach flipped over and over, turning her insides into mush.

The only thing that kept her grounded was the taste of her candy cane and the cold air that cooled her heated face.

"What's good around here? I haven't been exploring since I arrived."

Grace gestured down the street. "There's this diner that everyone loves. They serve the best apple pie. I wouldn't be surprised if they put something illegal in it." She chuckled, then sobered when she met his gaze.

Shoot. Another thing wrong? Riley had issues with alcoholism, but did he have problems with controlled substances too?

She took a bite of her candy cane and crunched it between her teeth. "They have a lot of other stuff too," she mumbled.

They entered Sal's Diner and took a seat by the front window. The few waitresses who were working hustled back and forth from the kitchen to the tables. Then one finally materialized at their sides and held out a menu. Her name tag said *Hope* and she poised her notebook with her pencil at the ready. "What can I get you two to drink?"

"I'll just have a water." Grace looked at Riley, who nodded.

"Same."

Hope nodded. "Coming right up." She hurried away and Riley set his gaze on Grace.

It was hard to keep her focus on her menu with him staring at her like that. Every time she glanced at him, his focus seemed to get deeper, firmer. Finally, she sighed and put the menu down. "What now?"

He shifted in his seat, then grabbed the napkin at his side. His nimble fingers unwrapped the paper holding it in a roll and he released his cutlery. "Why did you ask me to come to dinner with you?"

The pounding in her heart was so loud she was sure he could hear it over the hum of the guests in the restaurant. "Why not? We're all the way out here. I figured it would be nice to get something to eat that wasn't from the country club." She couldn't meet his eyes. How could she tell him that she wanted him to bring up the possibility of them dating again? Her curiosity had gotten the better of her.

It had come on suddenly. That was the only truth she knew. Each time she caught him staring at her had done something to tear down her defenses. She should have known better than to believe she wouldn't be worn down—especially with how much time they spent together.

"Grace."

She jumped and glanced at him that time. His lips twitched at the corners, and as much as she wanted to, she couldn't tear her eyes away from him. "What?"

"Yesterday you said we couldn't date."

Great. There it was. She knew he was going to point that out. Grace shrugged.

"Grace..." His voice held a hint of teasing. "I think we need to clear the air on this one."

The waitress placed two glasses of water in front of them. "Are we ready to order yet?"

Riley shook his head. "Not yet."

Hope placed the straws on the table. "Take your time. I'll be back around soon."

Riley set his eyes on her again. Why was it so hard to admit that she might have been jumping the gun on this whole no-dates thing?

Because she was right not to.

Brielle made it look so easy—doing something that wasn't quite right just because she wanted to. Grace took a deep breath and let it out, then reached for her straw and twisted the paper off it. "I didn't say we should start dating. I didn't even say this was a date."

"But it is."

She glanced at him once more. "Do you want it to be?"

He leaned back in his seat and appraised her. "You already know the answer to that."

Her heart fluttered again as she sat beneath his scrutiny.

He continued, "The question here is whether or not you're on the same page."

"I don't know," she murmured. "Do I think it's smart? Definitely not." She peeked at him. "But you caught me off guard. I can't help but wonder why."

Riley chuckled. "Why what?"

"Why me?"

His eyes narrowed and he leaned forward. "You're joking, right?"

She stiffened, looking around to see if anyone else was paying attention to her or her date. The residents of Copper Creek were notoriously nosey, and someone was bound to be watching her. "No. I'm genuinely curious."

He took ahold of her hand without warning and she jumped, nearly pulling away from him. Instead, she let him trace his thumb over her knuckles. His voice was low, and soothing. It was as if he was a different guy. "I've not had a serious relationship for an incredibly long time. In some cases it was because the girl I liked wasn't willing to date a soldier. Other times it was because I knew she couldn't handle what I was bringing to the table. I got used to the fact that I would never find a girl who I could spend the rest of my life with. It's just—too hard."

Grace's heart ached for him. The words that came from his lips just tore her apart inside. No one should feel like they were doomed to live their life alone. Especially not someone like Riley.

"But then I met you."

She had to hold in the snort that wanted to escape. She wasn't anything special. He didn't know what he was talking about. One day he'd realize that and would lose interest. But knowing that didn't dissuade her from wanting to see what it might be like to be with a guy like him. He was strong and brooding. But he was also sweet and sensitive. He was attractive, and he didn't make her feel like she was just some kid.

Riley continued. "There's something intangible about you that I can't put my finger on. There's no way to describe it in words. But if I were pressed, I'd say you are the first woman who has been able to tell me that I'm wrong."

"Surely you've dated women who have told you that you were wrong." Grace chuckled.

"Yes. But it's more than that. It's not the act of telling me I'm wrong. It's how you say it. It's refreshing. I don't know. None of that makes sense, does it?"

"Not really," she admitted. Carefully, she extracted her hand from his and leaned back in her seat. "So what then? You want to spend more time with me? That's it?"

The corners of his mouth quirked into a grin. "I'd like to think that dating has more perks than just spending time together. But yes. That's where things would start."

She swallowed hard. She knew exactly what he was referring to. She wasn't an idiot. But just the thought of letting him pull her into his arms set her heart aflame. She couldn't control the churning and waves that crashed within her.

Her gaze inadvertently drifted to his arms. His muscular form was more defined than most of the ranchers in Copper Creek. He must work out regularly. Of course, he probably knew how to do hand-to-hand combat of some kind. His tours of duty were likely filled with all kinds of stories that she would never hear. That concept terrified her, but she couldn't figure out why.

Grace clasped her hands in her lap. "Shane wouldn't approve."

"I figured."

"We'd have to get you a new therapist."

That made him go quiet. Up until this moment, she'd entertained the idea that she could do exactly what Brielle had modeled for years. Skirt the line and lie to those around her. She wasn't about to lose her job over a fling. And it wasn't in her character to sneak around, though the concept did present some interesting sensations inside her.

"Are you certain?"

She nodded resolutely. "It's not in my nature to break the rules like that. If you want to date me while you're here, then you need to find a new therapist."

His features darkened. "I don't want a new therapist."

"Then the line in the sand has been drawn."

"Are you ready to order now?"

Grace jumped, finding Hope standing at their table. How long had she been there? Had she heard their embarrassing conversation? Shoot. Was she one of the waitresses who liked to spread gossip in town?

Oh boy.

If she was, that meant they might be outed before they got back to the country club. Shane would most definitely reassign her if he got even a whiff of her being inappropriate with her client.

She shot out of her seat. "I'm sorry. We're not going to be able to stay." She pulled out a ten-dollar bill and tossed it on the table. "I'm going out to the truck."

What was she going to do now? She should have known better than to let Riley pull her from her morals. She should have never suggested dinner.

Grace pulled out her phone and dialed Shane's number. She needed to get out ahead of this if she wanted to ensure her reputation stayed in a good place. The second she hit send, she brought her phone to her ear. Then it was yanked from her grasp.

She sucked in sharply and spun around to find Riley with her phone at his ear. "Hello, Mr. Owens. It's Riley Scott."

Grace gasped again and lunged for her phone, but she was

too short and Riley was too fast. "What are you doing?" she hissed. "Give me back my phone."

"Yes, there's something important I need to discuss with you. It's about Grace."

She froze. Her blood ran cold. *No.* He wouldn't.

"I was planning on coming to your office to discuss this, but seeing as I have you on the phone, I figured I'd get this out in the open. I don't want a new therapist." He chuckled as his gaze landed on Grace and locked with hers. "I understand if you want to assign her to someone else, but I'm going to put up a fight. Yes, I know that doesn't make sense. I'm getting to that." Riley took a step closer to Grace, causing her to step back and bump into her truck. "I don't know how to put this other than to just tell you. I've developed an attraction to her—more than that. I have feelings for her." He was silent for a few minutes, and all Grace could hear was the mumbling sound of Shane's voice on the other end.

Feelings?

He had to be lying. But why would he lie about something like that to Shane?

Riley rested his free hand against the truck right above her shoulder. The gesture was far more intimate than she expected and her breath hitched in her chest. His firm voice lowered. "I understand your policies, and I respectfully disagree. I don't think it will hamper my ability to improve during our sessions. In fact, I feel the opposite. Miss Callahan is the single most amazing person I have ever worked with."

Shane's unintelligible voice buzzed through the phone again.

"Well, if that's what you think is best, then find someone new. But in the meantime, I will continue my daily sessions— *with* Grace Callahan." His eyes bore into hers as if he were talking to her and not to her boss.

It wasn't hard to gather how their conversation had gone.

Shane wasn't thrilled about Riley's confession. She was bound to get a conversation of her own. Riley was making demands, and Shane wasn't one to get bullied.

In all likelihood she might have just lost her job.

Riley hung up the phone and held it out to her. "There. It's done."

She stared at the phone in disbelief. "What have you done?" she whispered. "He's going to fire me."

"He wouldn't do that."

She glowered at him. "You don't know Shane like I do. He's got the perfect excuse to fire me. He doesn't have to find me a new client. He can just—"

Riley hooked his finger under her chin and tilted it upward. "He's not going to fire you. He's not thrilled about what I had to say, and he's looking for a replacement as we speak—"

"See? A *replacement*. You're my only client. There aren't any others who—"

"I'm not going to let you get fired."

"You don't have any control over that," she sputtered. "What are you going to do? Threaten to quit? You were here against your own will as it was."

Riley's eyes flashed with irritation. It was brief, but it was there, and it reminded her of the times when he'd lost his temper out at the club. She snapped her mouth shut, hoping her dark gaze would be enough to make him understand she wasn't happy with him either.

He dipped his face toward her, his eyes softening. "I may have come from nothing. But I made something of myself. You'd be surprised how easy it is for someone like me to throw some money around and make a difference."

She let out a huff. "Shane has all the money he needs. You can't manipulate him that way."

"I never said the money would be for him."

Grace stilled. "What do you mean?"

"Manipulating the business owner isn't the only way money can change a situation. Reporters love stories like this. If he fires you, we have an arsenal at our fingertips. Besides, who wouldn't love to write a story about a vet falling for the woman who helped him on his path to healing from PTSD?"

Whoa.

There was no way she had misheard him.

Having feelings for her and being attracted to her weren't nearly as big as falling in love.

This was all happening too fast. She couldn't breathe. Grace ducked out from where he had her pinned with his gaze and hurried down the sidewalk. He couldn't love her. Not yet. That was too crazy for even her to believe at this point.

"Grace. Wait," his voice followed her.

She ducked her head down, bracing herself against the cold wind that tugged at her hair and clothes. Shaking her head, she waved him off. "Nope. Not right now, Riley. I need to sort some things out."

He jogged up beside her. "I'm not going to apologize for anything I just said because I mean every single thing."

Grace shot him a disbelieving look.

Riley ran a ragged hand down his face. "Look, I'm not an idiot. I know that these feelings are just beginning. We don't even know if whatever this is between us will last the month. I'm not going to make the assumption that we're soulmates or anything. But I'm also not going to walk away from this place wondering if I made the biggest mistake of my life in not asking you out."

17

Riley

RILEY COULDN'T TELL if he was breathing heavy because he'd had to run to catch up to her or if it was because he was terrified that she'd tear him down.

One word was all it would take for him to regret everything he'd done and said in the last twenty-four hours. Not only did he risk losing her as his *sponsor*, but he also risked losing out on the chance to have something more.

He took a deep breath, then released it and let his shoulders drop. "I'm not good with my words. I have a hard time fighting for things that I want. All I know is that I want to be with you."

She certainly stared at him like she thought he was crazy. He couldn't blame her. From the first day they'd met, he'd been someone even he wouldn't want to be around. But he'd gotten out of his shell, and now he just prayed she wouldn't turn him down.

Grace stopped her escape and he had to hurry back to her

after going a little too far. His approach was slow as he strode toward her. He felt like he was approaching a skittish rabbit. She crossed her arms, her eyes narrowed. "I can't believe you took my phone."

He grimaced. "I'm sorry."

"And told Shane all of those things."

Riley gave her a pointed look. "That wasn't for his benefit."

She clamped her mouth shut. If it weren't for the cooler weather, he would have bet that her cheeks would have filled with color from his statement and not the wind. "I don't want you to do stuff like that."

"Noted."

She dropped her arms to her sides. "I guess there's no going back anyway. You can't take back what you said to Shane, and I know he wouldn't believe me if I said you were teasing." Grace looked down at her feet and shuffled her toe against the concrete before peering up at him. "I guess I just can't wrap my head around our age difference. That's the one thing that has me wondering if we're doing something wrong."

He chuckled and reached for her hand. His fingers played with hers before he wove his fingers between hers. "Sometimes it's best not to question something, especially when your heart is telling you to take a chance."

Grace snickered.

He glanced up at her, a frown creasing his brows. "What?"

"You said you're not good with your words. I'd say you're just fine expressing how you feel." She tilted her head, peering at him with her large eyes. "I'm probably going to live to regret this."

"Nothing in life worth having is going to be gained without some degree of risk."

She shook her head again. "I mean with Shane. Like I said, you don't know him. Even if I don't get fired, he's not going to let me off without a warning of some kind. He's probably going to ask me how long this has been going on."

"Well, that's easy. You just tell him the truth."

Grace laughed. It wasn't one of her soft, timid ones, either. She tossed back her head and her shoulders shook. Her laughter was so contagious that he chuckled right along with her. She shook her head as soon as her laughter died down. "You don't want me to do that. Based on how things started, I'd say a lie would be more believable."

"What are you saying?" he scoffed. "I was a perfect gentleman despite being attracted to you."

"You *weren't*."

He nodded, tugging on her so that she nearly stood touching him. He tucked a strand of hair behind her ear. "I knew you were something special. I just didn't know that I'd get a chance to be something more to you."

What he wouldn't give to kiss her—in that moment—on the street—in front of anyone who bothered to look. But the time just wasn't right. They'd gotten through the thick of it and came out okay on the other side.

He couldn't think of a happier moment than this one right here. The future was bright, and there was nothing he was going to do to jeopardize that.

Riley stepped backward, still holding her hand. "You probably don't want to go back into that restaurant, huh?"

She looked over her shoulder. "Yeah, not so much."

"What if I order something for us to go and we can eat it at my place?"

The hesitation was still there, but it wasn't as strong. Grace nodded. "Sure. Okay."

He gave her hand a small squeeze and stepped back. "You have anything you really like?"

Grace shook her head. "I'm easy. Surprise me."

Riley hurried back to the restaurant, and the moment he

entered the building, the air felt different. The hum of conversation died down and several people looked in his direction. That was strange. He headed over to the counter and pulled up a stool. "I'd like to place an order to go, please."

The woman behind the counter approached. "Sure, hon. What can I get you?"

Riley dragged a menu closer and scanned it for something he thought Grace might like. He pointed to a Philly cheesesteak sandwich. "I'll take two of those with fries."

"You got it."

The restaurant was still too quiet. The longer he sat with his back to the room, the harder it became to remain calm. The hairs on the back of his neck stood on end and his pulse accelerated. His fingers itched to reach for the gun in the holster at his side.

There were no threats here.

That's all he needed to repeat to himself.

Zero threats.

The stool beside him creaked and he jumped, his hand already wrapped around the grip of his gun.

"I would let go of that weapon if I were you, son." The man beside him placed a sheriff's hat on the counter. "I think we need to have a talk."

Riley released his gun and clasped both hands on the counter. "I'm not doing anything wrong, sheriff. I have a permit to carry that gun."

"That's not what I'm here for, but thanks for the heads-up."

His jaw tightened and he glanced around the room. "Am I correct in assuming that it might have something to do with those in this room?"

The sheriff leaned back on his stool and glanced around, a smile touching his lips. "One thing you learn real quick about this place is that they take care of their own."

"I fail to see what that has to do with me ordering a meal to go."

"It's not the meal that is the problem. It's who you were with that is."

Riley stiffened. "Grace?"

"That's the one." The sheriff gave Riley a pointed look. "You arrived with one of the Callahan girls, and then she left in a hurry. A few people saw you arguing outside. You want to tell me what that's about?"

Mouth hanging open, Riley let his eyes sweep through the restaurant again. "You're joking, right?"

"Unfortunately, I'm not. There have been a handful of unsavory folks who've come and gone from town in recent years. The folks here are just trying to make sure Grace is safe."

Riley snorted. "Do you have any idea who I am?"

"That's what I came here to ask you."

He scowled. "I'm a US Army veteran. I served my country for fifteen years."

The sheriff arched a brow. "Am I correct in assuming you're one of them veterans staying at Shane Owen's place?"

"Yes, sir."

"I thank you for your service, but you'll understand if I still need to ask you a few more questions."

Riley remained stiff in his seat. On the one hand it was nice knowing that Grace was looked after, but on the other, he didn't like being the one people were suspicious of. He frowned at the sheriff and gave him a short nod.

"Is there anything wrong?" the sheriff asked.

"I'm going to have to ask you to elaborate."

"The argument," he clarified.

Riley lifted his chin. "Ah. Well, only time will tell on that one."

The sheriff chuckled. "Humor me. Let me know what's going on so I can put these folks at ease."

"I don't think you have any right to something that isn't your business to begin with."

The sheriff's eyes narrowed and he peered at Riley with a stubbornness that was all too familiar. It must be something that was in the water.

Riley sighed. "I'm trying to date her. *That's* what's going on."

The man's face spread into a wide smile. It didn't even appear that he tried to hold it back. His lips twitched. "Son, you don't know what you just got yourself into." He patted Riley on his forearm and chuckled. "Don't worry. I'll keep your secret. The last thing you need right now is to have this whole town talking about the two of you." He shook his head. "Have a good evening."

Riley watched him walk away, confusion flooding his thoughts. What was *that* about?

The waitress arrived with a plastic bag and held it out to him. He paid for it, then headed for the door. The room grew quiet once more. Small towns were the worst.

RILEY LED Grace up to the front door of his small cabin and fiddled with the keys. This would be the first time he showed a woman—or anyone for that matter—his personal space. He gave her a small smile as he pushed open the door.

Holding out his arm, he nodded to the entrance.

Grace ducked inside and he followed after her, shutting the door behind him. She stood in the entrance, her eyes sweeping through the room from the small kitchenette to the even smaller living space. This cabin wasn't built to house more than one to two people. While it suited him just fine, it wasn't exactly the kind of place he thought he'd bring a girl to.

He stood beside her and gestured to the area. "Well, this is it. There's a bedroom through that door. The only bathroom is in there, so…" Riley rubbed the back of his neck and gave her a crooked grin. "You want to eat at the table or by the fireplace?"

Grace shifted her focus from one location to the next, then smiled at him. "I'm always up for a picnic."

"I'll get the plates." He made a beeline toward the kitchen and shot a look over his shoulder toward Grace, who was currently moving the small coffee table out of the way. "Do you have any blankets?"

He shrugged. "I don't know. The one on the bed?" He chuckled as she rolled her eyes.

"We're not using the blanket from your bed to eat on."

Riley grabbed two plates and put some silverware on them. He crossed the room and placed them on the coffee table with the food, then returned to the cupboards for some cups. By the time he returned, she was plating the food.

Grace sat across from him, her legs folded in front of her. She dropped her gaze to her plate and smiled as she tucked a strand of hair behind her ear. "This is strange, isn't it?"

It wasn't strange at all. This was exactly what he had hoped it would be. But he couldn't say that. Instead, he changed the subject. "How well do you know the sheriff?"

Her eyes lifted. "He's my godfather. Why?"

Riley's heart stuttered and he coughed. "What?"

She chuckled. "Did you meet him or something?"

"He was in the diner when I went to get food." Riley went over everything they'd said in their conversation. The sheriff hadn't indicated that he knew her any better than anyone else in town. His abnormal interest in Riley and Grace's interaction suddenly made a lot more sense. He hadn't interrogated Riley because the town wanted him to. They'd had that uncomfortable conversation because he had a vested interest in Grace.

Grace laughed again. "I know that look. What happened?"

Riley cleared his throat and heat crawled up the back of his neck. "Let's just say that he asked me some very personal questions, and now I understand why he'd be curious about that sort of thing."

"Now you have to tell me."

He shook his head.

She nudged him. "Come on. I need to know. Otherwise I'm going to be blindsided—especially if he tells my dad."

"I don't think he'll do that." Riley took another bite and chewed thoughtfully. "Though he did say he wanted to wish me luck."

Her expression flattened. "Riley. You need to tell me."

He bit back a smile. "You mentioned your dad was kinda strict?"

She nodded.

"What would he say if he knew you were dating me?"

Her eyes widened and she placed her plate aside a little too hard. It clattered on the coffee table, and she rose up on her knees. "What did you tell him?"

"It's not like I had a choice. He's the sheriff. I think he was about to arrest me if I didn't tell him."

She dragged her hands down her face. "You didn't."

"I just said I was trying to date you."

"*Riley*." She groaned and sat back on her haunches. "You told Michael that we were dating? You realize he's not going to keep it from his wife. And he most definitely won't keep it from my dad. You might as well have stood up in the middle of the diner and sang that you were in love with me."

He just stared at her. She painted a pretty picture, and had he not been such a private person, he might have been willing to do just that. "What if he doesn't?"

"Oh, he will. Michael likes to toy with us—and my dad. He's gonna get a kick out of telling my dad for sure. And then he's going to sit back and watch the show."

"Then I guess we better take advantage of tonight while we still can." He laughed when she gave him a dirty look.

Her eyes clouded over and she let out a sigh. "I knew this was going to be crazy. I just didn't realize it would be this bad."

"Bad? Hey, I resent that. I'll have you know I don't make a half-bad boyfriend."

She peered at him and snickered. "Oh yeah? What makes you so great?"

This conversation felt so normal. The banter, the smiles, all of it was what he'd been missing from his life for so long. He placed his plate on the coffee table beside hers and dusted off the crumbs. Then he got to his feet and held out his hand.

She stared at it and then lifted her eyes to meet his. "What?"

He emphasized his hand so she'd take it.

Grace let a little smile sneak out before placing her hand in his. Her hand was soft and warm. It fit perfectly in his own. The contact between them was both electrifying and magnetizing. There wasn't a doubt in his mind that they were supposed to be together—which was a strange thing to think because he'd never really thought much about finding a soul mate. But now that it was a real possibility, he was grateful to have the chance.

Riley pulled her to her feet and against him. He slipped his hand around her waist and let her body mold against his. Then pulled her into a dance. They swayed back and forth, and she let out a nervous laugh. "What are we doing?"

"What? I thought all you girls dreamed about dancing in the kitchen when there wasn't any music playing."

She laughed again. "You make a good point." It was then that she relaxed, resting her cheek against his chest. His heart pounded harder, more erratically. His grip on her hand tightened and he placed his chin on her head.

There was no music, no sound except the crackling of the fireplace beside them. But inside, he could hear a thousand love songs that told him he was right where he was meant to be.

18

Grace

Okay, this was happening. It was *really* happening. And each step she made closer to allowing herself to fall for him, the scarier it became. That was normal, right?

Grace could hear his heart beating in his chest, the way it seemed to beat to the song neither one of them could hear.

So Riley was a romantic. She never would have guessed. And he was willing to spill their secret to the sheriff so he didn't get dragged out of the diner for all the town to see. She'd have to have a talk with Michael to inform him he wasn't to breathe a word to her father about any of this.

There was still no guarantee that she'd end up staying with Riley. This was her first serious relationship. She didn't even know what she wanted in a guy.

Except Riley seemed like a pretty good option right now.

Dinner.

Dancing.

Firelight.

He hit everything on a girl's dream list, and it was so easy to just give in. Her whole body hummed with nervous energy and her heart beat in time with his.

She lost track of time as they swayed back and forth. At some point they'd stopped dancing altogether. Riley held her close and she let him. She'd never felt so safe and yet so thrilled at the same time. Her heart was split into two parts.

Riley shifted first. He pulled back just far enough that he could look into her eyes. "See? I make a pretty good boyfriend." The husky tone of his voice caused her whole body to go into overdrive. Her pulse went haywire, and her throat went dry.

"I stand corrected."

His eyes traced over her face, from her hair to her eyes and down to her mouth. She couldn't look away, so the best thing she could do was blink. She knew it was coming before it happened, which made the whole experience feel like it was going in slow motion.

Riley dipped his face closer to hers, his eyes searching, asking permission for what he was about to do. Her breath hitched in her chest and she tilted her chin upward, her eyes fluttered closed.

Then nothing.

Grace waited, expecting and hoping for his lips to brush over hers like the wings of a butterfly. She wanted to give him the same thing, to show him that she desired him as much as he desired her.

Then again, maybe he didn't.

She opened her eyes, finding him staring at her. His gaze was so serious, like he was weighing all the pros and cons of what he was about to do. She could see the hesitation in every line of his face. He wanted her. There was no doubt about it, but he was also worried.

Grace pulled away, crossing her arms tightly across her

chest. "You need to make up your mind. Do you want to date me or not?"

She didn't know what she expected, but it wasn't laughter. Riley moved toward her. "I want to kiss you more than I want breath itself."

Grace's eyes cut to his. "Then why don't you?"

"Because once I do, there is no going back."

"Isn't that the point?" she said with exasperation. "You fought so hard to get me to agree to any of this. I thought that this was the next logical step."

His eyes drilled into her. "You don't understand." Riley let out a hard breath. His chest rose and fell as if he was grappling with what he needed to say. "I know that if I kiss you, there's no way I'm going to be able to go back to the way things were before. I know I'm going to want more. And I don't know if you're ready for that yet."

Her whole body went numb. So this was far more serious for him than she'd expected. But if she were honest with herself, she'd admit that to a degree she *knew*. The strange part was that she wasn't as scared as she thought she'd be.

There was this feeling of peace that surrounded her whenever she was near him, along with the high of anticipation for what might be. Her patience was wearing thin. Grace wanted Riley to know she wasn't one of those girls who changed her mind just because things got hard. When she made a decision, she stuck with it.

Grace took two steps to close the distance between them. She placed her hands on either side of his face and tugged him down, closer to her. Pressing her lips firmly against his, she allowed herself to get lost in the sensations that crashed over her.

She'd never done something so forward. She'd never fought for what she wanted more than the typical work stuff. So standing here in front of him and pulling him in for a kiss wasn't something she had ever expected would happen any time soon.

It was dizzying and breath-stealing. The way her body reacted was like one of those science experiments gone haywire. Everything within her bubbled and surged into each other. Her heart thrashed in her chest, and she could no longer hear anything except her pulse roaring in her ears.

Riley's arms wrapped around her, kissing her with an unexpected gentleness that caused her legs to grow weak. She tilted her head up to catch her breath while Riley's eyes stared into hers and his thumb caressed her cheek.

His touch was gentle, making her feel as though she were fragile, cherished even. After everything he'd experienced in his life, she hadn't expected this side of him.

Riley was the first to pull back. Desire danced in his eyes, making her shiver with anticipation. So this was what it felt like to be wanted. This was what it felt like to throw caution to the wind and let her heart take her for a ride. It was terrifying, thrilling, and completely out of character, but she wanted more.

"What if I do?" he murmured, dragging her from her thoughts.

"What if you do what?"

"That bit you said about standing on the table and announcing I love you. What if I did?"

Her breath caught in her throat.

Love? How could anyone know they were in love with someone this soon? Then again, there were people who believed in love at first sight. That hadn't happened with them, but maybe this was real. She swallowed hard, shaking off the feeling of longing she felt for that to be true.

"You can't possibly know if you love me," she whispered.

"How would you know what I am capable of?" His palm cupped her cheek and his eyes delved deeper into her. "I've been around long enough to know what these feelings mean. And if you don't feel the same yet, that's fine. Clearly, I can't do anything about that. But it won't stop me from trying."

Her throat closed up, dry and hot. Tongue swollen and unwilling to engage in any sort of speech, Grace did the only thing she could think of. She stood on her toes and her lips barely grazed his. For whatever reason, she couldn't bring herself to confess any sort of feelings for him. That was a big step, even if the thought of having won his affection sent shivers through her.

They stared at one another for a while longer before he spoke again. "I guess that settles that."

She worried her lower lip. "I suppose it does."

Riley pulled her close once again, resting his chin on the top of her head. He let out a shuddering breath, and she grinned. This wasn't nearly as easy as he had made it out to be. And she liked him even more for it.

THE NUMBERS on the microwave that hung above the stove glowed a vibrant green, telling Grace she was past curfew. Well, it was after what her curfew used to be before her father lightened up.

The house was silent, having gone to sleep along with its occupants. Grace placed her boots by the door and eased it shut. If she could get to her room without waking anyone up, she would be able to save face. The last thing she needed was her nosey sisters asking her a million questions.

Worse, she didn't want her father knowing exactly where she'd been—and that was if she was lucky enough for her godfather to have kept quiet.

Grace tip-toed through the kitchen, still feeling like she was floating after the evening she'd had. On the outside, she had been able to contain the excitement she felt. But inside was another story entirely. Her stomach danced and her heart soared, blissfully unaware of the seriousness of her current predicament.

Her light steps took her from the kitchen through the living room. Just a short distance more and she'd be heading up the stairs, and then she'd be home free. She had to be extremely careful because...

"What do you think you're doing?" The click of a lamp flicking on was almost deafening.

Because of *that*.

Grace's hands flew to her mouth and she whirled around to find Brielle sitting smugly on the couch. She folded her arms, her eyes laughing with mischief. Glaring, Grace crossed her arms. "I could ask you the same thing."

Brielle shrugged. "I'm just sitting here."

"In the *dark*. Were you waiting for me? Honestly, Bri. Out of everyone here, I would have thought you were the *one person* who would understand—"

"Easy, tiger. I'm not going to turn you in. Though I'm not sure what dad would do if he knew you didn't get home until well past midnight." She sat straighter in her seat, then patted the cushion beside her. "But out of all our sisters, I didn't think you'd be the first one to break curfew."

"We don't have a curfew. Not anymore."

Brielle snickered. "Do you seriously believe that? Dad said we could start dating. He also mentioned that he would ease up a bit on the other stuff. But when did he ever flat-out tell us that we were—" She laughed again and sliced her hand through the air. "It's that veteran guy, isn't it?"

Grace stiffened.

"I know you never really said anything specifically about him. But I know it's gotta be him. Isn't he like in his forties?"

"He's in his early thirties," Grace muttered coolly. "And it's none of your business." She didn't take the seat that Brielle offered. She fully planned on heading up to her room before anyone else managed to walk in on their conversation.

Brielle sighed and got to her feet. She clicked her tongue as if she were chastising Grace on every single decision she'd made in her life that had brought her to this point. "No. That's where you're wrong. Do you know why dad changed his tune? It's because of me. Maybe a little bit of Constance. But mostly me. I'm the one who refused to follow the neat little path he had laid out for us. And I can almost guarantee I could put us back on it."

Grace narrowed her eyes. "You wouldn't do that to Faye and Eloise."

"No, I wouldn't. But what you're doing—risking everything —you'd be the one to turn this all upside down. If Dad had been the one sitting here tonight, what do you think he would have done? Do you think he would have let you just slip past him and go to your room?"

"I don't know. You tell me. You're the one who has more experience with this sort of thing." Grace regretted the words the second they left her lips. She pinched her lips together and waited for the inevitable fallout from Brielle. Whenever her dating history was brought up, she had a tendency to go on the defensive.

Surprisingly, she did nothing. Brielle blinked once, then let out a sigh. "I'm not trying to make you feel bad, I swear. I'm trying to help you not make the same mistakes I made. You don't want to prevent Eloise and Faye from finding the guys they want to marry. Dad is finally giving us some breathing room. Just..." She sighed again. "Just be careful, okay? That guy isn't from around here. We don't know anything about him."

"I know plenty about him," Grace shot back. "I know that despite being in the military and seeing some pretty nasty stuff, he's been nothing but sweet with me. He trusts me, and I trust him."

"I'm not saying you can't date the guy. I'm just telling you to think before you allow yourself to fall head over heels for him. Do you even know what his plans are for when his therapy sessions are over? Speaking of which, isn't it like some kind of conflict of interest for you to be dating him anyway?" Brielle moved around the coffee table and her voice softened. "I don't want to see you get hurt."

"I'm fine, Bri. I'm not a child, and I can make my own decisions."

"Of course you can."

"Then will you stop making statements that sound like you don't agree? It's late and I'm tired. I just want to get to bed. Tomorrow I have to visit with Shane about what is going to happen next. I'm probably going to lose my job as it is."

Brielle's features scrunched into a look of concern. "Is he really that mad?"

"No. He's not mad. But you're right. There's a conflict. But Shane doesn't have anyone else he would put me with. My client—Riley—he was the only person I was working with."

"And suddenly everything makes sense." Brielle chuckled.

"What's that supposed to mean?"

Her older sister shrugged. "Nothing. Not really. It just figures that he's the only guy you're spending all your time with lately. He's the *first* guy you've spent a lot of time with. Don't you think you should go on some dates with other people before you jump in without a life preserver?"

"Who says I don't have one?" Once again, Grace felt her defenses going up. "I thought you said you weren't going to interfere."

Brielle laughed. "I said no such thing. If you'll recall, I said you get to make your own choices. Did I start seriously dating the first guy I liked? Nope. And it turns out it was the best decision I ever made."

Grace gave her a disbelieving look.

"What? It is."

She shook her head. "None of us were fooled for a second when it came to James. We all knew you liked him. We just didn't know if you still did when he started dating Constance."

Brielle's mouth fell open. For a second Grace thought this might be the one thing that put her over the edge. She'd get offended and their little conversation would turn sour. But then Brielle let out a quiet laugh. "There are literally no secrets around this place, are there?"

"Guess not."

"You know what that means, don't you?"

Grace frowned. "What?"

"That your secret won't be a secret for long. Someone's gonna find out and—"

"Too late."

Brielle choked on her words. "What do you mean, too late? Did you tell someone already?"

Grace felt the blush creeping before she even got to say a word. She looked away, hoping the coloring wouldn't look so bad in the dim lighting. "Sheriff Michael was at the diner when Riley picked us up some dinner. Apparently, he pressured Riley into telling him exactly what was going on."

This time Brielle's laugh was loud enough that Grace was certain it would wake up at least a few of her family members. Grace's eyes grew wide and she shook her head, her finger coming to her lips.

Brielle snapped her mouth shut, but her laughter persisted. "Michael found out? Oh, you're in trouble. There's no way he'll keep this from Dad. No one would be dumb enough to keep this kind of thing from Dad." Her features sobered. "He's not gonna like that you're dating a guy who's so much older than you are."

"What does age have to do with it?" Grace demanded. "If Riley likes me and he doesn't think I'm too young... and if I don't think he's too old..."

Brielle shook her head. "If you were to ask me, I'd say love comes in all shapes, sizes, and ages. I don't see anything wrong with it. But think about why Dad had the rules he did. He wanted to control who we were dating so he knew that the guys we brought home were worthy of us—or something like that. If he finds out, you might as well break up with him right now."

Grace's frown deepened. "I'm *not* doing that."

"Then you better think up a plan and make sure it's a good one. Otherwise, this relationship of yours isn't going to get very far at all." Brielle brushed past her, leaving Grace alone with her thoughts.

Would her father really disapprove of Riley?

19

———

Riley

Riley sat in front of Shane. They were at an impasse. Somehow word about his date with Grace had gotten back to the guy. It was as if gossip in this town could move at the speed of light. On top of that, he was completely against Riley working with Grace considering Riley's developing feelings.

Shane's brows were lowered and his focus didn't leave Riley's face. "Do you have any idea what you're putting me through? This is supposed to be a reputable business, and you're making me out to be the laughingstock of the community."

"I wouldn't go so far as to say *that*." Riley shifted deeper into his seat. "It was just a date."

"I didn't give you permission to go on a date with her."

He leaned forward. "With all due respect, sir, you don't have that kind of power. I can date whomever I would like."

Shane shot out of his seat. The motion was probably meant

to startle him, but Riley remained calm and collected. "You are here under my supervision as ordered by the courts. I provide lodging and food, and you are supposed to follow the rules. Until I can find a replacement for you, I don't want you seeing Miss Callahan again."

Riley's jaw tightened. "I don't have to stay here."

The man in front of him swiped up a document from the table and waved it at him. "This court document says otherwise. If you fail to meet the guidelines that have been set out by the judge, I am required to contact law enforcement."

For all Riley knew, Shane was right. But there was a part of him that thought there could be some kind of allowance. He flexed his hands and leaned forward again, keeping his voice steady and low. "The judge required I get therapy because I wasn't coping the way I should have. I was drinking. And when I get drunk, I get belligerent." It hurt far more than Shane would ever know to admit that little truth. "Since working with Grace, I haven't felt the need to escape like I used to. Don't you think that is an improvement?"

"That's not for me to say."

Riley threw his hands into the air. "So what then? Because some people saw me at a diner having an argument with Grace, I'm not allowed to see her anymore? How is that even fair? You realize you can't keep me from her, right? I can track down her address and go visit whenever I want. I'm not a prisoner here."

Shane groaned and slapped the paperwork on the desk. "Why can't you just let me do my job? I don't run a freaking dating service. If word gets out that the guests who are here are dating their therapists, I might as well close up shop."

Riley snorted. When Shane shot him a dirty look, he sobered. "Look, we're not doing anything sordid. She didn't stay at my place, and I was a perfect gentleman."

A bark of laughter burst from Shane's mouth and he spun on his heel to pace behind his desk. "You don't know what it's like in this town." He peeked at Riley out of the corner of his eye. "These folks are the salt of the earth—or they can be. But before they trust you, they're going to judge every little thing you do and then talk about it." He let out a sigh and ran a hand through his hair. "Boy, they talk about it. There's nothing that happens here that isn't discussed at family dinner."

"So?"

"*So?*" He stopped and placed his palms down on the desk. "*So*, do you have any idea who her family is?"

Riley wasn't about to be intimidated by anyone if that's what Shane was hinting at. Whoever her family was, he'd happily shake hands and get to know them like any other person he'd met.

Shane dragged a hand down his face. "Zeke Callahan is the single most terrifying person in town when he wants to be. He's got the biggest property and the means to put anyone in their place."

"He sounds like any other guy I've met."

"And he raised seven girls all on his own. How do you think he's going to feel knowing that a guy like you is interested in the youngest one?" Shane let that question settle.

A small sliver of concern flooded Riley's gut. Shane made a good point with that one. Grace was the baby of the family. As such, she would be the one that Zeke would have the hardest time letting go.

Still, none of that mattered. If he could show Mr. Callahan that he loved her and he'd protect her, then what did age matter in the long run?

"See? I knew you'd understand." Shane's whole body seemed to relax as if he'd been in the middle of a strenuous workout. "I'm glad you're seeing reason. So let's get you set up with a new therapist, and after you're done with—"

"No."

"No?" Shane sputtered incredulously.

"No," Riley repeated. "I'm not going to work with anyone else. I've given it some thought, and I know that if you assign me to someone I don't know and don't trust, nothing will improve."

Once more Shane groaned. "Riley, there's nothing I can do. My hands are tied."

"Then assign me a new therapist, but Grace is going to assist. I'm not going to lose what I have with her." His heart was beating far quicker than should have been expected. He'd been in the field, staring down the wrong side of a gun and not been this terrified. If he lost Grace, he didn't know what he would do. There was just something about her that made him believe that living a happy future was still a possibility.

Shane studied him, his dark expression thoughtful. "I suppose that *might* work."

"It will work."

Shane scooted his chair to the edge of the desk. "But if I agree to this, there will be no public displays of affection while you complete your sessions. You will listen to your new therapist and do everything he says—*no* exceptions."

"Right. Of course." It was as if a weight had been lifted from his shoulders. At this point he'd agree to anything as long as it meant that he could still see Grace every day.

Yes, he'd have to figure out a way to meet her father and try to make a good impression, but for now, he had won the first of many battles.

The weary man before heaved another heavy sigh. "Don't make me regret this, Scott. I'm finally becoming a valued member of this community—"

"Yeah. I get it. Don't embarrass you."

Shane shook his head. "You misunderstand. It's *more* than that. For instance, if you choose to stay for that young woman, you'll figure out real fast what I'm talking about. Zeke Callahan is one of those quiet forces to be reckoned with. If I were you, I'd be careful. Maybe talk to Grace about meeting her father."

"I get it already," he grumbled. "No offense, but you aren't my therapist, and we're not even friends. If it's all the same to you, I'll take my chances and follow what my gut tells me I should do."

The man before him didn't look offended. At least not on the outside, but he also didn't continue talking. He turned to his computer, a nonverbal way to dismiss him.

Riley clenched his teeth as he got to his feet. What he wouldn't give to have one of his friends here. The members of his squad were the only ones he felt he could come to with stuff like this.

They would have loved Grace.

Then again, they might have called him crazy for chasing after a girl who was so much younger than he was.

He wandered out of Shane's office and headed for his cabin. Today he didn't have a session due to Shane's insistence that they get another therapist. Suddenly he felt more alone. Grace said she'd stop by after she helped her sisters with some of their chores at home.

Shane's words reverberated in his head, ricocheting against every side. As much as Riley hated to admit it, Shane had made a good point about Grace's father. If Riley had a daughter, he wouldn't want to hear about her boyfriend from some neighbor. It would be best to confront this issue head-on.

He had no idea how Grace would feel about it. He'd have to bring it up when she stopped by. Riley probably looked like a crazy person. The smile that crossed his face as he wandered down the path wasn't something he could control. He'd never been this happy. Maybe his quack of a therapist back home had been right. On top of confronting his demons, he'd been told to try to return to a normal life.

Both suggestions had fallen on deaf ears at the time. But

there might be a point in finding a girl he could spend his life with.

"What? No." Grace laughed.

Riley didn't know what she found amusing, but her answer had been the opposite of what he'd been expecting. "You *don't* want me to meet your father?"

She pulled groceries out of a brown paper bag and placed them on the counter. "You're serious?"

He rested his elbows on the counter, staring at her intently. "Why wouldn't I be?"

Grace placed her hand on her hip and snorted. "We just started—whatever this is. We've had like two dates, if that. You tell me. Does that sound serious enough to meet my father?"

How could he tell her he felt serious enough that he wouldn't mind going out to look for rings? Okay, he was getting ahead of himself. He could see that now. "I dunno. Shane said..." He shook his head. "Never mind. Forget it," he muttered.

He couldn't decide if he was more upset about the fact that she didn't want him to meet her father or that she didn't think they were serious. He was so out of his element. More than that, he was out of practice. Based on her reaction, he was taking things too fast.

She shifted, her arm dropping to her side, then leaned forward as well. She grasped his hands with hers while her eyes narrowed with curiosity. "You know I can tell when you want to talk about something, right?"

Riley ran his thumbs over her knuckles. "I guess that's a hazard of you having a therapy background."

Grace tilted her head slightly. She wasn't asking him

outright to talk. It was entirely possible that she wanted him to insist they don't.

He glanced up at her once more. Honestly, he *didn't* want to talk about it. Even when he hung out with his guys, they didn't *talk* or give advice. It was more like catching up with each other. Riley squeezed her hands. He might as well just get it out of his system. There were worse things she could be asking him about. Certain things that he'd keep to himself forever.

"I had a meeting with Shane today."

"How did that go?"

"That guy is a real piece of work, you know that?"

Her lips twitched, but she didn't comment.

"What kind of guy tells a stranger that he should meet the father of the girl of his dreams?"

This time she did smile. "What kind of stranger tells the owner of the therapy center he's using that he's developing feelings for the girl who's helping him get through his sordid past?" She looked away for a moment then her gaze bounced back to meet his. "Is that what this is all about? You want to meet my dad because of what Shane said?" It was the first time he noticed the tightness in her voice.

That's when the realization hit him over the head. "You don't want me to meet him."

She grimaced. "Not really. I mean, it's not why you think. This is new. I don't want to jinx it."

Riley frowned. His stomach twisted uncomfortably. The way she phrased it wasn't so bad, but the notes of uncertainty in her tone were enough to set his teeth on edge. For all her lectures on not hiding stuff, he could tell she was doing just that. "And yet your father probably already knows more about me than I know about him."

The wrinkle that formed between her brows would have been adorable if not for the reason it was there. Did she think he was an idiot and that he wouldn't put it all together? She'd commented on all this already. Shane was more direct, but he knew—there was no hiding their relationship from anyone now.

"Your dad. He already knows. What's the point in trying to keep it a secret?"

"He doesn't know. If he did, he'd have said something..." Her voice trailed off and she pulled her hands from his. "He would have asked about you or asked to meet you." Her eyes got a far-off look and she gnawed on her lower lip, then she nodded resolutely. "Yes. He would have said something if he knew. It's not like my dad to sit back and just let things simmer. He's much more direct than that."

"Don't you think it would be better to get out ahead of this? What do you think he's going to say when he finds out that I'm not only someone who's utilizing the services here, but that I'm so much older than you?"

She laughed, but it was strained. Her eyes darted away from him and she got back to work pulling the groceries for their dinner from the bag. "You're worrying about this too much. While he's still very direct, people like Shane are thinking about what he was like before he made all these changes to our family rules. They're scared of what he used to be. Not what he is now."

"Your tone doesn't instill much confidence." He stared hard at her, daring her to meet his gaze, but she didn't.

Well, if she wasn't going to facilitate the meeting, he'd have to figure out a way all on his own. Theirs might be a new relationship, but it was still one that was worth investing in. Back in the day, men like Riley would make their intentions known. Zeke sounded like an old-fashioned kind of guy. He'd probably appreciate the fact that Riley would come to him.

Grace would just have to accept that it was going to happen with or without her approval.

20

Grace

It wasn't fair. All Grace wanted was to slow this down, think things through. The second she had even a small interest in someone, everyone was breathing down her neck about it.

Brielle was telling her that she needed to be careful how she acted whether or not she announced to her father who she was dating. Apparently, her boss even had an opinion on how things should be handled when it came to her father—something that left her unnerved.

Now, Riley was telling her he wanted to meet her father.

What in the world was going on?

Wasn't that the kind of thing that happened after people had been dating for months? Not days? Sheesh. They had time. Riley wasn't going to leave any time soon. Why couldn't they just enjoy each other for a little while longer before the world came crashing down on them and reality hit them in the face?

Romance was supposed to be fun and exciting, not laced

with this strange feeling of expectation. She was still a young twenty-something girl who had her whole life ahead of her.

Grace was beginning to think maybe her father had it right the first time. Let her grow up.

And those were the thoughts that continued to plague her over the next few weeks. The voices kept her up at night. They were the first thing to fill her mind in the morning. Every time she looked at Riley during their sessions, all she could think about was how she might have jumped into this way too early.

She refused to let him come to her house. Yes, she was nervous about what her father would say. But she also didn't want her sisters giving their unsolicited advice. Not to him and most certainly not to her.

Besides those lingering thoughts of doubt, their relationship had continued to deepen. He shared a lot about what it was like growing up, as did she. They talked about high school and their career choices. Though Riley continued to avoid telling her exactly what he had to do when he was deployed.

Instead, he focused on telling her about the people he'd met and the friends he'd made. Grace had faith that one day he would finally tell her about the things that kept him up at night. He still dismissed the idea that talking about something made it better.

Grace grabbed her keys from her dresser and yanked a heavyweight jacket from a hook on the back of her door. They had to pick up his motorcycle today. Apparently, the repair issue had needed a part they didn't have in stock and it had finally arrived.

She hurried down the stairs and into the kitchen. Her father sat at the table with all of her sisters who were still living at home. Brielle and her father sat on one side, while Constance, Eloise, and Faye sat on the other. Grace reached over Faye and grabbed a piece of toast.

Her father wasn't eating. He'd probably had something

before he went out for the day. Her sisters, on the other hand, were having a later-than-usual breakfast.

"Aren't you going to join us?" Zeke looked up from a newspaper he held in his hand. His gray brows lifted slightly, and she couldn't see the rest of his face to tell if he was in a good mood this morning.

Grace took a bite of her toast and hurried over to the counter where she grabbed a glass and filled it with some orange juice. "I have to head to town this morning."

Faye straightened. "Ooh. I need something in town. I'll come, too."

"No."

All eyes turned to gaze at her and she cleared her throat. "I'm actually not going for myself. I have to take someone to town to get something." Her focus shifted to Brielle who seemed to be holding back a smile. Grace let her eyes widen pointedly at her, hoping she got the hint and would come to her aid.

She should have known better.

Faye's brows pulled together. "I don't mind tagging along. I'll even sit in the backseat. Let me just go get my things and I'll be ready before you know it." She left the room before Grace could tell her to stop and get back into her seat. She stood there forlornly in front of her family, hating the expectant looks on their faces almost more than the smug look that Brielle wore.

"Who are you taking to town?" Her father put the newspaper down on the table and picked up his coffee. "Do I know them?"

Grace shook her head.

Zeke arched a brow—a clear indication he didn't like the direction that this conversation was taking. He didn't say a word, but Grace knew what he was asking her with his eyes. He wanted details, and he'd be getting them one way or another.

Grace shot a look at Brielle who didn't bother meeting her

gaze. She merely picked up her fork and started eating the food on her plate once more.

"Is it someone from work?" her father persisted.

Grace sighed. "Remember that guy I was assisting with equine therapy services? It's him."

Understandably, her father's features tightened. "The army vet?"

She nodded. "His motorcycle is in the shop, and he needs someone to take him over there."

"Don't they have a driver service out there? I'm sure Shane has something the man can use. You shouldn't have to take him *anywhere*."

"I don't *have* to do anything. He's my—" Her eyes darted to Brielle who finally looked up. Grace had shied away from labeling Riley as anything other than her client when it came to their family. Miraculously, no one from town had deemed it a necessary tidbit of information to tell her father. Perhaps they were worried he would shoot the messenger. Even Michael had kept it under wraps.

She knew better than to believe her sisters hadn't heard rumors, though. She just didn't know if they believed it or if Brielle was the only one who knew for sure.

Grace cleared her throat. "He's my friend and he needed a ride." She tried to sound as nonchalant as she possibly could, but her voice still came out strained no matter how hard she tried to hide it.

Her father sensed her discomfort. It was written all over his face in the way his brows twitched to the tight line of his mouth. "How long will you be gone?"

Faye breezed into the room, a flushed smile on her face. "Ready."

Grace stifled a groan. "Are you sure you want to come? It's going to be boring."

"She's going. I didn't give you that truck so you could

monopolize it. You have a job that's off this property. That truck was your mother's. You remember the deal. If your sisters need a ride, you facilitate that." Her father picked up his newspaper, his earlier question apparently forgotten.

Eloise had lost interest in the conversation long ago. Brielle was the only one who seemed to stay interested enough to glance up every so often.

Grace sighed. "Come on." She didn't know how Riley would feel about having a third wheel. She didn't mind the extra visitor. She just didn't want Faye to end up telling their father what was actually going on. If Riley held Grace's hand, touched her... kissed her... then Faye would have an arsenal of information just from those innocent displays of affection.

Oh boy. This was not what she wanted.

The whole drive over to the country club, Grace itched to warn Faye about who Riley really was. But she couldn't find the words to tell her sister any of it. She couldn't exactly demand that she keep her mouth shut. People always wanted to do something more when they were told they couldn't.

So they drove in silence all the way up until they stopped in front of Riley's cabin. Faye moved to the backseat without waiting for Grace to make the request, and Riley exited his temporary home at the same moment.

His steps slowed and he glanced up at the driver's side window with curiosity. His brows furrowed. Then a small smile appeared on his face and he climbed into the truck. Without preamble, he twisted in his seat and glanced back at Faye. "Which one are you?"

She stared at him, confusion plastered on her face. Her eyes darted from him to Grace and back. "Pardon?"

"Which sister? I'm assuming you are Grace's sister. She hasn't let me meet any of you besides Brielle—"

"We should probably get going. Faye needs to pick up some stuff in town. That's why she's coming along." Grace backed out and headed toward the main road. "I'll drop you off to get your bike first, and that way, you don't have to go all over town on errands with us."

"I don't mind." Riley faced forward and reached for her hand like he usually did when they went on walks or a drive to town.

But Grace kept her hands glued to the steering wheel. She sensed more than saw his disappointment and confusion. It practically radiated off him. This wasn't going to be good. They had been getting along so well, and now this had to happen.

She knew exactly what he was going to say about all of it, too. He'd ask her why she was avoiding telling her family about him, especially since she had been trained to be a therapist of sorts.

Well, there was no easy answer to that question, and he didn't need one either. It was her choice whether or not she told her family. She'd do so when she was good and ready.

The tension in the truck continued to mount with each passing mile. Riley tried to make small talk with Faye, but all Grace could hear was a buzzing in her ears. The irritating sound only continued to make her headache worse.

By the time they arrived at the mechanic's shop, she was on edge and her teeth ached from clenching them.

Logically, she had no reason to be upset about any of this. She could try to talk herself out of it, but every time she did, her heart raced a little faster and her head pounded like someone banging against a drum.

Riley frowned at her. "I said I was fine to come along." He leaned closer to her and whispered. "Are you trying to get rid of me?"

She flushed as she shook her head. Then her eyes darted to where Faye sat behind him. "I just really didn't think you'd want to go all over town..."

"I don't mind, Grace. I want to spend time with you."

Faye shifted in her seat, and Grace could feel her stare on them. Well, the cat was out of the bag. There was no way her older sister hadn't caught on. To make matters worse, she'd probably ask Grace why she was trying to hide it at all.

And Grace had no idea how to answer that question.

"Tell you what, I'll go see if it's ready, and if they need more time, then we can run those errands, get some lunch, and come back." And before she could stop him, he pressed a quick kiss to her lips.

A searing heat washed over her and her blush intensified as he climbed out of her truck and shut the door. Grace squeezed her eyes shut briefly, then watched him head inside the building.

"Ohhhh," Faye murmured. "I get it now."

Grace whipped around and stared at her sister. "You don't get anything."

Faye snickered. "There's nothing wrong with dating someone. Remember? Dad doesn't care anymore."

Grace huffed. "He'd care about this one."

"Why? He seems nice."

She let her head fall back against the headrest. "He's great. That's not the problem."

"Then what is?"

Grace shut her eyes again. How to answer that question without sounding ridiculous? She couldn't even figure out why this was bothering her so much. Could the age gap be a bigger issue to her deep down? Was it his past? When they were together, she didn't have a problem with any of it. But trying to explain to someone else what she felt seemed so impossible. She sighed and twisted her head around to look at her sister. "How many guys have you dated since Dad said it was okay?"

Faye shrugged. "Only a few, I guess. Nothing serious, though."

"Okay. Have any of them been in the military?"

Her sister pouted out her lower lip in thought. "No. I don't think so."

"Were any of them a lot older than you?"

Faye blinked. "How much older?"

"Just answer the question."

"Grace, I don't interrogate the guys who buy me dinner. They're about my age. But Riley looks about our age, so what are you getting at?"

Her lower lip was getting raw with how much she'd been chewing on it lately. Grace turned forward in her seat again. "He's ten years older than me." She said it so quietly she didn't know if Faye would hear her correctly.

She shouldn't have been worried.

"Ten years," Faye squawked. "You're joking, right? You're barely legal."

Grace huffed and spun around faster this time. "I'm mature for my age."

They stared each other down until Faye's eyes shifted from Grace to something behind her, following that something until Riley opened the door and climbed in.

He beamed at them both. "Good news. The bike still needs a few more hours of work." His eyes bounced from Grace to Faye and back. "Did I miss something?"

Grace yanked the gearshift into reverse and backed out of the parking lot. Then she put both hands on the steering wheel and shook her head. "Nope. Everything is great." She glanced in the rearview mirror at her sister, who smiled much like Brielle had this morning. She was like a cat who had swallowed a mouse. There was no way she would keep this from her other sisters.

Brielle was great at keeping secrets. Faye could keep a secret, but she enjoyed telling her sisters every little sordid detail of something like this.

And Eloise could never keep a secret. By the end of the

week, no, by the end of the day, her father would likely know more than Grace had ever wanted him to.

Something mechanical in her truck squealed in protest and then died down. Riley frowned. "That didn't sound good."

"It does that," Grace muttered. "That's the thing that they can't figure out. But this truck still gets me from point A to point B. So who am I to complain?"

"We should get you a new one. I don't like the idea of you driving in this thing around town."

Grace chuckled dryly. "I'm sorry. But I don't have that kind of money. And my father doesn't give his money out freely. He expects us to work for our things."

Faye leaned forward. "Besides, this was our mother's truck. There's no way any of us would get rid of it."

Riley shot a look at Grace and she met his gaze. An understanding passed between them, and he nodded. "Understood. Maybe one day we can get you a replacement along with getting this thing fixed, and then you can give it to one of your sisters."

Faye settled back into her seat. "I like this one, Grace. I think you should keep him."

Riley chuckled and twisted around in his seat. "Well, I like you, too, Faye."

Grace could feel his eyes on her as they drove farther into town. He wasn't happy about something. The tension hadn't completely gone away—not even after Faye's comment. They'd have to figure out how to dispel it later. Right now wouldn't be an option. Not with Faye as their willing audience.

21

Riley

That tight, unyielding sensation filled his stomach. He felt like he was drowning again. The way Grace had acted when she arrived to pick him up had been startling at best. He'd thought they had gotten past the awkward beginning stages. In fact, he'd been considering bringing up meeting her father again.

But after the way she'd acted in front of Faye, he knew better. Grace had been hiding their relationship. He couldn't help but feel like she was ashamed of him. And who wouldn't be? She knew enough about his past. Why would she want to share any of that with her family and friends?

He was broken.

He'd come to this town solely because he wasn't following the law. What kind of woman would want to have a guy like him meet her father and sisters? Not a sane one.

Riley didn't deserve to have a girl like her. That much was clear. He just hadn't allowed himself to see the truth of it.

He chanced a look out of the corner of his eye toward her, and those desperate thoughts continued to drag him down into the depths of frustration and pain. She shifted in her seat and fidgeted.

If he wanted to do something to fix this, he'd have to finally dig his heels in and fight for it. Riley didn't know where she lived—that was the only thing holding him back. That and not having his motorcycle.

But now he had access to her sister. Faye might be willing to give him some extra information. He just had to get her alone. Somehow he knew that if Grace was nearby when he asked, she'd prevent him from getting anything from Faye and his plan would fail.

They found parking near the hub of town and everyone climbed out of the truck. The three of them wandered down the sidewalk. Riley reached for Grace's hand, half-expecting her to pull away from him the second he did.

Surprisingly, she let him lace his fingers within hers and she leaned into him. The sensation was reminiscent of their first date when they danced to no music, and a wave of peace crashed over him. Perhaps he'd been overreacting to how she was behaving.

He had to remind himself that while she was mature for her age, she was still young and with that came certain tendencies. Riley lifted her hand to his lips and watched for a reaction as he kissed the back of it.

A small smile touched her lips. Good. All was not lost.

"What do you say we get a coffee to warm us up?" Grace tilted her face toward him. "I think it will help me not be so on edge."

"Oh, is that what you call it?" he joked, loving the way her cheeks filled with a little color.

She gave him a playful shove. "I was thrown off a little when Faye asked to come. I didn't know how you would react."

"Me?" He glanced over his shoulder to where Faye wandered a few feet behind them. "I've told you before. I'd love to meet your family as soon as you'd let me."

Grace grimaced. "I really don't think that's a good idea yet. My dad is—"

He shook his head. "The longer you wait, the harder it becomes. We really should—"

"I'm going in here, guys."

They stopped and turned toward Faye, who had stopped beside a bookstore. "There's a new book I really want to get."

Grace offered her sister a wave. "We're going to get some coffee. You want some?"

Faye shook her head. "No thanks."

"Actually, a book sounds nice. Mind if I look around while you go get the coffee?" It was a weak excuse but possibly the only opportunity he had to get Faye alone long enough to ask her a few questions.

Grace glanced over to where Faye had just disappeared inside the store, then looked up at him. "Yeah, sure. I'll be right back."

He kissed her quickly on the cheek. "I'll miss you."

She shot him a funny look and shook her head. "I'll literally be like five minutes."

"I'll still miss you."

Riley watched her walk away for only a moment then he darted inside the store. He didn't have much time. An address should be easy, but he had no idea what Faye was really like. For all he knew, she'd try to give him the run-around just to mess with him.

He looked down several aisles until he caught sight of her and charged forward.

Faye glanced up at him as he neared and then past him. "Where's Grace?"

"She's getting coffee."

Her eyes were similar in only a few minor ways. They were clearly related, but the eyes that made him stay up at night spoke to his soul. Riley gave a sharp shake of his head, dispelling the distracting thoughts. "I need to ask you something."

She placed the book that she held back onto the shelf before her and grabbed another. "Okay."

"Has Grace talked about me?"

Faye froze.

Great. This was exactly what he had been worried about. Grace wasn't willing to invest in their relationship by sharing it with anyone in her family. Well, all of that was about to change.

Faye finally lifted her eyes to meet his. "We all assumed something was going on with her. She seems happier lately. And she came in late a lot more often than it just being work-related." She cocked her head to the side. "But you specifically? I'm sorry, no."

"She's happier?"

"Sure. She hums a song sometimes. She's more chipper. Though sometimes that just happens as it gets warmer. None of us like to stay cooped up inside. The winter can be rough."

Riley nodded and stood a little taller as he shifted his gaze to the door. "Do you think you could give me your address?"

"My address?" Her brows furrowed. "Hasn't Grace…"

The look on his face must have said it all.

"Oh." She folded the book in her arms against her chest. "Well, if Grace doesn't want you to have it, don't you think there's a reason for that?"

He sighed and ran a hand through his hair. "I just want to surprise her with something. That's all." It was the most logical explanation he could come up with. If he could get Faye to give him even a hint at where Grace lived, then he had a small shot at getting her father on board with them dating for the long haul.

Faye shifted her weight from one foot to the other. "I mean, is there a reason she'd keep it from you? Because I don't mind giving it to you if her reasons are really dumb." She let out a soft laugh. "My sisters can be kinda stubborn sometimes. It's in our blood."

"So I've heard. I've also heard you come by it honestly."

Her laugh was louder this time. "You mean our dad? Oh yeah. He's just as stubborn as we are sometimes."

The door to the shop opened and closed. He didn't even bother checking to see if it was the one person they were discussing. "The address?"

She nodded. "I'll write it down on a piece of paper before we drop you off." She wiggled her book in the air. "But it's gonna cost you."

"I'll buy you a dozen books if it means—"

"I got coffee," Grace sang out as she got closer to them.

Riley spun around and accepted the drink with a smile. Faye's smile was less hesitant this time. She turned toward the shelf and pulled two more books from the same author and stacked them in her arms, then held the stack toward Riley. "These are the ones I would recommend."

Grace leaned closer, eyeing the books, then she laughed and stared at Riley. "I didn't realize you liked reading."

"Yeah? Well, there's a lot about me you have yet to learn."

She tapped the cover of the top book. "Oh, I figured that much. But I *really* didn't expect that you'd enjoy reading about a love triangle set in a fantasy world with dragons."

His gaze dipped down to the book and then his eyebrows rose as he looked up at Faye. It was clear she was fighting back the smile that hovered just beneath the surface.

This better be worth it.

~

RILEY PULLED out Faye's chair and then Grace's when their errands were finally complete. They opted to eat at one of the nicer restaurants in town rather than risk being talked about at the diner. The absolute last thing he wanted was to be seen with *two* Callahans and have another run-in with their godfather.

He picked up the menu and glanced over it before he put it down.

"So, Riley, what branch of the military did you serve?" Faye asked.

Without missing a beat, he spouted off, "The army national guard."

"Wow. Have you ever been deployed overseas?"

"Yes..." he drawled, his eyes meeting Grace's. She'd probably be watching him to see if he was able to handle this conversation with her sister. Already his heart beat a little heavier. People who didn't know much about what he did never really liked the answers he could give them.

And ultimately, they never liked to find out just what he had to deal with on a daily basis.

The anger.

The guilt.

The depression.

"Where was your last assignment?" Faye reached for her glass of water and took a long sip.

Riley cleared his throat. This was a test. It would dictate how Grace viewed him. They were innocent enough questions. He ought to be able to answer them without feeling triggered. Thankfully, Grace had steered clear of his more recent stories. Instead, they focused on the things he enjoyed.

Unfortunately, everything that had happened in the last couple of years were what made him hate who he was.

He rubbed his hand down his face. "I served in a desert

location on a small base we shared with some special forces and CIA agents."

Her eyes widened. "Oh. I think I heard about that one. The president was pulling you guys out, right?"

"Faye—" Grace started, but Faye ignored her.

"I bet it was hard, wasn't it? Did you guys have to deal with a lot over there when the flu hit hard this year?"

Riley stiffened. Faye wasn't one of the normal curious individuals who only wanted to know if he had ever killed someone. She was actually informed. His throat tightened and he sought out Grace's eyes, but his vision blurred. "Yeah," he croaked, "it was a lot harder than anyone will ever understand."

"I can only imagine. I had a friend who was telling me some stuff he heard about closing down that base. Were you there when that happened? He was saying that—"

Riley shot out of his seat and his chair toppled backward, drawing the focus of everyone in the restaurant. Without another word, he charged toward the door. The walls were closing in on him and the sounds of all those voices calling for help overwhelmed his senses. He couldn't see or hear anything but the cries, pleading, begging.

Even when the cool air hit his face, Riley was stuck back where it all went wrong. He shut his eyes to push out the memories. Hot emotion burned in the back of his throat and behind his eyes, clawing for a way to escape. A sob bubbled up like molten lava and he swallowed it back.

No. Not now. Not here.

He vaguely realized that the door beside him opened and footsteps approached. "Riley?"

His head snapped up and he stared at Grace and Faye. Both of them looked completely terrified. Or maybe he was just projecting. That was something his therapist back home used to tell him he did. When the voices and the noises wouldn't leave his head, he'd picture them on the faces of the people who were around him.

Riley ducked his head, raking his hands through his hair as he took in several deep breaths.

A gentle hand touched his arm. "You can talk to me. You know that right?" Grace's soft voice filtered through the cacophony of sounds that continued to beat against him like the sound of a heavy storm.

She was wrong. He couldn't talk to her. He couldn't talk to anyone. Judgment came in all forms, and the only person he could trust when it came to these things was himself.

Himself and the few remaining members of his team.

Riley took one final deep breath and slowly lifted his head to gaze into Grace's concerned eyes. "I'm sorry," his voice cracked and he reached for her hand to give it a squeeze. "Sometimes I get a little claustrophobic. I don't have episodes often, but when I do, it's not pretty." It was the lie he told everyone.

Yes, when he had these panic attacks, the walls would close in around him. But it wasn't just a sense of claustrophobia. It was the feeling he would never escape what he'd lived through no matter how many days passed. No matter how far he ran.

He jutted his chin toward the building. "How about we get lunch before they give our table away?"

Her brows were still pinched and she exchanged a look with Faye before meeting his eyes. "You sure? We could go find somewhere to eat outside."

Riley nodded. "I'm sure."

Faye shrugged, then turned toward the door.

He moved past Grace while keeping her hand in his, but she didn't budge, causing him to turn back to face her.

"Riley."

"What?"

She pursed her lips for a moment. "That wasn't claustrophobia, was it?"

"Sure it was."

Grace shook her head, her hand tightening on his. "I know what claustrophobia looks like. I've had training. You were having a panic attack or an episode. Whatever you want to call it, you were reacting to Faye's questions. Is that what happened when you got arrested?"

He scowled at her. "No. Of course not. Random people don't just come up and ask me about my last tour." He'd been arrested due to his unhealthy habit of turning to alcohol to drown out those voices that screamed at him when it got too much for him to handle.

Riley swallowed again, his jaw tight. "Let's just go get some lunch and we can talk about this later." He tugged on her hand, but once again she didn't move.

"I think this is something we need to discuss. And somehow, I feel that you won't do that if I don't make you right now."

"Your sister is in there waiting. I'm not going to have a session out here on the sidewalk." It was getting increasingly harder to remain patient with her. And with each passing second, he became more and more aware of just why she would want to keep him a secret from everyone she cared about.

She was ashamed. Or perhaps she was worried about what he might do to embarrass her.

Riley released her hand. "Come eat or don't. I'm not going to stand out here like a crazy person." He strode toward the door and headed right back to their table, where Faye was seated. She pushed a napkin toward him and he stared down at it. Scrawled there in black and white was her address.

He grabbed the napkin in his fist and shoved it into his pocket before Grace could see.

His previous plan to speak to her father was currently up in the air. Grace had seen evidence he wasn't ready to climb out of the mud created from his despair. And Faye was her witness. Even if Grace still cared about him, it wouldn't take much for Faye to turn her against him.

The canyon of risk that lay between them had widened. If he had a shot at keeping Grace in his life, he'd drastically threatened that reality and all because he allowed Faye to delve into his past like he was some carnival freakshow and she had a ticket, bought and paid for.

race

GRACE GLANCED at Riley for what was probably the hundredth time. The three of them ate in silence, filling the void with menial small talk. Faye was doing most of the work, and while she was making an effort to keep her voice light and upbeat, the dismal tone came through like thorns on the stem of a rose.

This was not how today was supposed to go. They were going to get his motorcycle and then... what? She hadn't planned on going to lunch. She definitely hadn't planned on exposing his past in front of a stranger.

Granted, that part of the problem wasn't something she should be blamed for. Riley had been the one who'd let Faye ask him questions he wasn't ready for.

Then what was the point of the therapy sessions? Wasn't she supposed to be the person who helped him get through the hardest parts? He should have had enough practice by now.

She pushed some of her corn around her plate with the fork. They should just leave. No one was having fun right now. Grace felt more than one pair of eyes on her, and she couldn't bring herself to look at either of them. Her own irritation simmered. It had started small, but the more Grace thought about it, the more she realized she was out of her depth.

She wasn't a good enough therapist. And as far as their budding relationship went, how was she supposed to support him if she couldn't get him to talk to her?

Had she made a mistake?

She allowed herself a peek at him and found his gaze locked onto her. A small thrill shot through her. Based on that reaction alone, she should just allow herself to continue exploring their relationship, right?

They could take it slow—really slow. And when she was ready for them to move forward, they'd take that step.

A small smile tugged at his lips and he looked away. That's all it took. A smile and she was putty in his hands once more. Grace placed her fork on her plate and grabbed her napkin. She dabbed at her mouth and then stood. "I'm going to use the restroom. Then we can go get your motorcycle."

She strode toward the back of the restaurant. The bathroom was around a corner down a short hallway. Before she could slip into the restroom, a hand grasped her wrist. Grace spun around.

Riley's gaze smoldered. The desire was far too easy to read in his expression. He tugged her closer and slipped his free hand around her waist. "I'm sorry," he whispered.

"You're sorry?" Her lashes fluttered. "Why?"

He shook his head and let out a heavy breath. "I shouldn't have made a scene."

It wasn't really a scene. He'd had an attack. Why wasn't he acknowledging that? Was he still so out of touch with his struggles that he couldn't label what had happened? This was just another bit of proof that she might be in over her head.

Grace wanted nothing more than to help him. But how was she supposed to do that when he wouldn't let her?

The only reasonable explanation was that he was prepared to take it slow, just like she was. He'd get to a point when he could talk to her. At least she hoped so. She pressed her lips together tightly. Part of her wanted to tell him that very thing. They wouldn't be able to move forward in a relationship if he wasn't willing to let her in.

There was one big problem with that. She wasn't ready for something that serious. Not yet. And definitely not so soon after her father had made all these changes. Grace might not agree with Brielle on everything, but her older sister had made a decent point. Grace couldn't predict what her father might do. She didn't even want to think about what might happen if he rescinded his new rules.

Grace swallowed hard and smiled at Riley. She placed her palm against his cheek, letting her thumb trace over his cheekbone. "It's a good thing we have plenty of time."

His brows furrowed. "What do you mean by that?"

She lifted a shoulder. It was a touchy subject. To tell him he still had a long way to go would only cause more contention. "We got past the hardest part, right?"

Riley leaned into her touch. "I suppose we have."

"Then let's just go at a pace that makes sense." Nice and slow.

He dipped his face closer to hers, claiming her mouth with a deep kiss—one that curled her toes and made the hairs on her arms float. The fluttering of her heart started out slow, then sped up, thrashing around in her chest like the wings of a hummingbird.

Grace stood on her toes, throwing her arms around his neck and shoving aside all the fears and worries that plagued her.

Time was the answer. It had to be. No one was perfect. Everyone had problems. They could get through this as long as they worked on their communication. This afternoon was just a small setback.

GRACE LEANED against her truck as Riley spoke with a pretty young woman in coveralls. If it weren't for the simple ring on that woman's finger, Grace might have been jealous. Who was she kidding? She *was* jealous.

Could that be a sign that she wanted Riley more than she was ready to admit?

Nah. That was ridiculous. She knew she had feelings for him. She knew she wanted to spend more time with him. And everything about his pain and the stuff he had to work through... that could be worked on. No one was perfect.

Riley glanced at her over his shoulder and she smiled at him, giving him a little wave. Nothing worth having was easy to get. At least that's what her father had said on more than one occasion.

The man who stood a few yards away could be that thing worth fighting for.

That giddy feeling inside her continued to occur even when he wasn't anywhere near her.

"Whatcha thinking about?"

Grace jumped and shot a look to her side where Faye all but hung out of the window. "Nothing."

Her sister shook her head, a knowing smile crossing her face. "That look ain't nothin'. I might not be in a serious relationship, but I can tell when something's going on."

Grace rolled her eyes. "You know something's going on because I literally told you so."

"No. You said you were dating the guy. You didn't say you were in love."

Grace stiffened. Every bone and muscle in her body went rigid and she didn't dare move. Hairs stood at attention on the back of her neck as if wanting to jump in on the potential of where this conversation was about to lead.

"No comment, huh? That's fine. If I had to bet, I'd say he knows he loves you."

She spun around so fast she tweaked her neck. "He has no idea whether or not he loves me."

Her sister's smile widened further. "So he's told you."

"No. He hasn't said any such thing."

"But I bet he hinted at it."

Grace groaned. "I thought we'd grown past the teasing part of talking about our relationships."

"Never," Faye said with a short laugh. She sent a quick look in Riley's direction. "Why haven't you told him where we live?"

Grace shot her a surprised look. "He told you that?"

Faye shrugged. "Maybe."

"What did he say?"

"You answer my question first."

Grace turned away from her sister, her arms folded. "I don't have to tell you anything."

"Same goes for me."

She sighed. "Would you tell someone you've just started dating where you live?"

Faye snorted. "You really don't know anything about dating, do you? Of course he'd know. How else would he know where to come to pick me up for our dates? How would he know where to send the flowers or love notes? The only reason you don't tell a guy you're interested in where you live is if he's some sociopath or something."

Almost immediately, Grace's thoughts shifted to the outburst Riley had at the restaurant. He wasn't a sociopath. She had zero concerns about him doing anything that would hurt her or anyone else, for that matter. But what made this conversation worse was the fact that Faye made a good point.

Boyfriends usually knew where to go when they were dating someone. Had Grace been unreasonable?

She glanced once more over at Riley. Her eyes swept over his tall, strong silhouette. What was holding her back? She couldn't think of any reason besides the fact that she was terrified their relationship wouldn't last. It made sense that she didn't want to risk everything so soon, right?

"To answer your question, he didn't say anything. He just mentioned he didn't know where we lived, and I thought it was strange, that's all." Faye retreated back into the truck and settled onto her seat.

Great. Now she had to figure out a way to tell Riley why she didn't tell him where she lived. She still wasn't ready for him to have that information, and she was quickly realizing it had nothing to do with feeling safe.

No, it had everything to do with how she felt about the seriousness of their relationship. He'd have to be patient with her just like she was being patient with him.

She pushed away from her truck and slowly made her way over to Riley and the mechanic just as another mechanic came out. He was dressed in blue coveralls that were smudged all over with grease and dirt. His white shirt had seen better days, and his face was just as filthy. But he had the most striking blue eyes that she had ever seen. They were as blue as the summer sky on a cloudless day.

He wiped his hands on a rag and held one out to Riley. "Mr. Scott, you've got some motorcycle there. Have you ever considered selling? I've been in the market for one of them for a while."

Riley shook the mechanic's hand and chuckled. "Absolutely not."

The man laughed with him. "I don't blame you. She sure is a beaut." His gaze landed on Grace. "You must be one of the Callahan girls."

Her brows furrowed and she shifted her focus from Riley to the woman to the mechanic again. "I am."

His smile broadened. "I've lost track. Which one are you?"

"I'm sorry, have we met?"

The mechanic tilted his head. "You were probably in middle school when I left for college, so I don't suppose you would have remembered me. Name's Adam."

Her eyes widened with recognition. "I remember. You were one of the football players at the high school."

His chest puffed out and his eyes flashed with pride. "That's right. I was the quarterback."

The woman snorted. "Of course you were the quarterback." She rolled her eyes and headed back inside. "Don't take too long. Your dad wants us to get to work on one of the Keagan's tractors out back. Shane Owens is footing the bill, and it's got top priority."

Adam jutted his chin toward the motorcycle. "We figured out the problem. You had a…"

Grace studied Riley out of the corner of her eye, pretending that she was listening to the boring update being offered on the motorcycle. There must be something really wrong with her if she wasn't willing to let Riley hang out with her at home. If he'd been some local guy, he would have already known where she lived. Ha, it wouldn't be hard for him to figure it out anyway. All he'd have to do is ask around. Everyone and their dog could tell him where the Callahan's ranch was located.

So why couldn't she just admit she was wrong and tell him to come over?

Her father, that's why.

She still had no idea where her father would stand on this situation. Grace could imagine her father wouldn't be thrilled about Riley from the start. The meeting could range from awkward silences to full-blown shotgun escorts off the property.

Grace had been smart to tell him no. She needed to have a long talk with her father about what Riley really meant to her.

Her thoughts shifted to what Faye had said about Riley loving her. If she was right about that, then Grace needed to figure out right quick how she felt about him. She might be old-fashioned and prefer to take things slowly, but she wasn't about to lead him on.

"You ready?"

She jumped and looked up at Riley. "What? You want me to ride with you?"

He shot a look over to his bike and chuckled. "I wasn't suggesting that, but now that you mention it—"

"No."

Riley's lips curled into a crooked smile. "Rain check, then." And before she could tell him he shouldn't be kissing her in public, he brushed a kiss to her sensitive lips. Tingles erupted and her knees went weak.

She might not love him yet, but she was quickly arriving there. It was like she'd been spending her days riding a horse alongside a train. But now she wasn't on the horse anymore. She'd managed to jump aboard that train and was flying faster and faster toward the place where he was.

Love might not be far off.

23

———

Riley

The next couple of days were a little rough, but then they usually were after Riley allowed things to build up like they had at the restaurant. That sort of thing was perfectly normal. Sometimes issues could get to be a little much, but once they blew over, it was fine.

Except this time, it was a little different. He couldn't shake the feeling that he'd done something wrong. Even though Grace wasn't acting any different, he could sense something had shifted and that made it harder to get over the hurdle.

On top of those uncomfortable thoughts, Riley had to deal with his new therapist. The only one who finally had availability in his schedule open up was an older cowboy. He didn't talk much, but the disapproving glances he gave Riley whenever he showed Grace even an ounce of affection had Riley on edge.

If Shane was okay with his relationship, then this guy should be too. Riley wasn't doing anything wrong.

This train of thought almost always set him back. Grace still hadn't invited him to her home. She hadn't allowed him to pick her up for a date. He hadn't met anyone besides Brielle and Faye. For the life of him, Riley couldn't figure out what held her back. Her father was bound to know about him by now. Wouldn't it just be better if he got to know her family now before people started talking?

With each passing therapy session and every dinner they shared, that was the one issue that continued to bother him. As much as he tried to ignore it, he couldn't deny that Grace was either scared of taking the next step or she simply didn't want to.

The napkin with her address had been folded up neatly and he kept it in his wallet. With Faye's help, he could take the situation into his own hands and show her he wasn't scared of her father. Riley was ready.

He'd spent far too long alone, and Grace was the one he wanted to spend the rest of his life with. There was a chance she just needed a little nudge.

Riley looked over to Grace where she sat on the edge of the corral fence. Today was colder than it had been since he'd arrived, and her nose was an adorable shade of pink. She'd said she had some errands to run today so she couldn't stay after their session. Perhaps he'd have a chance to head out to her place and finally meet her father face-to-face.

"That was good. You've got some natural talent with horses."

Riley swung his gaze around, finding Bud's hard eyes on him. His new therapist followed his gaze over to Grace and then back to Riley. He leaned on the saddle horn and nodded toward him. "Take Dolly around the corral a few more times and then we'll head in."

"That's it? We're just going riding? No talking? No forcing me to confront my demons?"

Bud arched a brow. "Do you *want* to talk?"

"Well, no… but—"

"Then enjoy your ride and stop making goo-goo eyes at young Miss Callahan."

Riley clenched his jaw. He could spit back any number of retorts, but he thought better of it. Bud clearly didn't have any interest in what Riley had to say. As much as he preferred this kind of hands-off therapy, Riley couldn't help but feel he was missing out on something.

He chanced another look over to Grace, then pulled his horse around. The steady plodding beneath him soothed the sense of instability he felt. He refused to think the insecurity he was experiencing had to do with his PTSD. He was on edge because of Grace. That was it.

After all the sessions with her, he felt he'd convinced her he was doing well enough to have his sessions passed off. He would be cleared of his court-ordered reasons for being here, which meant the shadow of his PTSD wouldn't loom over him. Grace wouldn't be able to force him to talk out anything if she thought he'd gotten past the worst of it.

As soon as his final session was over, they could shift into a more normal relationship. That's all either of them needed. No more of this focus on what he was or wasn't struggling with.

"A little faster," Bud called out to him.

Riley glanced over his shoulder and gave the man a nod. Maybe working with Bud wouldn't be so bad. These were more like riding lessons than therapy sessions. There was a normalcy about it all and the stress he carried melted away.

Once his ride was over, Grace climbed down from her perch and walked beside him. He reached for her hand, lacing his fingers within hers. Bud walked a few yards ahead of them and Riley slowed his pace so the old man couldn't overhear their conversation.

He brought her hand up to his lips and murmured. "I was thinking about something."

"Yeah?"

"Maybe I could come to your place and meet the rest of your family."

She stiffened. It wasn't in the way she held his hand—but rather the way her face tightened and her mouth formed a strained line. Grace didn't meet his gaze right away, but when she did, the forced smile did nothing to assure him of her feelings for him. "You know I care about you, right?"

Riley ground his teeth back and forth. "Sure," he muttered.

"Don't you think that's a little fast?"

He stopped and faced her. "Fast?"

"Yeah. We've only started dating. We have a lot more to learn about each other before we move to that point, don't you think?"

Except she was wrong. He *knew* what he wanted, and that was Grace. Staying in this state of limbo only caused more frustration. He swallowed that ugly feeling down. "When do you think you might be ready for that?"

"Me? It's not just me." She peeked at him, then looked away. "It's both of us. I..."

"You two coming?" Bud had stopped and he stood in the doorway of the barn with his arms folded. "I told Shane I'd help out with these sessions, but if you're going to be using this time for your personal relationship, then I'm going to have to reconsider."

She reached forward and grasped his hand. "I'm not saying never. Of course I want you to meet my family. I just want to make sure we're both ready." Grace dropped his hands, then grasped Dolly's lead rope before leading her toward the barn without another word.

Once again, he felt lost. When he'd made up his mind to introduce himself to her father, he'd been in control. He'd figured out a solution for the way he was feeling. Back in the day, men would approach the fathers of the women they were interested in just to make clear their intentions.

That couldn't hurt. A quick five-minute meeting wouldn't make anything worse than it already was. The last time he'd followed orders without challenging them, he'd been broken. That wasn't going to happen again. Grace didn't know what was best. She didn't have the experience he had. She might be smarter when it came to certain things, but in this case she was wrong.

Based on what Shane and Michael had said about Zeke Callahan, Riley was only making matters worse by staying away.

He shoved his hand into his jacket pocket and took the folded napkin out of his wallet. The plan was still on. When Grace left, he'd take a short ride to her family's place and see if her father was around to visit with him.

Theirs would be a short conversation where Riley could assure Zeke that he only had the best of intentions.

RILEY SAT on his bike at the edge of the Callahan's property. He'd lost his nerve the second he turned onto the winding road that would ultimately take him to Grace's home. He was out of his depth. He'd probably been out of his mind, too.

What had gotten into him that he'd decided to come here without Grace?

He placed both hands on the back of his neck. It wasn't too late to turn back. As much as he still believed this was the right decision, it was likely too soon.

Well, not too soon for him. He'd gladly go out and buy a ring if it meant securing a future for the two of them.

A heavy-sounding vehicle rumbled behind him and he

froze. The next thing he knew, a truck pulled up beside him and the passenger side window rolled down.

The gruff man in the driver's seat was probably one of the most intimidating men Riley had ever encountered in his life. He wore a cowboy hat that shaded his eyes, and his firm jaw was set in a tight, hard line. "You lost, son?"

Riley's first attempt to speak came out barely audible, forcing him to clear his throat. "No, sir. I'm here to meet with Mr. Callahan."

The man's gaze swept over him before lifting to his face once more. "You looking for a job? Did Adeline send you? I keep telling her we're fine."

Before Riley could correct him, the cowboy sighed.

He gestured up the road. "Well, follow me. I'll give ya an interview, but I ain't making any promises."

Riley held up a finger and his mouth opened, but no sound came out. The cowboy he could only assume was Grace's father drove forward, leaving Riley in a cloud of dust. Riley waved his hand through the air to disperse the floating particles, then started his motorcycle. At least he hadn't been kicked off the property yet. He had a reason to be here. If all went well, he could tell Grace she had nothing to be worried about and they could move on to the next step in their relationship.

Control.

That's what he'd been missing from his life since retiring from his service in the military. He needed to find that balance again, and taking charge of his relationship was just the ticket.

Riley drove far enough behind the truck to avoid getting a mouthful of dirt but not so far behind that Zeke would lose him. They crested a hill and he had to stop or risk his safety.

The large house that loomed before him wasn't just some small cottage. It wasn't like anything he'd expected for a rancher to own. But then again, it was supposed to be big enough to raise several daughters.

There was a large porch that wrapped all the way around the building and the architecture made it look like it belonged in a storybook rather than a ranch out in Colorado. Grace was regular small-town royalty. No wonder the whole town gave him the stink eye when they saw the two of them together. More pieces fell into place as he continued thinking back to his conversations with the sheriff and Shane.

Shoot.

He'd made a grave mistake. He shouldn't be here. He should have listened to Grace when she said to take it slow.

Riley twisted around to look back at the road from which he'd come. What if he turned back and went home right now? Maybe Zeke wouldn't recognize him when Grace finally felt ready to tell her father about her boyfriend.

Okay, that was a stupid thought.

Of course Zeke would remember. Grace wouldn't take *that* long to come around to his way of thinking. For all he knew, he'd be here within the week to meet him.

He'd done it now. This really was a very bad idea. What was he supposed to tell her father? That he loved Grace and he had every intention of marrying her?

His whole body went hot and cold all at once. He wanted to marry her. That was the one truth he could say without a doubt in his mind.

He was deeply in love with her. What other reason did he have for being all the way out here to speak to a man he'd never met before in his life? Riley was either crazy or in love.

Probably a little bit of both.

All he could do was hope he didn't screw this whole thing up.

Riley balanced on his bike and put it into drive once more. He came up beside Zeke's truck just as the man was climbing out of his vehicle. Zeke didn't smile. He didn't offer any kind of upbeat conversation. All he did was grunt and gesture toward the porch. "It's not my usual setup but seeing as my daughter sprung this on me at the last minute, it's all I can offer you."

Riley shook his head. "You misunderstand, sir. I'm not here for—"

"Are you looking for work or not?"

He stood a little straighter. Technically if he were to stay, he'd be looking for work. Shane had told him there might be a scenario in which he could work there. But being here with Grace sounded even better. Riley straightened his shoulders and nodded. "I'll be needing a steady job here soon."

Zeke fixed him with a strange kind of look—one that said he had no idea what Riley could mean, but at the same time he wasn't willing to make him explain. A man looking for a job wouldn't be hunting unless he needed something at that moment. At least that was how Riley did things.

Riley shoved his hands into his jeans pockets and waited. It was as if the two of them were in a standoff. What was supposed to happen next? Zeke was the interviewer here.

Thankfully, Zeke made the first move. He jutted his chin toward the porch. "Well, go on then. Take a seat."

Riley lurched into action, climbing the few steps to the porch before taking a seat.

Zeke settled beside him, removing his hat and placing it on his knee. "What experience do you have with horses?"

"Sir?"

"Son, I don't got much time on my hands today. I'm only giving you this interview because if I don't, I won't hear the last of it from Adeline. I don't know where she found you, but if she thinks you're worthy of my time, then I'm not going to question her. Now, answer the dang question."

Riley swallowed at the lump in his throat. "To be honest, I don't have a lot of experience with horses."

Zeke's eyes narrowed as his eyes drilled holes right through Riley's soul. He'd been in any number of dangerous situations over his life, but right now, Riley was the most scared he'd ever been. Zeke leaned toward him only slightly. "Then why are you on my property?"

He had two choices. Answer honestly—even if it meant getting the wrath of Zeke Callahan to rain down on him. Or he could plead his case for a job and then pretend it was a coincidence that he had an interview with his girlfriend's father before meeting him.

The second option sounded so much better than the first. But he knew better.

Riley scooted to the edge of his chair and swallowed again. "Actually, sir, Adeline didn't send me." He didn't think it was possible, but the darkness in Zeke's expression worsened.

Without a word, he got to his feet and headed for the front door of his house.

Riley stood, unsure of what he should do. Was he supposed to follow him? Explain his reasons for being there?

The door banged open and Zeke emerged with a shotgun pointed directly at Riley. Instinct had Riley reaching for his own firearm at his side—something he hadn't brought with him. He lifted placating hands and took a step back. "Whoa. I can explain. I'm actually here for a good reason."

Zeke jerked the barrel of the gun toward the steps. "I don't know you. No one sent you. That means you don't belong here."

"It's Grace," he blurted. "I'm here about Grace." Riley stumbled down the steps and fought to regain his balance the second his feet hit the earth below.

The man hesitated, though he didn't lower his weapon. "Is she hurt?"

"What? No." Technically he had no clue. Just the suggestion alone had his heart racing erratically. "I don't think so," he amended. "I came here to speak to you about my intentions."

Riley had expected to throw Zeke off enough that he'd lower his gun, but the man was on a mission.

"What are you talking about, boy?"

"I love your daughter."

Zeke didn't move for what felt like several minutes but was, in reality, only a few moments. Then he threw back his head and laughed. "Do you have any idea who you're talking to?"

"You're Ze—Mr. Callahan, isn't that right?"

"I'm that girl's father, and you—" His dark eyes swept over Riley. "There's no reason you should be within fifty yards of my daughter. I suggest you get your head on straight and head back to where you came from."

Riley's adrenaline finally kicked in. He straightened his shoulders and lifted his chin. "I'm in love with your daughter, and one day I'm going to marry her. I only came here as a courtesy to you."

"Son, if you were so important to my daughter, why isn't she here?" As if his words were enough to summon Grace all on their own, her familiar truck materialized over that small slope in the road. Zeke still had his gun trained on Riley as his eyes shifted over to the vehicle closing in on them.

It came to an abrupt stop beside Riley's motorcycle and Grace jumped out of the truck. "Riley! What in heaven's name are you doing?"

24

———

Grace

Grace charged forward, driven by terror and elation. Riley had gone against her wishes and just shown up at her house. Part of her swooned over how romantic that sounded in her head.

But then reality splashed her with a bucket of ice water. This wasn't romantic. It was controlling and overbearing. They'd discussed this. And she'd told him *no*.

Well, she'd told him *not yet*.

"Daddy! Put that gun away."

Her father didn't budge an inch. She let out an exasperated sigh as she stormed toward the two men.

"Grace—" Riley started.

She held up her hand. "Not now."

"But—"

Grace whirled around and faced him, making sure her body was the one thing between her father and the man that she knew she had deep feelings for. "What are you doing here?" she seethed. "We talked about this."

Riley's whole body remained stiff and prickly. She could easily imagine trying to give him a hug and getting stabbed by the invisible quills he had protruding from his body. He spoke low through gritted teeth. "*You* talked about this. I didn't agree."

She threw her hands into the air. "Seriously? What were you thinking? Do you even realize just how bad this invasion of privacy really is? You can't just show up at my house. I don't know how you got my address but—"

"Faye gave it to me."

Grace smacked her forehead with her hand. "Of course she did."

"Grace?" Her father's hard voice pulled her from the conversation, forcing her to turn around to meet his gaze. "Please tell me this is a joke."

She sighed again, then shook her head. "It's not a joke."

Zeke's focus shifted to Riley. "He's one of them, isn't he?"

"*Them*?" Riley attempted to move around her. The venom in that one word was enough to set her teeth on edge.

"No offense, son, but if you're one of those folks down at Shane's place, you have no logical reason to be interested in my daughter. I appreciate your service, but I forbid anyone with your background to be romantically involved with her."

"*Dad!*" Grace gasped.

Zeke finally lowered his gun and held it at his side. "It's got nothing to do with him specifically. I'd say the same thing if he was a deputy's sheriff. I changed the rules about you dating. Don't make me regret it."

She felt weak. This was exactly what Brielle had been warning her about. As far as she knew, the age difference hadn't even come up yet. How could her father be so short-sighted as to generalize people with similar backgrounds to Riley's?

Grace could sense Riley's fury building, almost as if heat

was coming off him in waves. She needed to diffuse this all before something really bad happened. She could have a discussion with her father later. He would be the easier one to handle.

Right now, she needed Riley to know exactly how he'd overstepped so he didn't do it again. Great. She was entering autopilot mode. The therapist inside her was already trying to fix this problem when there were bigger issues at play.

Her head was spinning and her whole body had betrayed her. This wasn't how things were supposed to go. Grace stared at Riley, her gaze holding his firmly. "I need you to leave."

Shock filtered across his face, then he worked his jaw. It was like she could see his thoughts in real time. He was planting his feet firmly and he didn't want to go. Didn't he see the gun? Why wasn't he willing to listen to her?

"Riley, *now*." For a moment she thought he would verbally refuse. She didn't know what she would do if that happened—especially if Riley said "no" in front of her father. Everything was out of control. "I'll meet you at your place in a half hour."

His eyes darted to Zeke then back to her. She knew him well enough to read the argument in his gaze. Riley didn't want to leave for whatever crazy reason he had in his head. She groaned as she slipped her arm through his and propelled him backward.

"I can't believe you did this to me," she said.

"Me? What about you?"

She stopped and stared at him. "What?"

His voice remained low and his demeanor was relaxed, but the intensity in his gaze had flickered to life, and within those depths, she saw a fire she wasn't sure she was prepared to combat. Anyone not part of their conversation would look at the two of them having this conversation and they'd think it was just a normal exchange of words.

They would be so wrong.

Riley's eyes flitted to her father, who was likely watching with rapt interest from the porch. "You didn't want me to meet your father," he accused.

"And you wanted to? I had good reasons. He pointed a gun at you," she said, throwing her arms in the air. "But that's not the issue right now."

"Isn't it?" He let out a derisive chuckle. "From what I can tell, the biggest issue has everything to do with you and your fear of commitment."

Her head reared back and her defenses went up. "I am not afraid of commitment."

He snorted. "Yeah? What do you call it when one person in a relationship isn't even willing to say they love the other? When that one person doesn't allow their partner to meet anyone they consider important? I've only met two of your sisters, and I have a feeling that wasn't something you were all that thrilled about in the first place."

Her heart was going triple speed, and the shock that had sprouted to life in her stomach had quickly morphed into something far more poisonous. "I call that being cautious and realistic."

"What do you have to be cautious over? You know who I am. With that folder of information Shane has on file, you probably know me better than anyone on the planet. From the sounds of it, you had zero interest in sticking it out with me."

She sucked in sharply. There was a tiny voice in the back of her head that told her to drop it. He needed to cool down. And she needed to think about whether or not this relationship was worth it.

But then that small voice was swallowed up by a whale of desperation. She cared about him—more than she had cared about anyone else in her life besides family. And if he didn't get this PTSD sorted out, the rest of his life would end up failing him.

Grace's eyes narrowed and she forced her voice to remain in a constant unemotional tone. "This isn't about me. This is about you."

His brows lifted.

"You overstepped."

"I—"

She held up her hand and shook her head. "Let me finish. We are in a committed relationship. You asked me about coming here, and I told you no." He needed to acknowledge that there were boundaries he still needed to follow no matter who he was dealing with in a particular moment.

He huffed. "Yeah, because you're ashamed of me."

"What? No, I'm not."

Riley waved his finger at her, then gestured toward her father. "You think I'm damaged. I'm sure your father shares that sentiment. Both of you take one look at me and see the scars and the results of trauma and war. But instead of accepting and appreciating what I did for you—for this country—you keep me at arm's length."

Once again, the control she had over this situation was spiraling. He'd latched on to one of his biggest insecurities and was running away with it.

"Both of you are a bunch of hypocrites. This whole planet is full of hypocrites. All of you think you can just put us in a box, throw some food, money, and therapy at us, and we'll be okay. Guess what? We're not. We go through hell and back, carrying all of you on our backs to keep you safe and unaware of the dangers that surround us every single day and what thanks do we get?"

Grace moved closer to him. "That's not what I was saying at all. I should have known better. You needed more time to get to the root of your issues."

"Issues?" he said. "I don't have issues. I'm *fine*. I was doing just fine before I met you, and I'll do just fine when I leave. I didn't need you to prop me up because there was nothing wrong with me in the first place. That judge who sent me here was an idiot, and he didn't appreciate what I've done."

"Riley—"

"No. I'm not going to stand here while you tear me down and make me feel like this is my fault. I didn't do anything wrong. Any man in my position would wonder why you didn't want me to meet your family. Any *ordinary* man. I'm just the poor sap who thought you could look past the panic attacks and my history to see what was beneath it all." He stomped toward his bike and sat down. He shoved his key into the ignition and the bike whirred to life.

In no time he was down the road and over the crest of the hill. He'd disappeared.

"Get in the truck."

Grace jumped, then spun around to stare at her father with wide eyes. "What?" At some point he'd wandered off his perch on the porch and stood beside her.

"I want to have a word with Shane."

If possible, her eyes widened even more and her mouth fell open. "Why? Shane has nothing to do with this."

"Shane Owens is the reason for this." Zeke turned toward the house, gun still in hand. "Shane let this happen."

She huffed, scrambling after her father. "Shane had nothing to do with any of this."

Zeke shot a look at her out of the corner of his eye. "Is that so?"

"I'm not dating Shane, Dad. I'm dating Riley."

His expression hardened. "Based on the way you two were talking, are you sure about that?"

She dragged her attention back to the road where Riley had left. Her father was right. At this point, she wasn't sure if they were. He hadn't outright said that they were breaking up. For all she knew, his rant was just a long venting session about issues that still needed to be resolved.

Grace forced herself to the present and charged after her father. "You're not going to talk to Shane."

He chuckled. "You can't tell me what to do."

She grabbed his arm and swung him around. "And you need to learn that you can't tell me or any of us what to do."

Zeke stared at her hard. He'd been doing so well with relaxing the rules; she probably shouldn't have poked the bear. He was still her father and someone she needed to respect. His opinion mattered.

But that didn't mean he could control her life. She needed to make her mistakes and learn from them just like anyone else. Grace shook her head. "You're not. Because this has nothing to do with you, I made my choices and I get to deal with them. I wanted to date him."

His features softened slightly.

"And for the record, Shane wasn't all that pleased that we developed feelings for each other either. The age thing for sure bothered him."

"What age thing?"

Her eyes widened and she released him. "It doesn't matter. What matters is that Riley needs me. He needs someone who knows how to listen and get him through the rough spots. Didn't Mom ever do that for you?"

At that moment she saw it in his eyes. His resolve faltered.

"Riley is just a man like any other. He has things he's working through, but at least he's doing that. I don't know many who would actually stick it out when they've been told to get therapy. That takes a different kind of strength, and he should be respected for it too."

Her father rubbed the back of his neck and he looked away. "Sometimes I forget that you're not my little girl anymore.

You've grown up and matured into a lovely young woman. Your mother would be so proud."

Grace's heart tightened, making it more difficult to breathe. "Thanks, Dad," she murmured.

Zeke shook his head and tossed his gun slightly to get a better grip on it. "Fine. I won't go talk to Shane. But if anything happens to you, I'm holding him liable."

"Dad! Nothing is going to happen to me. Riley—"

"Loves you, I know."

She snapped her mouth shut. That's not what she'd planned on saying. She wasn't there yet. Love was a big commitment—bigger than agreeing to date someone. She wasn't ready to admit something like that. When she finally said those words, she wanted to know without a single doubt in her mind that she meant them. She wanted to ensure that the person she said those words to would know just how much weight a proclamation of love meant.

Her father placed a firm hand on her shoulder. "I can tell he cares about you. But I don't think he's ready for you yet."

Brows pulling together, Grace frowned with confusion. "You don't think he loves me?"

"Oh, I'm sure he does. But there's a difference between the first breath of love and the kind of love a man has when he knows he will sacrifice everything for her."

Grace's stomach dropped. Was her father suggesting that Riley was merely infatuated with her? Was she right to withhold saying those three special words?

"From the looks of it, Riley is still working through some things. His heart is juggling those feelings and the feelings he has for you. At some point he's going to miss, and a ball will fall to the floor." He put a hand on her shoulder. "I don't want that to be you."

She bit down on her lower lip, emotion filling her throat. She didn't want it to be her either. Her father might not be suggesting that she break up with Riley, but it sure felt like he was telling her she needed to take a break and let him sort things out for himself first.

Zeke released her and headed toward the house without another word, leaving her cold and alone with her tumultuous thoughts.

25

Riley

Riley pulled sharply into the country club's parking lot. Gravel spewed angrily from beneath his tires, reminding him he needed to tread carefully or end up with those tiny stones tearing into his flesh. He turned down the small road that led to the cabins, barely keeping his emotions intact.

All his thoughts from his latest encounter were attacking him like a swarm of hornets. They dove at him, stung him until his confidence had been torn in two, leaving him raw.

Grace hadn't defended him. She hadn't been willing to see what he saw, no matter what he'd said to her. On top of that, she continued to push him down whenever he clawed himself to his feet by telling him he was still struggling.

He wasn't struggling.

Everyone had bad days and good days. He might have a different way of dealing with things, but he was doing better than most.

Granted, he hadn't been sleeping well. And his drunken misconduct hadn't been one of his finer moments, but he was fine.

Fine.

Boy, that word was beginning to sound strange even in his head. It was like it had become this foreign substance that didn't exist in this dimension.

Angrily, he tore his helmet from his head and dropped it to the ground before storming into his cabin. Every nerve, every fiber of his being itched with indignation.

He'd seen it in the way her father looked at him first. The man didn't have to utter a single word. It was clear Riley wasn't good enough for his daughter, and he never would be. And Grace had probably been influenced by him. That was likely the reason they didn't have a shot at a lasting relationship.

He should have known better than to allow himself to fall for a girl like her. She only saw the damage. She would never forget the things he'd said or the way he acted around her family.

The whole situation ripped through him, and he snapped. Riley ducked down, swiping everything from the coffee table onto the floor before he upended it. Wood cracked, splintering with the force of the momentum.

He stared at the mess, his shoulders heaving. Then all at once, the fire left him. He crumpled to the floor and leaned against the couch. His face rested on his knees and he let out a sob. The weight of everything pressed down on him. His most recent tour. Grace. Her father. All of it culminated in a stew of pure defeat.

The words he'd spewed at Zeke bounced around in his head, mocking him. He wasn't a hero. He didn't do what he should have done when he'd had the opportunity to make a change. He wasn't good enough for Grace.

The best thing he could do for her right now was to

distance himself from her. They both needed to cut ties before everything became ten times worse.

Riley sat in that position, letting out all his anguish until he fell asleep. By morning, his body ached, but his mind and soul were numb. He knew what he had to do, and he wasn't ready for it.

He got to his feet and looked at the mess he'd made. It could have been so much worse. He'd have to survey the damage before he left. Chances were high he'd be replacing that coffee table. But that didn't matter. Nothing mattered anymore except to get his sessions done and leave this place.

"You're kidding." Shane peered at Riley from across his desk. "Not even a few weeks ago, you were insistent that Grace was the key to your successful therapy sessions. Now, you don't want her there at all?"

"That's correct," Riley muttered.

"Obviously, I need to know why. Has something happened between the two of you? Was she inappropriate? Has she broken any confidentiality agreements—"

"No. She hasn't done anything wrong. We're just... not dating anymore."

Understanding immediately filled Shane's face. Followed by a hint of pity.

Riley stood to his feet abruptly and turned away. He paced a few steps, then stopped. "I don't want to discuss this. I don't want you to fire her. Find someone else for her to help or... I don't know. You probably have other jobs around here she's suited for. I just don't want her in my sessions anymore." He waited for an argument—any response, really. Shane didn't seem like the kind of guy who would just let this sit. He'd already intervened too much with all the advice he'd felt obligated to shove down Riley's throat.

But Shane didn't say a word.

He turned to face Shane. "You won't fire her, will you?"

Shane had his steepled fingers to his lips, and the only thing that moved on his face was his brows and his eyes as they shifted toward Riley. "I'm sure I can figure something out. You will complete your sessions with your current therapist?"

"Sure. Whatever."

Shane dropped his hands and nodded. "Okay. You're running late for your group session."

That was it? No lecture? Nothing about the fact he was making the worst mistake of his life? He should be grateful. As it was, he didn't know if he was strong enough to stand his ground when it came to Grace. Not having to see her again would make things so much easier.

~

"Riley, do you want to share?"

He glanced up. His gaze swept through the group and he lowered his scowl to his hands. "Nope."

"Is everything still going well? The last time you shared, you were excited about the prospect of your future and possibly staying here in Copper Creek."

His glower intensified and he refused to make eye-contact with anyone. "Plans change."

"Oh?"

If Riley wasn't already so close to completing his mandated time here, he would have launched from his seat and stormed away. He didn't need any of this. Everyone sitting in a circle talking like a bunch of little chickens was ridiculous. None of it helped anyone.

"What are your plans when you're done?"

"I'm going home."

"I'm sure that will be nice." Kevin turned to another poor unfortunate soul who sat in their circle. None of this mattered. The people sitting here could talk all day long, but it didn't change what happened to them. It didn't make things better. They would all remember the thing that turned them into the people they currently were.

Riley crossed his arms and half-listened. He was stretched out on his chair with his ankles crossed, but then he nearly fell out of his chair when the main door opened and Grace entered the building.

Her eyes met his briefly before she headed toward Shane's office.

Straightening, he fought the burning sensation in his face. He hadn't expected Shane to call her so soon. She didn't look happy. That was understandable, considering they had broken up. He couldn't deny that it gave him a small amount of satisfaction to know that she hadn't bounced back.

The group around him got to their feet and started folding up the metal chairs they sat on. He stumbled to his feet, grasping the back of his chair and just as it folded, Grace materialized. Riley bit back a yelp.

Grace had her hands on her hips. Her eyes flashed with fire, and her face was flushed like she'd been doing some sort of strenuous activity. "Broken up?" she seethed. "You told Shane we're broken up?"

Riley glared as he yanked up the chair and took it over to be leaned against the wall with the others. "What did you think our last conversation meant?"

"That you were upset. Not that we were broken up. I thought you said you were serious about us."

He whirled around to face her. "I was. The problem, though, is that you clearly weren't."

"What?" Her head reared back and she blinked at him.

"Why do you think that? I spent almost every evening with you."

His heart was beating at an irregular pace. The knots in his stomach churned and bumped into other things. He felt cornered, blocked in and unable to move. Lungs burning, aching for air, he brushed past her.

Grace's footsteps followed after him. "I don't understand you. I've never seen someone so intent on getting someone to like them only to toss them away the second something hard happens."

He spun to face her again, fury boiling within him. "You don't get it, do you? This isn't about something hard. This is about the fact that I care about you a heck of a lot more than you care about me. I can't believe I allowed myself to think you could be capable of loving me the way I love you." His eyes swept over her from head to toe. "You're practically a child. What do you know of love?" He stormed away, expecting that she would just let him escape. That's all he wanted right now. Escape.

But she didn't.

Grace hurried after him, and when he caught a glimpse of her, he noticed the moisture brimming in her eyes. "I may be younger than you, but I know better than to throw away something just because it's not what I was expecting. You might think this is about me, but you need to take a good long look in the mirror and see what's really wrong here. You're running because *you* don't think you're good enough. It has nothing to do with me." She blinked, causing a tear to slide down her cheek. "And as for the declaration of love?" She huffed. "I've never dated anyone seriously. I'm not going to say I love someone just because it's expected. He's got to earn the privilege of hearing it." She spun on her heel and charged toward the back door in the direction of the barns.

"You're not my therapist anymore. You don't get to be part of my sessions." He called it out over the low rumble of voices in the immediate area and immediately regretted it. Grace stopped where she stood, her hands down at her sides clenched into fists.

People stopped their talking, making the room almost deathly quiet. Slowly, Grace turned around to face him. "I'm not your therapist anymore," she repeated. "But I have a new client who happens to need me right now." With those final words, she slipped out the door.

Several eyes turned to look at him. Their expressions ranged from disgust to mild curiosity. Some of these people knew Grace well enough, and of course he would be the bad guy.

Riley dragged a hand down his face. This wasn't how everything was supposed to go. Grace was supposed to be his person—the one who accepted him for who he was despite all the scars.

His jaw tightened and he turned his scowl to the floor. He couldn't miss any sessions or he'd be required to stay here even longer than he already had. It was time to get this whole thing over with so he could leave and never look back.

Riley marched toward the same door where Grace had disappeared. By the time he ended up on the trail leading to the barn, she was already at the structure and heading inside.

He should wait. Outside, there were plenty of places to hang out until Bud was ready—unless Bud was already in the barn and waiting for him to saddle Dolly.

Who was he kidding? There would be no avoiding Grace. She worked here, and this was where he would continue living for the next few weeks.

Riley muttered a curse and stomped all the way to the barn. Upon entry, his gaze immediately found Grace. She was crouched down in front of a little girl with blonde hair. The girl clung to a young man—maybe her father. She stared at Grace with wide eyes as Grace murmured something to her and gestured toward the horse in the stall they stood next to.

As he watched, his heart tore a little more. By now it was probably in shreds lying at the bottom of his chest, unable to be patched together. He wasn't an idiot. He'd fallen hard for Grace. He'd wanted everything to be perfect, but there was one problem.

This was the real world, and people like him never ended up happy.

Riley's eyes shifted to the young man as Grace straightened. He smiled at her and the smile she gave him only made Riley's stomach sour further. He'd seen that look before. The guy was smitten already. Turning toward Dolly's stall, Riley gripped the door with both hands hard enough for the wood to dig into his palms.

Irony. That's what this was called. Just like in the army, Riley was replaceable. And by the looks of it, the man beside Grace wasn't damaged goods like he was. He had a kid. He probably had a good job. And he had every opportunity to make Grace fall head over heels for him.

"Ready for our session?" Bud arrived and opened the stall across the aisle.

Riley shot him a dark look.

"Having a bad day?" Bud glanced down the aisle to where Grace stood with the small family. "Looks like Grace has other arrangements this afternoon."

An expletive escaped Riley's lips and he stormed toward the door. When he got outside, he swore again. Pacing back and forth, he contemplated what Bud would do when he went back inside. He'd have to apologize. Bud wasn't the one he was upset with. It was himself. Riley was the one who had made this mess, and he deserved to be miserable.

Bud emerged from the barn a few minutes later and leaned against the doorway. "Well, that was something."

Riley froze in his place and looked at Bud.

"You feel better?" Bud asked.

"No."

"You gonna go riding today? Or are we skipping?"

Riley's shoulders slumped and he frowned at Bud. "You're not going to lecture me?"

"Why would I?" He jerked his chin toward the interior of the barn once more. "Come on then. We need to get those horses saddled if we're going to head out on the trail."

26

___

Grace

Was she supposed to feel hollow—like she'd lost a piece of her heart? Is that what it felt like to break up with someone?

Grace glanced over her shoulder as Riley left the barn. Her eyes met Bud's only briefly before he followed. What she wouldn't give to follow the two of them and find out what was wrong. Riley needed her and not just as a therapist.

But he didn't want her. Not anymore. He'd made that perfectly clear. So even if she was still drawn to him and she felt the need to help him through whatever he was having struggles with, she couldn't do a thing about it.

She turned back to the little girl she was supposed to help now. "Your brother says that you like to draw horses. Is that right?"

Kristin nodded but remained halfway hidden behind her older brother.

Grace smiled at her. "It's okay if you don't want to talk.

Sometimes I feel the same way. It's nice when we can have some quiet, don't you think?"

Kristin looked up at her brother, and he squeezed her shoulder before he let out a soft chuckle. "Kristin has an expressive speech delay, but she can understand everything just like a typical kid. She's really shy because it's hard for people to understand her. She sees a speech therapist, but they thought coming here would be a good idea to help her express herself more."

Grace rose to her feet and shot Kristin another smile. "Sometimes getting to know a horse is just the thing to help people out. I'm going to get a saddle for you. Then we can pick out a horse that isn't being used."

Her eyes drifted toward the door once more as she strode toward the saddles. Riley hadn't come back yet. Had he left for good? What was she thinking? He'd basically kicked her out of his life. He didn't want her worrying about him. She needed to move on. That was the smart thing to do.

It didn't matter how much her heart ached and how distracted she was; Riley wouldn't be part of her life. She blew out a breath to calm herself and lifted the saddle before turning around to head back to her new client.

Out of nowhere, Riley materialized and they collided. The saddle slipped in her fingers. She had to catch it to keep it from falling to the ground. Her wide eyes lifted to meet his then she scowled. "Excuse me, Mr. Scott."

Riley stiffened. She couldn't tell if it was her tone, the look on her face, or the way she'd called him by his last name that threw him off. But it didn't matter. She shifted to move past him and his arm came up.

"Grace—"

She didn't let him finish his sentence as she pushed past his arm and strode toward her new clients. Dust flew into the air as her boots carried her across the barn floor. The way her heart hammered in her chest heightened the way her other senses interpreted everything around her. She could hear even the smallest movement Riley made behind her. The smell of the barn triggered memories of their time shared here, but that wasn't the strangest part. She could have sworn she could taste him—like she was reliving their kisses in real time.

Her throat closed up and her vision blurred until she closed her eyes to shut it all out. When she opened them, Tyler was staring at her with concern shining in his eyes. His features were pinched together and he took a step toward her to take the saddle from her hands. "You okay?"

She swallowed, nodding but unable to speak. A reaction like this was foreign to her. She'd never experienced anything like it, but there was no time for her to examine what it meant. Plastering a smile on her face, she turned her focus to Kristin again. "Let's pick out that horse."

"SHE'S DOING GREAT, don't you think?" Tyler strode beside her as she led the horse around the corral. The sun was shining, making it an unseasonably warm spring day. They had opted to remain outside rather than heading into the indoor arena.

Riley had gotten back from a short trail ride and was in an adjacent corral with Bud working on communicating small things to his horse.

"Miss Callahan?"

Grace jumped. She blinked at Tyler, chastising herself for watching Riley in the first place. "What?" Her cheeks flushed with embarrassment. She was supposed to be focused on helping Kristin right now. After this session, Tyler would probably go to Shane and tell him she wasn't cut out for this gig.

Tyler's brows pulled together. "You okay? Cuz really, if you need to take a break, I can stay by her side."

"Oh, I couldn't do that. I'm supposed to—"

"I won't tell anyone. I signed a waiver anyway, right?" He chuckled. "Go take a breath. I'll stay right here just in case she needs me."

She didn't know what prompted her to release the lead rope that Tyler grabbed from her hand, but she did. He practically shoved her toward the side of the corral, a wide, reassuring smile on his face.

Grace leaned up against the fence and watched as Tyler encouraged his sister. Kristin reacted with her own wide smile.

"He's cute."

She was startled again and turned to find Dianna behind her. Arms folded atop the corral fence, Dianna nodded toward Tyler. "Is he single?"

Grace scowled at her sister, ignoring the question. She probably knew that Grace's relationship with Riley wasn't doing so well. Technically, it didn't even exist. Grace didn't have any interest in starting another romantic chapter any time soon.

"I heard about what happened with Riley," Dianna's soft voice broke through Grace's thoughts, and it took every ounce of self-control not to react. "I'm sorry, Grace."

"Yeah, well, I should have known better than to fall for someone I was trying to help."

"There was nothing wrong with developing feelings for him."

Grace arched a brow. "Really?"

Dianna snickered. "Well, I didn't say there was anything *good* about dating him either."

And that was the problem. Grace was inexperienced, and she'd made a stupid choice. She'd opened her heart to someone she shouldn't have. From the very beginning she'd been hesitant. So why hadn't she just listened to her instincts in the first place?

"So you gonna flirt with him?" Dianna's teasing voice only served to irritate Grace further.

"I'm not going to be dating anyone anytime soon. Maybe I won't date at all."

"Oh, come on. Don't do that."

"Don't do what? Be smart for once?" Grace shot a look in Dianna's direction once more, finding her smile had faded. She sighed. "Sorry. I didn't mean to suggest that you dating Tristan wasn't smart. I just..." She what? There were no excuses. She'd known what she was getting into when she started to fall for Riley. And she'd gone and thrown caution to the wind anyway. "You know what? It doesn't matter. Riley wanted something I wasn't ready for, and I needed something from him he wasn't ready to give. That's life, and life is hard." She crossed her arms as if the gesture could shield her from the ache in her chest that returned with a vengeance.

"Even if you don't think you want to *date* anyone, you really should at least consider hanging out with someone. If not with the new guy, find someone in town. You have to get back on the horse and figure out what you want—what makes you happy."

"Yeah. Maybe."

Dianna reached over the fence and squeezed her shoulder. "It'll all work out the way it's supposed to. You'll see. I have to go pick up a few things I left here. See you at home, okay?"

Grace nodded, gritting her teeth against the emotion that threatened to boil over and escape her throat.

Starting a new client today was probably a bad idea. But there was one thing Dianna had said that made sense no matter how much Grace hated it. She needed to get back out there so she could get her mind off Riley and move forward. She'd never been one to hold onto the past.

Her gaze flitted to Tyler again, finding him glancing in her direction. He smiled, and she offered a half-hearted one in response.

He wasn't a local, but he wasn't from out of state either. He'd been the one to drive Kristin here for her sessions from a neighboring town. One date. Would that be so bad? She just needed a way to slow the heartbreak that was currently happening inside.

~

"I CAN'T BELIEVE you said yes." Tyler pushed her chair in as she settled at the table. His button-up shirt was rolled up to his elbows and open at the collar—a different look than how he usually dressed at the country club.

When she looked at him, she didn't get that tingling sensation in her stomach. She couldn't tell if that was because, even after two weeks, she still felt numb or if it was because she simply didn't feel the same for him as she did Riley. One corner of her mouth lifted in a small smile. "I suppose I had to reward your persistence."

He chuckled, lifting his menu to look at the food offered at the steakhouse. "Kristin really likes you. She talks about you all the time."

Warmth spread through Grace's midsection. "I like Kristin, too. She's a sweetheart." While the young girl still didn't speak much to her, she was a fantastic listener. It only took a few sessions for her to master riding on her own, though Grace made sure either she or Tyler remained close.

The man seated across from her was sweet, too. There was just one problem. No matter how much Grace dove into work, no matter how much Tyler flirted with her, she still couldn't get her mind off Riley. He was the one she wanted to be with even after the way things had ended.

She tried to rationalize that he was just the first guy she had kissed and he was the first one she fell for, so it made sense she would have a harder time letting go. But that didn't help her move on like she'd hoped.

So now she sat in front of a guy who was *nice* but wasn't anything like the man she'd fallen in love with.

There was no going back from that. And if she were honest with herself, she didn't want to go back. If she only had the chance at finding love once in her life, then this was it and she'd failed.

"What are you in the mood for?"

She poked her head up. "Hmm?"

"What would you like to order?"

Grace glanced at the menu. "Probably just the six-ounce steak with a side of potatoes." She studied him as he perused the menu. He was too nice of a guy for her to lead him on. They'd spent enough time together for her to know that she wasn't interested in anything romantic with him. In fact, she continued to compare him to the one person she'd prefer to be with.

Maybe he'd realize she wasn't worth a second date as well. Then she wouldn't have to turn him down.

But something told her she wasn't that lucky.

27

———————

Riley

*R*iley released the bridle and slung it over his shoulder before moving to unbuckle the saddle. He'd hoped that Grace's new little client's sessions wouldn't overlap with his, but after two weeks it was clear he was destined to see her every single day of his miserable life while completing his sentence.

He'd come in early from his practice in the hopes that he wouldn't have to bump into her. But as much as he wanted to avoid her, there was a part of him that lived for the short moments when he got to interact with her.

It was this never-ending cycle where he tortured himself with what might have been. The man who came with the little girl every day clearly had a thing for Grace. And why wouldn't he? She was amazing. And from the looks of it, she was even better with children than she'd been with him.

There was just something about seeing her with that little girl that could melt a guy's heart. His jaw clenched and he shut his eyes against the frustrated fury that built in his head. His progress during his sessions had seemed to come to a standstill.

Bud would have him go riding, they'd come back, and he'd go back to his cabin. There was no pressure to talk, no progress to be had. It had gotten to a point where Riley didn't know what he was supposed to do next.

Laughter spilled into the barn as Grace wandered in with a horse and her little entourage. At least she appeared to be happy. He could rest easy knowing he'd done something right. She didn't need him in her life dragging her down.

They passed the stall he was in, and as they did so, the young man with her placed his hand on the small of her back —a gesture far too intimate.

What happened next wasn't expected, and Riley only made sense of it after Bud held his arm out to stop him. Riley shot a dark look in the older man's direction, but Bud only shook his head.

Riley blinked, looking down at Bud's arm as it continued to prevent him from exiting Dolly's stall. One more glance down the aisle where Grace had walked, and he backed into his stall again.

"Smart choice," Bud murmured. He slipped the bridle he held onto a hook and his eyes followed the group who had arrived. "You made your decision."

"You don't know what you're talking about," Riley muttered. He didn't choose any of this. He'd picked Grace—she was the one he had wanted to start his life with. "She made hers."

Bud laughed. "If that's the way you see it, I understand now why you're in therapy."

"What's that supposed to mean?" Riley shot back. "You can't make someone love you. It doesn't matter how hard you try. You can't change the way people look at you when you've been through what I've dealt with."

Bud sobered. He gave Riley a stern look, then he removed

his hat and placed it on a nearby hook. "Son, I'm only going to say this once, so you better listen and listen good." He raked a hand through his hair and moved closer. "I served our country too, and for you to suggest that you're only one of a few men who dealt with conditions that weren't ideal is shortsighted."

Riley stilled. Bud had never given him his credentials, but Riley had assumed that he was similar to Grace. He'd probably taken some college classes or did some service at a church that "qualified" him for this position.

Bud pulled at his collar until he retrieved something from beneath his shirt. On a chain dangling from his fingers were two dog tags. "Marine Corps. From what I remember, I was active duty when you joined the army, but I retired about five years later." He tucked the tags back into his shirt and crossed his arms on the stall door. The lines on his face seemed to deepen in real time as his voice lowered. "It ain't easy—what we do. Civilians will never fully understand some of the horrors we have to go through, and that's just a fact. But that doesn't stop them from trying."

He gave Riley a meaningful look. "The good ones always do. You're always going to carry this burden. There's no way around it, no way to forget. It's your cross to bear. But does that mean you have to keep it locked away in your heart for an eternity?"

Riley didn't know how to respond. He was still reeling from the fact that this was the most Bud had ever spoken to him since they'd started.

"The answer's no, son. You shouldn't keep it locked up. Because what happens when we let an infection take root? It festers until we have no choice but to cut it out." He glanced toward Grace. "She's a good one, and you let her slip from your fingers. That's on you. A girl like her? She's got a pure heart."

The scowl returned to Riley's face. "She didn't want me."

A quiet curse slipped from Bud's lips and he shook his head. "Lord, I pray I wasn't this pig-headed." He tilted his head from one side to the next, then set those stone-like eyes on Riley once more. "How in heaven's name do you know that? Did she say it?"

"Not in so many words..."

Bud shook his head. "That's not what I asked. Did Miss Callahan tell you she didn't want to be with you? Did she tell you that it was too hard to love you?"

"That's just it. She didn't say she loved me!" Riley snapped bitterly. "Not once did she say those words to me."

"Well, did you?"

His mouth opened, then snapped shut. He couldn't remember if he had actually said those words specifically. He had to have. It wouldn't make sense for him not to tell her how much she meant to him. Then again, he had always been really bad with expressing himself. Riley gritted his teeth and mumbled, "I'm not sure."

"Well, that's beside the point. The point I'm trying to make is that I heard about your little break-up scene. You told her you were done. It wasn't the other way around."

Riley's mouth fell open. The scene at his group session had been terrible, but he didn't remember all of that information being available to the public.

Bud waved a dismissive hand at him. "People talk, son. Whether it happened at the club or someone let it spill at the local bar, it doesn't matter. What does is that you made the conscious decision to walk away. There's only one question you need to ask yourself."

"And what's that?" Riley muttered.

"What do you do to win her over again? What was it that held her back? Answer those questions and you might just have a shot at mending this whole thing." He pulled away from the stall door and crossed the aisle toward the stall where his horse was housed.

Riley stared after him, a mixture of emotions ranging from

bitterness, heartache, fury, and shock blending together. How could this complete stranger know so much about this sort of thing?

"I went through it too, son." Bud turned around, catching him staring.

"What?"

"I lost the love of my life. I wasn't lucky enough to get her back. Don't make the same mistakes I did."

"I don't get it," Riley stammered. "Why are you a therapist if you went through all of that? Why aren't you as disillusioned as me?"

Bud laughed again. "I found a path that brought me joy. I didn't like talking about my experiences either. I also didn't feel the need to be *fixed*. But there are other people out there who need someone to listen. That's what I give them. Do what makes you happy. That's all the good Lord wants for any of us." He nodded toward Dolly. "Now, brush her down so we can get out of here."

RILEY FIDGETED at the foot of the stairs in front of Grace's house. He'd been standing there in the dark for at least an hour. No one had come or gone from the residence yet, but he was sure if anyone knew he was there, they'd be sending him off.

He fumbled with his hands and stared at her front door as if that would be enough to get her to come out. He hadn't had the guts to knock yet. Not after what he'd said to her at the country club. But he knew he needed to apologize. He needed her to know what was in his heart, no matter how hard it was to say.

Swallowing hard, Riley pushed down all the feelings of inadequacy and self-loathing. Bud might be well-adjusted now, but he didn't appear to be as happy as he might have been.

Riley ran a ragged hand through his hair and climbed the

stairs, his heart heavy. He rapped his knuckles on the door, then stood back. If Zeke was the one who answered, there was a good chance a shotgun would be pointed at his chest just like last time.

The wait stretched on for what felt like an eternity and he nearly headed back to his motorcycle when it finally opened. Faye stared at him with surprise. Her eyes darted out along the property before being brought around to his face. "Riley, what are you doing here?"

"Is Grace home?"

Her face fell. "I'm sorry. She's not. Grace went on a date—"

Light flashed against the house and the sound of tires on gravel reached his ears. He turned, shading his eyes from the headlights, then turned back to Faye. "Looks like she's back."

Grace climbed down from the driver's side door and shut it firmly. She froze, probably when she noticed him on the porch. But then she moved into action and hurried up the steps. Her eyes met his, then landed on Faye. Before she could ask her sister anything, Faye disappeared inside.

A sigh burst from Grace's chest and she folded her arms. "What do you want, Riley?"

So many thoughts, so many words filled his head. How was he supposed to make her believe him? Riley's fist bounced against his leg and he looked away, unable to bring himself to say what he knew he needed to while looking into her eyes. "Can we talk?"

She cocked her head and shifted her weight from one foot to the other. For some reason, her silence made it that much more difficult.

He cleared his throat and lifted his gaze to meet hers. "I'm sorry," he croaked.

"You're sorry," she repeated.

Riley nodded. "I'm sorry about how we ended things. I should have—" He clamped his mouth shut and heat crawled up his neck. "I'm in love with you, Grace. I want you back. I want a second chance to show you I can be better."

She stared at him until time had slowed and all he could hear was his blood roaring in his ears. The moment of truth wasn't coming fast enough.

"Please say something," he said.

Grace's brows creased. That wasn't a good sign. Even when she was worried or upset, she was beautiful. He'd missed being able to talk to her. But more than that, he missed having her in his arms.

"No."

All of his insides dropped, and the blood drained from his face. "What?" he asked hoarsely.

She pressed her lips together in a tight line. "I can't date you. Not right now." Emotion filled her eyes and a tear slipped down her cheek. She placed her hand against his cheek, allowing him to lean into it. "I can't because I love you, too, and our relationship can't be the thing that stands in your way of confronting your demons." She took in a shuddering breath. "You need to work on yourself before we can see where things might go together." A quiet sob escaped her lips and she dropped her hand. "I hope you can understand."

His first instinct was to let the fire of fury that came to life within him loose. He wanted to thrash and yell, acuse her of treating him differently because of who he was.

But Bud's words came back to him.

What would you do to win her over again? What was it that held her back?

Anything. He'd do whatever it took to start over.

He swallowed hard, extinguishing the fire monster that lived in his chest. Nodding because he didn't trust his voice, he reached for her hand and pressed a kiss to her palm. "Okay," he whispered.

28

———

Grace

Two weeks later

*G*race hurried down the stairs, pulling her hoodie down over her head. She skidded to a stop in the kitchen and grabbed a piece of bread before tossing it in the toaster. Riley was going to be here any second, and she needed to be ready or they were going to miss the sunrise.

"Where do you think you're going?"

She screamed and spun around to find her father sitting at the kitchen table. "What are you doing sitting in the dark?"

Zeke tilted his head slightly. "Sometimes it's quieter when the lights aren't on." He rose from his seat and strode toward the kitchen sink. His mug was placed in the sink with the other dishes before he turned to face her. "I'll ask again. Where are you going?"

"Riley and I are going for a ride. He wants to see the sunrise from…"

Zeke's dark expression gave her pause.

"What?"

"You're still spending time with that man?"

She groaned just as the toaster erupted with the slice of bread. She snatched it, then stood beside her father to butter it. "You know I am. I don't know why you act surprised every time I do something with him."

"He's treating you right?"

"Dad, we're not even dating. Not technically." They hadn't even said they loved each other since that night two weeks ago. "For now, we're just friends."

Her father huffed. "I don't believe that for a second. Maybe you should step back and reevaluate—"

"*Dad.* Nothing is going on between us. And if something does start again—"

"I'll be ready with my shotgun."

"*No,* you won't." Grace tore off a corner of her toast and chewed it thoughtfully. "Dad, I'm going to say something, and I want you to keep an open mind. I *really* like him. Okay, I love him. But I'm being careful this time. We're being careful. Riley knows he needs to be to a certain place before we take that next step, and he's just not there yet."

Her father muttered something under his breath. "He's not good enough for you."

"I guess it's a good thing you don't get to choose who I spend time with. He's an honorable man. You two just started off on the wrong foot."

"He hurt you, and I don't want to see that happen again."

Grace pushed the last bit of toast into her mouth. "We all make mistakes, Dad. Life is messy, and it's okay for things to be messy sometimes." She leaned up and pressed a quick kiss to his cheek. "Don't worry about me, Dad. I'm fine." With a little wave, she hurried out the door and sprinted toward the barn. This would be the first time she'd officially invited Riley to her home. This would be the first time he'd meet her horse and get to see the world she grew up in.

And boy, was she a nervous wreck.

It hadn't taken long for her to open up to Riley again. Even with the things he'd said. There was no logical explanation for that except the fact that she could actually see a physical shift in the way he acted around her.

For one, he wasn't nearly as pushy as he once was. It was as if they had just started over. He didn't try to kiss her, the hugs they shared were purely platonic, and they didn't talk about relationships at all.

Grace tossed the pad over her horse's back, followed by the saddle. She was running late. If they wanted to get out of there on time, she needed at least one horse saddled before he arrived.

Just thinking about him gave her goosebumps. It was the weirdest thing. Now that the pressure was off, she found herself wanting to be with him like they had been before. When they talked, she found herself leaning closer to him. When their hands brushed against each other, she fought the temptation to hold his hand.

Confessing any of that to her father was a very bad idea. If he knew, he'd shut this whole friendship down in a second.

Then where would she be?

Riley wasn't even making advances. After his confession of love, he stuck with their agreement. For all she knew, he wasn't ready for anything yet anyway.

Grace stepped back to examine the saddle. Telling Riley that she was quickly falling down the rabbit hole when it came to having feelings for him wasn't going to happen either. She'd made a commitment to herself. When Riley was ready to confide in her, that's when she'd tell him—even if it took years.

Footsteps echoed down the long aisle from the barn's entrance. She moved to the edge of the stall and poked her head over the half-door. Riley's familiar form approached, and that thrill returned.

He glanced over his shoulder toward the entrance, then let his eyes sweep through the structure before landing on her. One side of his mouth quirked up and he gave her that crooked grin that she was so fond of.

She folded her arms over the top of the door and rested her chin on them. "Hey," she said.

"Hey." Riley propped his shoulder against a nearby pole and gestured toward the barn. "This is some place you got."

"It's not as big as Shane's, but it does its job."

"I don't think there will ever be anything as big as Shane's." He chuckled. His eyes seemed brighter somehow. She couldn't remember exactly because the change had occurred over the course of several weeks, but Riley looked better—happier. He looked good.

Grace straightened and pointed to another stall. "You're gonna be riding Bandit. He's Faye's horse." She chuckled. "He's nothing like Dolly, but he's a good listener. I think you'll like him."

Riley swung his focus back to her, that smile of his making her legs weak, turning them into jelly. She'd chastise herself for falling into this trap a second time, but every time she attempted to put herself in her place, she remembered that none of these reactions were present when she had gone on a few dates with Tyler.

He tilted his head slightly and a soft laugh filled the space between them. "What are you looking at me for?"

Her eyes widened and her brows shot up. Heat seared her cheeks as she forced herself to tear her gaze from him. "I'm not. Nothing. Just—let's get Bandit ready so we don't miss this sunrise. It's gonna be the best—"

"Grace..."

She returned her focus to him. "Yeah?"

"Thanks."

"For what?"

Riley shrugged. "All of it. I wouldn't be where I'm at without you."

Her throat closed up. This was the closest she'd come to hearing him admit her sessions had made a difference. That small compliment was enough to set her heart into overdrive. She didn't know what to say. How should she respond to something like that? "You're welcome," she wheezed. Well, that didn't sound quite right. She was making herself out to be an embarrassment. If she wasn't careful, he'd realize he'd been better off when they'd been apart.

They made quick work of setting Riley up on Bandit and set out on the trail. It was still fairly dark outside, but the weather was cooperating. Their horses plodded side-by-side and the only sound that could be heard was that of their horseshoes hitting the earth beneath them.

Grace peeked at Riley and every single memory of the intimate moments they'd shared burst to the surface. The gentle way he could hold her in his arms, the soft kisses he brushed to her temple, the way his gaze made her feel like the only one in the room.

For the life of her, she couldn't think of a single thing that would be so bad he would be worried about sharing it with her.

And yet, he still refused to tell her any details as to why he didn't feel he deserved to be happy. It was still an issue they skirted just so they could see each other regularly. The baby elephant had grown into adulthood, and now it traveled with them wherever they went.

Riley caught her staring and shook his head as a smile stretched across his face. "How did your dad react when you told him I was coming?"

She made a face.

"That good huh?"

Grace peeked at him out of the corner of her eye. "He'll warm up to you."

"Yeah, I'm not counting on it."

She gave him a pointed look. "You shouldn't say that. He's gonna have to accept the man I fell in love with eventually. It might as well be sooner rather than later."

It wasn't until she noticed the strange look on his face that she realized what she'd said. Her eyes rounded and her breath hitched in her chest. As often as she'd reminded herself to keep her feelings private, she'd let it slip anyway.

"Riley, I—"

"I love you, too, Grace." They entered the clearing where they planned on watching the sunrise.

She snapped her mouth shut before taking a deep breath and murmuring, "You do?"

He tugged on the reins, pulling Bandit around in front of her and cutting her off from leading the horse away. Riley climbed down from the saddle in such an effortless way that it looked like he'd been doing it all his life. He held out his hands to her, offering to help her down. "Of course I do. I can't even remember the moment I knew I was in love with you, but it's never left. That feeling has been the one thing propelling me forward, pushing me to be better."

Grace placed her hands on his shoulders and he slipped his hands around her waist before he helped her to the ground. His touch lingered and his eyes drilled into hers while they stood there in the dim lighting of the rising sun.

"I will never not love you, Grace. I'm not capable of that. It's just that sometimes I get it in my head that one day you'll leave. When you find out what I am, the kind of things I had to do…" His voice cracked. "I've never wanted to risk losing you over something in my past. There are skeletons in my closet."

"I'm not scared," she whispered. Her hand dropped from his shoulder to cover his heart. "I know you're a good man.

What are we if we can't make mistakes and learn from them? That's a world I don't want to live in. Besides, whatever it is you're worried about, it happened when you were on duty. You had to follow orders. Sometimes we aren't given a choice."

"There's always a choice, Grace. I just think I made the wrong one."

Her brows furrowed. "You can tell me about it. I promise no judgments. I'm not going anywhere." She became distinctly aware of how close they remained—the way his hands at her waist felt. A tingle raced through her like a shooting star just before daylight.

His expression broke and he stepped back, releasing her. "I've kept it bottled up for so long..." He turned his back to her and let out a heavy breath.

"You don't have to talk about it if you don't want to..."

"No. You're right." He shot a look over his shoulder toward her, then sighed again. "My last assignment was overseas in a desert country I'm not supposed to name—right when there was a peace treaty between the president and a militant political group."

That didn't sound so bad. Treaties were supposed to be good for everyone, right?

"Our mission was to support the armament of AH-64D Apache attack helicopters. But during the treaty, no US troops were allowed to engage with local nationals."

His words jumbled in her head, only parts making sense.

Riley's voice broke and he looked away. "During that time, an unfathomable amount of the country's national army were attacked and executed, and we weren't allowed to protect them —all because of that treaty."

She sucked in sharply, the picture starting to come together. Chills swept over her body. She couldn't imagine being in that situation.

"The body count grew daily. There was nothing we could

do. The radio calls ended with silence as they were killed, screaming for help." A sob burst from his chest and he covered his face with his hands. "I could have helped, Grace. So many innocent people, and I did nothing."

Grace reached out to him as if her touch could heal the scars he wore. His shoulders shook and he slumped down onto the ground. This wasn't how their ride was supposed to go. She collapsed beside him, wrapping her arms around his shoulders. "It wasn't your fault," she whispered.

His harsh breathing settled and his hoarse voice broke through the silence. "Our mission was to send US assets home, stay the course, don't save the local nationals even though it was within our abilities." Riley looked up at her with red eyes. "I came home knowing I could have saved hundreds of lives, but I was forced to focus on shutting down all of the bases instead."

"I'm so sorry," she whispered. Her words sounded so trite, so hollow. It wasn't any wonder that he'd struggled with this information. She wished she could convince him that he didn't have to carry it all on his shoulders. But that would be like telling a cow that it didn't have to graze. This was a part of him that had been carved deep into his soul. No one would ever truly understand.

Riley stared straight ahead, his eyes glazed over. He sniffled, then wiped his face with the back of his hand. "No civilian will ever know what it is like, trying to sleep as mortar cannons are going off right outside their sleeping quarters." He glanced up at her. "And that really bad virus made it ten times worse. If someone even sneezed, they were sent off to be tested for it. And if they got flagged for it, they were sent away to an isolation camp for two weeks and left alone as their insanity took over. We were being attacked from all sides."

Tears burned behind her eyes and one slipped down her

cheek as the full weight of everything he'd been through came down on her.

They sat there, the sun cresting the hills in the distance. The silence suffocated her. The therapist part of her wanted to say something, give him advice on how to deal with it. Perhaps that was one of the reasons they weren't supposed to push their clients to talk details. But he wasn't her client.

He was the man she loved.

Grace tightened her arms around him, holding him close as if she were the only thing that could protect him from the world. "You are the strongest man I know," she said quietly.

Riley glanced up at her with surprise. His brows pulled together and he tugged at her, pulling her to sit in his lap. "I failed all of those people."

She shook her head, placing her palm against his cheek. More tears spilled down her face and she forced a sad smile. "You did what you were ordered to do. You weren't the one making the calls. We don't know why God allows such terrible things to happen... but we can count on him to bring us peace when we need it most."

His hard expression softened. "I've been thinking about God. And I think he must have sent you to help me." Riley's gaze dipped lower, shifting to her lips for the briefest of moments before he locked his eyes with hers. Then he gently brushed his lips against hers.

He tasted of salt and desperation, his kiss suddenly claiming her for his own. She gave into him, throwing her arms around his neck, kissing him deeply and with her whole heart. Nothing hung in the balance between them now. It felt like they were one.

She pulled back, her forehead pressed against his. "I love you, Riley. Every smile, every tear, every scar. I need you to know that."

Riley nodded, his eyes shutting tight. "I love you too," he whispered.

There was no need to discuss where things would go from here. He'd bared his soul to her, and she'd been there to pick up the pieces. They might have gotten to this point a little backward, but she knew in her heart they were finally on the same path, moving toward the same dream.

29

____

Riley

Six months later

Riley fingered the small velvet box in his pocket as he stood in front of the Callahan house. His heart thundered faster than the hooves of a hundred wild horses.

He was finally where he wanted to be.

He had *finally* found his place in the world.

When the depression still caught him off guard, Grace was usually there to be a sounding board. The support she offered always brought him back from the brink.

The small black box in his hand had been purchased two months ago, and it had taken every ounce of self-control to hold onto it and not propose to Grace on the spot. But there were a few things he had to get sorted out before he would allow himself to take that step.

And today would be that day.

He swallowed hard, shoving the box back into his pocket.

Riley hurried up the steps, taking them two at a time, then he knocked on the door. Grace would be at the club for the next two hours at least, which gave him plenty of time to confront the one obstacle in his path.

The door swung open, revealing Zeke's immovable form. He eyed Riley with the usual disdain. Six months and the man still didn't seem to like Riley, though his disapproval had appeared to shift into something resembling tolerance instead. "Grace isn't here," he said gruffly.

"I know. I came to speak to you."

Zeke arched a brow.

How was it that a man could unnerve him with one change of his expression? No wonder why Shane seemed to be terrified of getting on his bad side.

Riley gestured toward the chairs they'd occupied the last time he had spent some one-on-one time with the man. Zeke followed his gesture, then returned his eyes to Riley before squinting his eyes and striding past him.

At least he didn't bring his gun with him.

Seated on the edge of his chair, Riley fidgeted with his hands. "Sir, as you're aware, I've been dating your daughter—"

"Just get on with it, Scott. You're here to ask if I approve of you marrying my daughter."

Riley snapped his mouth shut.

"Well? That *is* why you're here, is it not?"

He nodded.

"Then convince me."

"Sir?"

Zeke leaned forward and his voice lowered, sounding more like a growl than anything else. "Why should I let you marry my daughter?"

A lump formed in Riley's throat. If he were honest with himself, he'd admit he didn't think he'd get *this* far. He actually expected Zeke to run him off like he had the last time. Only now, he knew Grace wouldn't come to his rescue. He swallowed, but it did nothing to alleviate the pressure.

"I love her."

"So?"

Riley blinked.

"Do you know how many men I would have to listen to if I accepted 'love' as a good enough reason to marry one of my daughters? Love means nothing if the man behind that word is willing to throw it around like his boots after a long day's work."

Riley grimaced. Zeke was right. He'd confessed his feelings before and then immediately broke it off. "You're right," he said.

Zeke's brows lifted and he settled back in his chair. Riley's words must have caught him off guard.

"The love I have for your daughter is a small part. I can't live without her. She fills a part of me that has been missing for longer than I even realized. While I find that to be the utmost importance in this situation, there's more." He peeked at the gruff man. If Zeke gave him a chance, he wouldn't waste it.

"Go on."

The excitement that accosted him next propelled him forward. His heart beat harder and his blood rushed faster. "I have never met anyone as exceptional as your daughter. She's done so much, and her future spreads out before her with loads of potential. I knew if I ever wanted to have a chance to be with her, I'd have to find a way to close that gap. That is to say, I'd need to make some changes to be worthy of her."

He grunted. Riley couldn't tell if it was a good thing or a bad thing.

"You recall, I came here to partake in the therapeutic services offered over at the country club. I've since completed what was required by the judge, and I've continued attending the group sessions on my own."

Zeke lifted that brow again. Was he marginally impressed

by that statement? If he was, he'd be pleased to hear what Riley had up his sleeve.

"While I don't necessarily need to work, I've chosen to explore a career that will help pay forward everything Grace has done for me. I've been taking some courses and I begin training next week. There's an opening at the club—Kevin—the gentleman running the group sessions—he's moving, and Shane has agreed to have me run that part of things."

Once again, Riley couldn't tell if Zeke was impressed or just curious. The lull in conversation tugged at Riley, making him even more antsy.

"If you give me your blessing to marry your daughter, I swear I will take care of her, love her, cherish her—"

Zeke held up his hand but didn't say anything right away. His eyes remained hard and his mouth was tight. Finally, after what felt like an eternity, he let out a heavy breath. "Do you know what it's like to raise seven girls?"

Riley blinked. That was clearly a rhetorical question, but he couldn't figure out how Zeke wanted him to respond.

Zeke lifted his gaze to Riley, and for the first time, Riley saw something different. Exhaustion. "They turn into women, you know. And after that, there's nothing you can do to stop them from what they want to do. I could tell you no, right here, right now. I could demand you leave my property and never come back as I point my shotgun at your chest. But it wouldn't stop Grace from doing what she wants to do."

"I'm aware of that, sir. You'll recall, I didn't come here asking for permission. I want your *blessing*." Riley sat a little straighter. "Family is everything, sir. I don't want to tear a rift in the fabric of your family any more than I want to see Grace get hurt. You're right. She'll do what she wants, and most of the time I'm just along for the ride."

Zeke's face broke into a smile and he chuckled. Did that

mean he was going to be on board with this? Was he giving his blessing?

"Sir?"

The man before him sobered somewhat. "My daughters are headstrong, that's for certain. But they have big hearts, and I can tell Grace has loved you since the moment she met you. There's a shift that happens, you know? She might not have realized it, but I could see it." He clapped his hands on his knees, then got to his feet. "It was nice seeing you, Riley."

He shot up from his seat. "Does that mean—"

Zeke turned toward him. "You have my blessing, son. Don't squander the opportunity it gives you."

"No, sir!"

It wasn't until Zeke had shut the front door that Riley realized he hadn't referred to him by his last name. Zeke had called him "Riley." If that wasn't progress, then he didn't know what was.

30

Grace

Grace reached out and patted Kristin's arm. "I'm sure going to miss you."

Kristin smiled brightly at her before she launched forward and wrapped her arms around Grace's neck.

A grunt escaped Grace's lips when their bodies collided. She let out a laugh and gave Kristin a hug. Her eyes lifted to Tyler and Kristin's parents, finding them smiling down at her.

"Kristin has really loved coming here," her mother offered. "She's loved every minute of it, and that's all thanks to you."

Grace couldn't hide the joy she felt as she pulled back from Kristin. "Don't forget how smart and wonderful you are. People will love you as soon as they get to know you."

Kristin nodded and moved to stand beside her parents.

Catching movement out of the corner of her eye, Grace glanced in that direction to find Riley hovering a few yards away. He wore a crooked smile that sent her heart skipping.

Kristin's family said their goodbyes and then wandered away, leaving her standing alone.

Grace shoved her hands into her jeans pockets and rocked back on her heels. Riley still hadn't moved from his place, and she snickered. "Well, are you going to come to me? Or are you making me come to you?" she called.

His smile deepened as he propelled himself toward her. "I wouldn't dream of making you do anything."

She draped her hands around his neck and pressed a kiss to his lips. "I didn't think I'd be seeing you until tonight for our date."

"This couldn't wait."

Tilting her head slightly, Grace studied him. That's when she noticed the small tremors. His cheek twitched and he shifted slightly in her embrace. Even his hands shook a little where they held her. "Is everything okay?"

Without a word, he stepped back and dropped onto one knee, then pulled out a ring. And it was perfect. The modest stones were arranged in a way that didn't appear too gaudy. The main stone was a perfectly shaped square. And the whole thing was set in glowing white gold.

A gasp ripped from her throat. Around her, people who were passing paused or stopped completely. She dragged her focus to Riley, willing her heart to slow down so she didn't have a heart attack. "Riley, what are you doing?"

He cleared his throat, his eyes never leaving her face. "You make me happier than I can ever remember being. I knew it from the first time you spoke. For me it has always been you and no one else."

It was as if an electric current flowed between them, connecting them in a way that had never happened before. His words resonated within her right to her core, and she couldn't bring herself to speak for fear it would dissipate like fog on an early spring morning.

Riley shifted his gaze to her hand, his brows lowering. "I'm not perfect, but I'm trying to get better. And I know you deserve more—"

She dropped down to her knees, forcing him to meet her eyes. "Deserve *more*?" She shook her head with a huff. "You are *all* I will ever need." She held his free hand firmly within both of her own. "I love you, Riley Scott."

The corners of his mouth quirked. "Grace Callahan, will you marry me?"

"Yes, yes, yes!" she replied.

They rose to their feet as one and stared into each other's eyes. The smile she wore radiated the happiness she felt.

"Are you going to kiss me or what?" she said, raising her brows.

Riley chuckled. "I want to kiss you more than I want breath itself."

Grace's lashes fluttered, a sense of déjà vu inundating her senses. She cocked her head and repeated the question she'd given him back before they'd shared their first kiss. "Then why don't you?"

The corners of his lips twitched, then lifted. "Because once I do, there is no going back."

"Good." Grace pulled him down, firmly kissing him, claiming him as her own. There was no way she'd ever want to go back. She was right where she wanted to be.

EPILOGUE

Two weeks later

Grace stomped into the kitchen and threw her cowboy hat onto the table. Faye jumped and Brielle rolled her eyes, but neither of them asked her what she was upset over. Of course they wouldn't care. They didn't have to deal with the awful truck that continued to leech money from her.

"I have to take the truck back to the mechanics. Again."

Brielle glanced up from her phone only briefly. "You said you wanted it. This is part of taking care of an antique."

"It's not an *antique*. And I don't want it anymore. Honestly, I'm about ready to sell it to the Cullen's for parts."

Faye gasped. She jumped out of her seat and hurried around the table. "You can't do that. It's Mom's truck."

Grace sighed. "I don't even remember her, Faye. I can't hold onto something like this when it's causing so many problems for me."

Faye shook her head. "You can't get rid of it."

"Faye. I have literally sunk thousands of dollars into that heap of junk to keep it running for the past year. I'm to the point where I just can't take it anymore."

"I'm sure Riley would help fix it up for you."

Grace scowled at her sister. "Just because we're engaged doesn't mean I'm going to be asking for money for something like this. In fact, he said we could go look around for a replacement today. That's not how I wanted to spend my Saturday, but the way I see it, I have no other choice."

"I'm not going to let you sell it. You can't," Faye continued to insist. "If you don't want it, give it to me. We can take it to the mechanic, and I can ask him what needs to be done."

Grace studied her older sister. Faye had always been the sister who put more value on memories and objects that reminded her of happier times. She was only about a year older than Grace which meant she had about the same memories of their mother. But for some reason, she didn't want to let go even two decades later.

"Fine. You come with me to drop it off at Cullen's and *you* work out what you're going to do. But if you give up and decide to sell it, I get half."

Faye's expression brightened. "Deal."

"I'm going to call Riley. We can meet him over at the shop." Grace shook her head with a mild form of disbelief. Faye would change her tune. Especially after she heard how bad it was straight from the horse's mouth.

Faye hurried out of the kitchen and Grace glanced in Brielle's direction. She thought that Brielle would have fought for the truck more than Faye, seeing as she had more memories of their mother.

Brielle must have felt Grace's eyes on her. She looked in Grace's direction then put her phone down. "What?"

"I didn't say anything."

"No, but you're looking at me like I did something wrong. Did Shane tell Riley I broke up with him?"

Grace blinked and her mouth dropped open. "You were still seeing him?"

Brielle groaned. "Sorta? Not really. I mean, we had that moment at the Christmas thing. And then we might have seen each other a few times over the last several months…"

"Brielle! You can't just string a guy along like that."

Her sister gasped. "I wasn't *stringing him along*. He knew I wasn't interested in anything long-term. He was fine with it." Brielle dropped her gaze and shifted in her seat. "It's just not gonna work between him and me. I'm not built to be the kind of girl that hangs off the arm of a wealthy man. It's just not me."

"But you kept going on dates with him."

She snorted and the corners of her lips curled upward. "I'm also not the kind of girl to say no to a free meal or a night of dancing."

"Brielle." Grace laughed.

Her sister shrugged. "It's fine. I finally told him enough. Not gonna go through that and get attached. Time to see what else is out there." She got to her feet. "Good luck with the truck."

"It's not mine anymore. I don't need any luck."

"I said what I said." She grabbed her phone and strode out the door.

What a strange comment.

"I'M SORRY, but this truck isn't worth saving." Adam Cullen wiped his hands on a grease-stained rag before tossing it over his shoulder. He wasn't who Grace had expected to speak to. Bridget was working on a different vehicle and Adam's father was out running errands.

She vaguely remembered Adam from when she was in

grade school. He'd left town right out of high school about five years ago. The fact that he'd returned was more than a little strange. From the gossip in town, she'd heard he didn't want to be stuck in Copper Creek all his life.

Faye elbowed her in the ribs and she let out a yelp.

"What did you do that for?"

"He's talking to you."

Grace grimaced and looked at Adam. "I'm sorry, what were you saying?"

"It's not really worth fixing, but if you wanted to rebuild the engine and the transmission, you'd have something that could last another twenty years easy."

Faye gave her a pleading look.

"I'll let you three talk it over. Let me know when you come to a decision."

Grace shook her head. "This is all on you, Faye. You have to figure it out if you want to fix it."

"I'm not working like you are. I can't afford to pay for something like that."

Grace shrugged, then crossed her arms. "This is what I was trying to say. Some things aren't worth saving because they're just not."

"Grace." Riley's soft voice gave her goosebumps. "We could help."

"No. I don't want you wasting your money on something so... frivolous."

Riley's eyes bore into hers as if he were telling her some kind of big secret, but she couldn't grasp the code to decipher it. He turned to Faye. "I can help out a little bit. I'll get the parts for you, but the labor is all up to you."

Grace gasped, and before she knew what was happening, Faye had thrown her arms around Riley to give him a big hug. "Thank you so much." She hurried over to the reception counter to speak with Adam.

Turning toward him, Grace fought the urge to yell at him. But the second she met his gaze and saw that silly little grin on his face, her fury melted. "Why did you do that?"

He pulled her close and she had no choice but to wrap her arms around his neck. "Because I can."

She snorted. "That's not a good reason to spend your money."

Riley glanced over to where Faye was talking with Adam. "Nothing does us much good being locked away where no one can see it. Not our past, not our feelings, not even money. I'd rather see it do some good."

His words gave her chills. "Have I told you how much I love you?" she whispered.

"You can always say it again." He cocked his head, his eyes dancing with amusement before they grew serious. "Because *I* love *you*."

Those words that she'd once refused to utter to anyone other than her family now easily slipped from her lips. She stood on her toes and kissed his nose. "I love you more."

Hello reader,

Did you enjoy Grace and Riley's love story? Then you don't want to miss what's next with the Callahans...

Faye Callahan would give anything to get her late mother's old truck running again. The only problem? She's broke—and far too busy helping her family on the ranch to make money.

Adam Cullen has just taken over his dad's auto shop in Copper Creek and isn't exactly thrilled to be back in small-town life—until he meets a certain pretty barrel racer.

When Adam offers to fix Faye's truck in exchange for horse-riding lessons, their deal sounds simple enough. But soon, hearts get tangled, and sticking to the plan becomes a whole lot harder than either of them expected.

Don't miss the flirty fun and slow-burn sparks in *Dating a Cowgirl, Callahans of Copper Creek Book 5!* The paperback books are available at **nataliedeanbooks.com** and other retailers.

ABOUT AUTHOR - NATALIE DEAN

Born and raised in a small coastal town in the south I realized at a young age that I was more adventurous than my conservative friends and family. I loved to travel. My passion for travel opened up a whole new world and new cultures to me that I will always be grateful for.

I was raised to treasure family. I always knew that at some point in my life I would leave my storybook life behind and become someone's mother, someone's aunt and hopefully someone's grandmother. Little did I know that the birth of my son later in life would make me the happiest I've ever been. He will always be my biggest achievement. The strong desire to be a work-from-home mom is what lead me down this path of publishing books.

While I have always loved reading I never realized how much I would love writing until I started. I feel like each one of my books have been influenced by someone or something I've experienced in my life. To be able to share this gift has become a dream come true.

I hope you enjoy reading them as much as I have enjoyed creating them. I truly hope to develop an ongoing relationship with all of my readers that lasts into my last days :)

www.nataliedeanauthor.com

 facebook.com/nataliedeanromance